MURDER BY DEGREES

A Mystery

RITU MUKERJI

SIMON & SCHUSTER

New York   London   Toronto   Sydney   New Delhi

Simon & Schuster
1230 Avenue of the Americas
New York, NY 10020

First Simon & Schuster hardcover edition October 2023

SIMON & SCHUSTER and colophon are registered trademarks of Simon & Schuster, Inc.

For information about special discounts for bulk purchases, please contact Simon & Schuster Special Sales at 1-866-506-1949 or business@simonandschuster.com.

The Simon & Schuster Speakers Bureau can bring authors to your live event. For more information or to book an event, contact the Simon & Schuster Speakers Bureau at 1-866-248-3049 or visit our website at www.simonspeakers.com.

Interior design by Wendy Blum

Manufactured in the United States of America

10 9 8 7 6 5 4 3 2 1

Library of Congress Cataloging-in-Publication Data has been applied for.

ISBN 978-1-6680-1506-3
ISBN 978-1-6680-1508-7 (ebook)

The Whole of it came not at once —
'Twas Murder by degrees —
A Thrust —and then for Life a chance —
The Bliss to cauterize —

The Cat reprieves the Mouse
She eases from her teeth
Just long enough for Hope to tease —

—Emily Dickinson

PROLOGUE

Her breath was soft and ragged. She crouched against the column and closed her eyes, placing her flushed cheek against the stone as if she could draw strength from its bulwark. Despite the cold of the night, rivulets of sweat dripped down her back, the wool dress soaked through.

She had slipped from the back of the carriage when he stopped to water the horse. She heard his shout of anger behind her, but she fled unseeing. The row houses and factory shops stood dark, their window lamps extinguished at this late hour. She fled through the silent lanes, sensing his relentless presence somewhere behind her.

She had come to the edge of the city street and could feel an opening in the space around her. She saw the outline of the trees and a hill above, a stark silhouette against the night sky. She knew this place, an entrance to Fairmount Park. It was familiar, a place of respite where she could walk and admire the view.

She ran into the park towards the river's edge. The curved paths led to picturesque fountains and by day, the river terrace was full of people enjoying a leisurely stroll. Now the expansive lawns and the well-tended shrubbery were a landscape cloaked in darkness, the amorphous shapes looming and fearful.

The moon rose above the river, casting light on the expansive sur-face of the water. She could see the waterworks on the promontory above the dam. The upper river stretched away into a placid pool, the surface smooth as slate. She could hear the soft rush of water as the waves poured over the dam.

It had been a mistake to leave the streets. She needed a place to hide.

She ran into the first pavilion, her footsteps echoing in the cavernous space. It was like a Greek temple of antiquity. The graceful buildings stood in a line, their stately columns gleaming in the moonlight. It was the province of a fairy tale, a ballroom empty of revelers. She could have been an elegant princess awaiting the first waltz, the drape of her gown trail-ing across the floor. But she stumbled, her legs weak and aching from the strain of exertion.

The buildings were an ingenious screen for the turbines that churned the river water day and night, purifying it for the city's water supply. Underneath her feet she could sense the steady creak of the wheels turn-ing. She knew there were doors leading to the wheelhouse. If only she could get below.

She reached the first door. Please, dear God. She turned the knob urgently. It was locked. She rattled it frantically, pushing her shoulder against the heavy frame. It was stuck fast. She ran to the next building and tried the door there. It was the same. She suppressed a sob as fear pressed on her chest like a weight.

She came to the final landing above the dam. There was nowhere left to run. She stopped at the railing and leaned forward. She could feel the fine mist of the water as it fell in a graceful arc below. The current was swift below the dam and the foaming waves churned as the river continued its path. How many times had she come here to watch, mesmerized by the many patterns of the water.

She took off her coat and shoes and climbed up on the railing. Her toes gripped the edge of the precipice. She allowed herself a moment of freedom, outstretching her arms. Her heart was pounding from the chase. But this place would hold no more fear for her; instead, it would be the site of her blessed release. She clasped the locket around her neck, pressing it tight in the palm of her hand.

She willed herself to look back. He was there, just as she knew he would be. She could not see him in the darkness. He was shrouded in a cloak with the hood pulled over his face. But he realized what she was about to do. The specter coalesced in terrifying form, running towards her. She lifted herself with her last remaining strength and jumped.

Part One

HISTORY OF PRESENT ILLNESS

1

Dr. Lydia Weston glanced discreetly at her watch. Her patient, Delia Townsend, sat on the examination table. With each deep breath, Mrs. Townsend's corsets creaked in protest. She lifted her chin in stubborn protest as she recited a litany of concerns.

"This fatigue consumes me. After breakfast, I feel ill-suited to do anything. I could lie down and sleep for hours. Perhaps I need a tonic?"

Lydia placed her stethoscope on her desk. Privately she thought that Mrs. Townsend should take some exercise, but she kept this to herself.

She took out her prescription pad and wrote as Mrs. Townsend disappeared behind the chinoiserie screen to dress.

Lydia sighed. She had a stack of patient notes to write before the day was done and Mrs. Townsend's concerns were nothing new. But the patient needed time to fully voice her complaints or else the visit would take twice as long.

An iron tonic would be little more than a placebo, Lydia thought. She had done a thorough exam as she always did: listening to the heart and lungs, palpating the abdomen, noting normal vital signs. An extensive laboratory evaluation had revealed nothing suspicious.

Mrs. Townsend reemerged, elegantly dressed in a cream silk taffeta that pooled at her feet. Lydia knew they were fortunate to have wealthy patients who sought treatment from a "lady doctor"; these patients' ability to pay provided much-needed revenue to support the work of the clinic.

Mrs. Townsend fastened the buttons at the top of her bodice. Her jeweled rings slipped atop gnarled joints, brown age spots mottling the backs of her hands. Lydia could see that her hands shook as she struggled to do up the buttons. No doubt severe arthritis was causing considerable pain. Lydia felt a stab of compassion as she watched the older woman take a deep breath and patiently begin again. Lydia knew wealth conferred no immunity from suffering. Mrs. Townsend's only daughter had died of rheumatic fever the year before and many of her visits stemmed from the void of loss.

Lydia handed over the prescription.

"If you like, you could try a daily tonic. But I would recommend light exercise. Start with a half-hour walk daily. It will make you feel better," she said gently.

"I suppose it can't hurt," Mrs. Townsend admitted.

"I would also suggest taking off your corset." Lydia could not resist a chance to dispense this advice. "It is a terrible constriction to the abdominal organs and can impair your breathing."

The remark was greeted with silence. Then Mrs. Townsend ventured, "Well, I don't know. It doesn't seem proper to be without a corset . . ."

"Please try it. I will look forward to our next meeting," Lydia said as she ushered Mrs. Townsend out of her office.

The Spruce Street Clinic had been founded by a group of doctors from the Woman's Medical College, fervent idealists who believed that medical care was not the sole province of the rich. It served a thriving working-class community and many of the shopkeepers, seamstresses, and livery drivers that Lydia had treated in the early days were still her loyal patients. Lydia met people from all walks of life, many her own age, who had endured unimaginable trials of sickness and loss.

The building had been a small textile factory, and the industrial flavor was still evident. The knotty pine boards on the floor were burnished to a sheen from countless boots trudging through the rooms in all weather. The former factory floor was divided into exam rooms and a reception hall. The upstairs floor could function as a small hospital ward, with a few beds for those whose conditions required more intense monitoring. There was an airiness to the waiting room, with its high ceilings and large windows. The walls were painted white, adorned with a few bland landscape paintings. It was as if the décor was an afterthought. The simplicity reflected the attitude of its founders: this was a serious place of work and it needed no distraction from the mission it served.

As she walked back down the hallway, the sound of Lydia's footsteps echoed through the empty rooms. She was alone, the last group of students having left a few hours before. The oil lamps were turned down and tepid gaslight from the street filtered through the mullioned windows in the hallway.

Lydia closed the chamber door behind her and paused for a moment at the mirror above the sink. She adjusted a few dark hairs back into place, tucking the mother-of-pearl pin in at a rakish angle. She stepped back in approval: the dark eyes held only a trace of tiredness. Her silk brocade dress was simple but to a studied eye, of the utmost elegance; the gold threads woven into the fabric glinted in the dim light. She touched the ivory brooch that sat over the top button. Lydia wore all black on her teaching days but allowed herself one memento, a cameo brooch with an elephant figure in the center. It was a gift from her English mother, from her own childhood in India. Lydia was never without it. Ganesh, the bestower of blessings and the remover of obstacles, watched over her always.

She turned up the lamp, casting light into the corners of the room. She pulled her Kashmiri shawl tight around her shoulders, the itchiness of the wool tickling her chin and the movement releasing the familiar smell of sandalwood. The office was sparsely furnished as it was used in rotation by all the doctors. But she carried all she needed in a capacious leather bag as she moved nimbly between her roles as professor of medicine at the Woman's Medical College and attending physician.

She sat at the desk and removed a notebook from her bag. The cover was embossed in gold type—L. N. WESTON, M.D.—and she opened it to review her schedule, taking pleasure in the busyness of the day. It was the beginning of the autumn term and she felt the excitement of a fresh start just as the students did. She had spent the morning giving lectures at the college and the afternoon here at the Spruce, supervising medical students. After the initial years of study in the lecture hall and the laboratory, they were eager to examine patients. Lydia taught them how to take a history, how to do a clinical exam, how to ask probing questions so as to hone in on a diagnosis. The Pennsylvania Medical Society was still adamant in its opposition to their work, barring women physicians from many of the city's teaching hospitals. Out of necessity, the college had created its own spaces to teach, and the clinic was one of them. She ticked off the names of the patients she had seen this afternoon. But she had circled one name, Anna Ward, and placed a question mark by it.

It was close to six o'clock. Anna had missed her appointment by several hours. It was unusual for the fastidious young woman. She was a chambermaid for a wealthy family in the city. No doubt she had been delayed in her work. But Lydia could not suppress her unease. When had she last seen Anna? It had been some time.

THEY HAD FIRST MET AT the Spruce Street Clinic's monthly educational series, a rotating talk on topics like nutrition and hygiene. On those nights the doors remained open after hours and the benches in the waiting room were lined up in a row. The attendees sat shoulder to shoulder as if awaiting the latest performance at the penny theater. Lydia's usual lecture choice was on the benefits of exercise, though it might have appeared condescending to lecture a roomful of laborers on such a topic. But she could preach with the passion of a zealot on its restorative powers. In the aftermath of her father's death, the depth of her grief was like a dark well from which she could not emerge. It was the walks through the quiet woods of Concord and the bracing swims in the deep cold of the pond that had brought her back into the physical world and to herself.

Some in the audience sat at rapt attention while others appeared to be doing penance for an unknown crime, staring ahead blankly. Many were present under some duress, referred by their doctors or the sanitary inspector. Lydia always forged ahead with her usual enthusiasm. At the end of one particularly spirited talk, a young woman had approached her. Her plain servant's garb was evident. Yet the dress was crisply laundered, the lace of the collar faded but not frayed.

"Thank you, Doctor." The young woman shook Lydia's hand. She held up a small book. "I have been taking notes. It makes me feel as though I am in school again!"

"Are you a student?"

"If only! No, I had to stop my schooling when I went into service. But now you are giving me the chance to learn again."

She introduced herself then as Anna Ward and asked thoughtful questions. Lydia was touched by Anna's interest and genuinely curious about what had brought her to the clinic. The girl's demeanor conveyed a quiet pride.

Soon after, Anna became Lydia's patient. The young woman was fatigued and profoundly anemic, beset by the demands of her job and poor nutrition. But she heeded Lydia's advice, taking the iron supplement diligently. After she finished treatment, Anna kept returning for simple complaints. But instead of discussing medical problems, Anna would pepper Lydia with questions about how she had obtained her education. She attended the lectures at the clinic regularly, absorbing the knowledge offered to her. Lydia was surprised to find herself drawn in, giving advice on the best reading rooms in the city libraries and even loaning her own precious volumes. She felt a kinship with this young woman who wanted to educate herself.

Lydia found the note in her schedule. She had seen Anna at this month's lecture. Sometimes Anna would arrive early to help her set up the coffee and sandwiches, always a popular draw for the audience.

But on the last evening Lydia saw her, Anna had come long after the talk had finished. The room was empty. Lydia had been collecting her papers, ready to leave for the evening. She had been interrupted by the sound of urgent pounding on the front door.

Lydia had raced down the hall. A girl stumbled through the doors and fell forward.

"Anna!" Lydia cried in shock as the girl lifted her head. Her face was gaunt, iridescent veins straining against pale skin. Her hat fell onto the floor and Lydia could see her hair plastered in greasy strands against her forehead. Anna crouched on the floor with exhaustion.

"Dr. Weston, how clumsy of me. I must have slipped on the threshold. I-I-I am fine, just let me stand up for a moment."

Lydia guided Anna across the waiting room. The girl slumped against one of the wooden benches.

"Stay here."

Lydia returned with a glass of water. Anna's hand shook as she brought the glass to her lips.

"Thank you. I am sorry that I missed the lecture. It has been a busy day at the house and I couldn't get away."

Lydia extended her arm to the girl for support. "I am glad you are here now. Come into my chambers. It will be better there."

She motioned for Anna to sit on the exam table. Before the girl could protest, Lydia took her stethoscope from her medical bag and started an exam. Lydia observed Anna in silence as she held her finger on the radial pulse, bounding and quick. Anna's cheeks were flushed, the skin suffused a pale pink. Lydia watched the girl's chest wall rise and fall with shallow rapid breaths. Did she have an infection of some sort? Had she taken an ill-advised tonic? Many of the cheap "cure-alls" sold at the apothecary were heavily dosed with alcohol, an immediate panacea to those desperate for good health. Or was she just exhausted from work and her body showing the toll?

Anna sat up slowly. She reached into her bag and drew out several volumes.

"Just as you said, I enjoyed the Tennyson poems most of all. I wanted to bring the books back to you. I understand how awful it could be to be parted from these good friends." Anna hesitated, her lip trembling.

"You needn't return the books so soon," Lydia began.

"I must, Doctor."

"Is something else troubling you?" Lydia asked.

"It is nothing. I just feel tired," Anna said.

"But it is more than that."

Anna shook her head. "Usually I can right myself. I eat a little more at breakfast or steal a rest when Mrs. Burt is not watching."

The girl could be ill. But it was her behavior that was so puzzling. Lydia felt as though she was speaking to a stranger, the conversation stilted and evasive.

"Why did you come to see me today?"

Anna looked up at her, the dark eyes full of sorrow.

"I am afraid," she said quietly.

"I know it can be frightening to feel sick and not understand why," Lydia said.

"It is not that, Dr. Weston . . . there is something else . . ."

"Tell me what is wrong and I can help. You must trust me." Lydia put her hand on the girl's wrist as a gesture of support.

"No, I am sorry . . . it was a mistake for me to come here." Anna wrenched her hand away abruptly.

Lydia drew back in surprise. It was as if the girl was caught in a struggle with herself.

Anna closed her bag and stood up. "Thank you, but I must go. They are waiting for me back at the house."

"Wait! Are you able to walk home? Let me get you a hansom."

Lydia hurried after her into the waiting room. But Anna did not look back. As she crossed the threshold, Lydia called after her. "You only need to send me a message and I will come."

But it was too late. Lydia looked out the front window. The opalescent sky held the last vestige of twilight, but the street was in darkness. On the road, carriages clattered by, their lighted lanterns swinging at the sides. The street was crowded with people hurrying to get home. It was a dark, roving mass of humanity and Lydia could barely make out the individual shapes. Anna had disappeared into the night.

THAT VISIT HAD BEEN ALMOST a fortnight ago. Lydia had not seen Anna since. There could be many explanations for her absence. Perhaps Anna had felt better, an illness resolved or a worry lifted. But Lydia could not shake the feeling that something was wrong, that she had too casually dismissed that last meeting.

The lamp drew down to its embers. Lydia always carried a few volumes of literature to have on hand for a moment's respite. She reached into her bag and took out a book, hoping it would calm her mind the way reading usually did. It was one of the books that Anna had returned to her.

Lydia hadn't noticed that a page was marked. The corner of the paper was folded down and someone had etched a pencil mark next to the poem.

I shall not see the shadows,
I shall not feel the rain;
I shall not hear the nightingale
Sing on, as if in pain:
And dreaming through the twilight
That doth not rise nor set,
Haply I may remember,
And haply may forget.

2

Sergeant Charles Davies of the Philadelphia police enjoyed his morning coffee break almost more than anything else about his job. It gave him great pleasure to sit at his desk and have the steaming drink brought to him in a porcelain cup and saucer, a biscuit perched on the edge. He had started life with little and that he enjoyed a ritual as civilized as this would have surprised those who knew him then.

"Good morning, Charlie." Inspector Thomas Volcker strolled through the double doors of the station, his walking stick swinging at his side.

Leave it to the boss, Davies thought. It was half past seven in the morning and Volcker was impeccably dressed in a gray houndstooth jacket and matching cap. He looked fit for a leisurely stroll on the promenade, not a day of work at the police station.

"It looks like the grand jury will return a murder charge in the Barrett inquiry," Volcker said.

"Really, sir?" Davies looked up.

They had spent several weeks diligently building the case. Barrett was a blacksmith with a prosperous business on Spring Garden. He had been found in his workshop, bludgeoned to death. Davies would never forget that gruesome crime scene. The victim's skull had been reduced to a bloody mass from the force of the beating, a macerated pulp of skin and hair and bone. The force of the blows had sent gelatinous brain matter and bright red blood spattering onto the walls and the rafters. The close quarters and stifling heat of the late August day had attracted flies and other vermin immediately. Barrett's wife had confirmed that he indeed had three gold teeth, else they would have had difficulty identifying the body. The coroner's report, "death by compression of the brain from blunt trauma by person or persons unknown," hardly seemed necessary.

It appeared to be a straightforward case of robbery and assault, albeit a brutal one. The safe had been open and empty of the week's wages.

The adage to never speak ill of the dead had not applied in this case, Davies thought. The victim had been universally despised and witness after witness testified to the fact that he had been a liar and a scoundrel who regularly cheated them of money. He was ruthless in his business practices. There was no dearth of suspects. But the chief inspector had encouraged them to drop the case after fruitless hours of interviewing turned up no solid lead. It was like so many of the violent and senseless deaths they investigated, too difficult to obtain a conviction.

Yet Volcker had refused to give up. The savagery of the beating was too much, he said, too personal. He and Davies had redoubled their efforts, questioning each witness again. They had scoured Barrett's bank records. It turned out the distraught widow had been withdrawing large sums from the account and transferring the money to a bank in Chicago. She also quickly cashed in the claim on Barrett's substantial life insurance policy. When brought in for questioning, she confessed that she and her lover had planned the murder. He was a former employee of Barrett's and had relished carrying out the brutal beating.

"Yes, it is a win. The district attorney has more questions for us. Finish up the report and we will pay him a visit this morning."

"Yes, sir."

Davies liked Volcker. They had worked together for five years. He knew his boss to be an honest officer who had come from modest circumstances like his own. But the inspector was regarded with suspicion by others. He was different from the usual breed of policemen, set apart from the clubby fraternity by his fastidious dress and old-fashioned manners. Davies's friends in the force who were promoted marveled at his loyalty. "Surely you want to get ahead, Charlie? Leave the old boy behind." But he wouldn't. Volcker was not beholden to the cronyism that was rampant in the department, the yes-men who did the bidding of the political bosses and City Hall. What Volcker lacked in brilliance he made up for in sheer persistence. They had solved many crimes like this, by following through on every imaginable lead until Volcker was satisfied.

Davies sat at his desk writing up the report. But the morning's peace had been ruined by the arrival of "an old codger who won't let up," as the desk officer explained. "A naval captain, sir. He says he has something important to report. He demands to see you and he won't take no for an answer."

When Davies came into the anteroom, he could see at once that Henry Logan was no crank, only slightly winded from the sharp pace at which he had made his way to the station.

"Slow down, sir, allow me to get your name and address," the desk officer was saying.

"Slow down!" Logan shouted. "How can I slow down when there is a woman's body lying out there exposed!" He eyed Davies coming around the front of the desk. "At last, someone in authority."

Davies put up his hand in supplication. "Please, sir. You must understand we need to follow procedure. If you could tell me what you saw."

"It is a young girl, dead in the river. I found her body, just off a bank of the Schuylkill, in Wissahickon Creek. I pulled her out of the water, not half an hour ago. She has drowned." Captain Logan's words were rapid-fire.

Volcker had joined them.

"We can't waste any more time!" Logan said angrily. "You must come at once."

"Right. No rest for the weary then," Volcker said. "Please take us there."

3

⌐⌐⌐⌐⌐⌐

"Well, if it isn't Dr. Harlan Stanley. How goes teaching young ladies the art of chopping up dead bodies?"

The voice was booming and unwelcome, and several people in the Academy of Music's crowded lobby turned to see the source.

It was a Tuesday evening and the glow of oil light cast the room in a gauzy dreamscape. Society ladies chatted discreetly, their silks rustling as they edged against the carpet. The gentlemen were clad in evening dress, with the occasional gleam of gold from pocket watches or a bejeweled tiepin. Inside the main theater a gilded proscenium of Mozart flanked by the muses of Poetry and Music adorned the top of the stage; on either side tiered boxes rose and met in a semicircle around the theater. The hall had opened in 1857, the interior of the building modeled on the Teatro La Scala in Milan. It had been designed in Philadelphia by the architectural firm of Napoleon Lebrun, in homage to European sensibilities. Since then, it had hosted lectures and public meetings, even the Republican National Convention. But the space was never as beautiful as on a night like this, filled with music. Tonight a rich program of Beethoven and Brahms was on offer.

Dr. Joseph Bledsoe slapped a meaty hand on Harlan's arm and squeezed it hard.

"How are you, old friend? I presume Woman's Med is treating you well?"

"Quite well," Harlan replied. "I am as busy as ever. And you?"

"One cannot complain. At the University of Pennsylvania, we are privy to only the finest students and teaching facilities."

"Have you met my friend, Dr. Lydia Weston?" Harlan asked.

Bledsoe said nothing. He gave Lydia the briefest of glances, a look of utter contempt.

"I have not." He nodded to her.

Joseph Bledsoe was one of the most vociferous critics of Woman's Medical College. He wrote frequently on the supposed incompetence of women physicians, expressing his view that the weaker sex lacked the temperament to withstand the rigors of medical training, prone as they were to fits of hysteria. Lydia knew him by reputation, a prominent surgeon with a practice that catered to the wealthy. He and Harlan had been classmates at Jefferson Medical College thirty years before, but the similarity ended there.

He pushed his face up closer to Harlan's, a sharp smell of whiskey on his breath.

"After all these years, I still marvel at the career you squandered," he said.

Lydia wondered what Harlan thought. The insult seemed to barely pierce his consciousness.

"We must follow our path as best we can. Please give my regards to Marianne and the children."

"And please do the same for Anthea." There was nothing more to say. Bledsoe retreated into the crowd.

Harlan turned towards Lydia. "I think we have earned ourselves another drink."

The doors to Broad Street were open and the cool night air wafted in, giving relief from the dense cigar smoke. Lydia could hear the pleasing sound of glasses clinking at the bar, amidst the rise and fall of conversation.

Harlan stood just over six feet tall. His jet-black hair was streaked with gray and his broadcloth suit looked as freshly laundered as it had been when he donned it in the morning. His imposing presence belied his kind demeanor. He was professor of surgery and anatomy, one of Woman's Med most senior faculty members. He was also an avid concertgoer, and after a long day in the operating theater he often sought refuge in music. Lydia stood with him at the bar as he poured a glass of claret from the decanter. His movements were deliberate, the glass filling slowly with the dark liquid.

"Lydia cares for you far more than I do," Anthea Stanley said good-naturedly as she joined them. "I couldn't stomach a moment's conversation with that boor."

Like her husband, Anthea was an accomplished physician and professor at the college. She was petite but of generous proportions, kitted out in emerald green silk. Anthea believed that an impeccable sense of style was required armor to face any situation life might present. Her broad face was flushed, and a tendril of hair escaped from her neat bun. She watched as Lydia took a sip of wine.

"You are pensive this evening," she said.

"Forgive me. I am tired," Lydia said.

"You may hide from others but not from me. What is troubling you?" Anthea said.

Lydia put her glass down on a table.

"Yes. I didn't come tonight for the music. I hoped to find you here to discuss a patient."

Lydia told them of Anna's missed appointment and the strange meeting that had occurred almost a fortnight before.

"With these young girls, it could be any number of things: money worries, an unsuitable courtship . . . They have no means of dealing with any of it, so it all manifests as aches and pains and mysterious fevers. I think you are wise to give it time. She will appear again as though nothing happened," Anthea said.

Anthea was right. The life of a young servant was tenuous at best. There was little security and circumstances could change in an instant, with employment abruptly terminated due to a family's finances, or an illness or death.

"But if you are worried, perhaps inquiries could be made with her employer or her family," Anthea said.

"I would caution against that," Harlan interrupted. "Lydia's involvement may put the girl in an even more vulnerable position."

Anthea blew out her cheeks in exasperation. "If the girl is in trouble, the only way to find out is to go to the place she lives and ask questions."

"Give it a bit more time. So many of these crises pass over," he replied.

"The longer she waits, the more likely the girl will get hurt or be lost for good," Anthea remarked.

They all knew from experience how many of these stories ended, young women desperate to escape a life of drudgery. Their naïve forays into the city often ended disastrously with illness or degradation.

"There is something in particular that bothers you," Anthea probed.

"She bears her responsibilities with grace. They don't seem a burden to her," Lydia said. "Her brother is bed bound. Their older sister stays with him day and night. From what I gather, her wages support the family. She would never abandon them."

"I have no doubt you have given Anna much," Harlan said gently. "But you cannot give in to worry. It will serve no one."

"Besides, you must focus on your teaching and clinical duties." Anthea was never one to mince words. "God only knows what this might turn out to be. It is hardly proper for you to be involved with seamy police business."

Lydia could not suppress the flash of anger.

"Come now, Anthea. I would say it is a bit late in the day to worry about appearing ladylike."

Lydia had been a physician for more than ten years and done all manner of grisly work without flinching, venturing into the tenements alone to assist at a difficult birth or to treat patients in the throes of a last painful illness. She had assisted in surgeries, her arms aching from the strain of holding retractors in place as the surgeon performed an amputation, warm blood soaking through the hem of her apron. She had done countless dissections on corpses procured from potter's fields, all in the name of medical education. Many in polite society would argue that her own activities bordered on criminal.

"Don't be cross with me, dear Lydia. You know I keep your best interest at heart," Anthea said. She took her friend's hand and squeezed it.

Lydia looked at them both, feeling the familiar sense of comfort in their presence. She had known them since her first days in Philadelphia, when she had been placed in Anthea's advisory group as a medical student. They had been her foundation at a time when she had been alone, uncertain about her ability. The Stanleys had given her the warmth of their friendship and now she had a daughter's familiarity with their home, having spent countless holidays with them. They were the closest thing to family that she had.

"I know," Lydia relented. "But something was troubling Anna deeply and I didn't pursue it. It would have been so easy for me to do so."

"I think this puzzle sounds like just the thing for our Inspector Volcker," Harlan said.

Harlan also did consulting work for the police, performing autopsies in cases of suspicious death. Through work on investigations, he had developed a relationship with a police inspector, Thomas Volcker. Lydia knew he considered Volcker a friend.

"He could send a constable round to the employer's house. It would be better than going there on your own. I will speak to him myself," Harlan said.

4

A bleak sun pierced the fog. The walking path veered up at this point in the river. A simple fence served as a border between the path and the steep hillside covered with dense foliage and loose rocks. Captain Logan told them he often walked from the boathouses after morning exercises with his rowing club. He had found the body in the water, butting up against the rocks. He led them straight to the riverbank where he had pulled the body up.

The day had turned colder with a punishing wind whistling through the trees, whipping up off the water.

"Sir, there is no one in the immediate vicinity." The uniformed officer stopped short as he came to the huddled mass of the body. He blanched as he saw the victim's face.

"Very well." Davies's voice was stern. "Make sure that you let no one through on the footpath."

Davies knelt and reached out to finger the wool fabric of the dress. His ruddy cheeks were flushed with the cold. The wind seemed to stop short when faced with the commanding bulk of his frame.

Whoever she was, she had been young. He could see how lucky they were that Logan had been first on the scene. There were no additional footprints visible, only the broad swath of dirt where the wet skirts of the corpse had been dragged out of the water.

Volcker examined the body from all angles. The skin on her face was grotesquely bloated, with a waxy sheen. It was a leering monster staring back at them, the eyes and mouth edematous slits, dark tendrils of hair clinging to the face like tentacles.

The edges of the dress were torn. Volcker lifted the hem of the skirt. It was sodden and dense.

"Tell me your thoughts, Sergeant," Volcker said. He crouched by the body, balancing on his heels. He looked like a huge bird that had come to perch, with his beaked nose and thin arms folded over his chest in a watchful pose.

"Well, sir, from a preliminary search of the area, it appears to be a suicide. The clothes and the body are soaked through. The skin appears bloated, so she must have been in the water for some time," Davies said.

Volcker nodded.

Davies continued. "The area upriver is secluded. It is unlikely she would have been noticed by any walkers on the path. The current is faster and the water much deeper. She could have drowned quickly if that was her intent and then the body floated downstream."

Volcker opened the small case he had brought from the station house. It contained a few tools useful for crime scene investigations. He removed a folded cloth and motioned to Davies to take hold of one corner. Together they snapped the cloth into a taut sheet. They set it down next to the body.

"I'll need your assistance here. Take hold of this side. On my count of three," Volcker said.

It was like lifting a great boulder, as the water had soaked through the thick fabric. They staggered from the unexpected weight as they positioned the body on the cloth.

It will be a devil of a time getting identification, Davies thought. It was difficult to distinguish any facial features. Who knew how long the body had been in the water? But the hands, the skin smooth and taut, indicated the youth of the victim.

"What do you make of the marks on the face, Sergeant?" Volcker pointed.

Davies could see faint, serpiginous tracks on the cheeks and forehead.

"It is likely done from rocks and branches in the river, as the body came downstream, getting caught along the way," he said.

"Possibly. What makes you so sure it is suicide?" Volcker said.

Volcker's probing always made Davies feel uncertain. He shifted his feet from one side to the other.

Davies looked up. "Could she have been harmed before going into the river?"

"It's too early to say. The body needs to be examined more closely."

Davies sighed. It had been appropriate to investigate Logan's inquiry as the first officers at the scene. This part of Wissahickon lay in their jurisdiction, part of the city ward encompassed by their station house. But if the girl had died in the water, it would be the responsibility of the river police. Surely this was simple enough: a drowned girl, no doubt driven to the act by luckless circumstances. There would be nothing more to it. But he knew what would happen next: the body would be taken to the morgue and he and Volcker would scour the area for clues to the girl's possible violent death.

He watched Volcker circle the body and crouch again.

"Look at this, Davies," he said.

Volcker held up a pale hand for examination.

"If she had gone through the tumult of the river, her hands would be scratched. Compare this to her face, where there are multiple abrasions—how could this be?"

Davies's interest was pricked. He knelt to take a closer look; the fingernails were neatly cut, with no dirt beneath them. No sign of struggle or disruption. Volcker regarded him.

"A young lady comes to the river to end her life," Volcker said.

"She knows it will be unlikely to meet someone on the path," Davies continued. "If she goes in upriver, it will take time for the body to float down and be discovered."

"Exactly. The body would be more likely to get caught up in branches, rocks, all manner of debris that is churned up by the current."

"Thus the scratches on the face," Davies began.

"Precisely."

"So the drowning would be immediate. The body would submerge and then the damage to the face would occur as she traveled down, catching debris," Davies said.

"If that is how she died, then why do her hands remain untouched?" Volcker asked.

5

Lydia stepped off the omnibus a few blocks from the medical school. This was her usual practice; walking was a way to clear her mind before a long day of teaching. The neighborhood was so different from the narrow cobblestone lanes and leafy paths of the Old City, where she lived. There were offices of the railroad interspersed with neat brick row houses. At the corner of Ridge Avenue was a marble works and a lumberyard, the industrial flavor of Philadelphia on full display. She didn't mind the grittiness at all. Sometimes she would dodge workers as they spilled onto the footpath, balancing the roughhewn planks destined for the planing mill across the street, her boots crunching on the sawdust and wood shavings underfoot. She continued along the broad avenue of North College, passing along the stone wall that bordered the spacious grounds of Girard College, the charitable institution and school for orphaned boys.

But it was the building at the corner of Twenty-Second Street that sparked a fresh sense of pride each time she encountered it. It had an elegant redbrick façade and tall windows that fronted the street. It had opened this year, to house the classrooms and laboratories of Woman's Medical College of Pennsylvania. Just next door was Woman's Hospital and the clinics of the Dispensary, the city block now a seamless campus for the faculty and students to carry out their work. How far they had come since the college's inception in 1850, with six Quaker physicians as the founding faculty and a small group of students, in rented rooms at the back of a house on Arch Street. One of those former students, Dr. Ann Preston, had become dean of the college in 1866, and since then an unbroken line of women physicians had held the post. Here was the heart of the revolution.

Lydia climbed a few steps into the main lobby. She stamped her boots against the parquet floor to ward off the cold. She could see groups of students milling around. They were dressed in somber hues of black and gray, a uniform fit for serious work. But the beginning of term had the festive air of a family gathering, the palpable energy infectious. It was a time of reunion as students caught up with one another on work and travels. She nodded and smiled to several colleagues, chatting in small groups.

She had a few moments before the start of the lecture. She perused the large bulletin boards, where posters bore testament to a robust social life, advertising performances at the Walnut Street Theatre, pleasure boating on the Schuylkill, and excursions to see exhibitions at the Academy of Fine Arts and the Franklin Institute. She saw the printed announcement for the 1875–76 session.

The weekly schedule delineated lectures in the basic sciences like gross anatomy, chemistry, physiology, materia medica, and general therapeutics. The college had adopted the Progressive Course, a more rigorous three-year course of study, moving beyond the vagaries of the antiquated preceptor-apprenticeship system. It was a curriculum that stood on par with those of Philadelphia's most venerable medical schools, Jefferson Medical College and the University of Pennsylvania. Lydia noted the clinical schedule, the practical training that was the foundation for the medical degree, providing experience in the hospital wards, the operating theater, and the ambulatory clinics. She saw with satisfaction, along with the expected Woman's

Hospital assignments, a new name: Pennsylvania Hospital clinics. The bland notation conveyed nothing of that triumph, a culmination of years of struggle to secure teaching privileges at the storied public hospital.

Lydia's lecture notes were at the ready. She paused for a moment, her hand on the doorknob of the lecture hall. She could hear the excited chatter of many voices. She pushed the heavy glass-fronted door open and stepped inside. There was a generous space in the front of the room, the "pit," with an examination table and chairs as well as large chalkboards adorning the front walls. This room and its twin on the second floor were the crown jewels of the structure. Twice a week the clinical faculty in medicine and surgery presented cases in demonstration clinics. Patients were brought before the class, thorough histories and physicals were done, and the cases were discussed in detail.

She looked up at the rows of wooden seats, reaching to the top of the room. Today the hall was full. She recalled sitting on the edge of her seat as a student herself, craning forward to hear every word of lecture, her portable desk perched on her knees. Her kind heart had been pierced by the sight of the unfortunate patients, paraded in front of them in the name of education. At the time, she felt it was a terrible show. But to her professors, clinical diagnosis was paramount. They could recall how close in recent memory it had been possible to receive a medical degree without having touched or examined a patient. The students would obtain tickets to the lectures of favored professors, and Lydia was surprised to find herself in this group.

"Good morning, ladies." The noise settled down, papers rustling and pens at the ready. She looked out at the sea of faces, their attention on her.

"This morning we shall be discussing a case involving a thirty-year-old woman with progressive shortness of breath and leg swelling," she said. "Our patient is a young mother who first noted these symptoms after she gave birth to her fourth child."

The side door opened and the patient was ushered in. The students fell silent as they watched the young woman walk slowly across the stage, wheezing with exertion, each step laborious. She used a cane and paused to take in ragged breaths. Her pale hair was pulled back but heavily streaked with premature gray. She was small, but due to the fluid retention, she appeared grotesquely round. Her face and belly were swollen with two thick, woody legs protruding. Lydia watched the audience's faces, their rapt attention a mixture of pity and fascination. Nothing could compete with the sheer drama of the clinical cases; it was one thing to read an account of disease in textbooks, but there was no replacing the visceral experience of seeing, hearing, touching the patients. She had presented all manner of affliction: lupus, apoplexy, phthisis; men and women of all ages, but it was always the young ones that left the indelible mark.

Lydia stepped forward to take the patient's hand, careful to make eye contact. She spent hours revising her lectures and putting the patients at ease about what to expect. She had carefully prepped this patient and introduced her by name, Catherine Porter. Lydia elicited a social history, a few personal details of the life of this young woman, not much older than many of the students. They had to see that this was not a specimen on display, to understand the courage it took to expose oneself in all one's human frailty before a roomful of strangers. Mrs. Porter was dressed in a cotton singlet with a robe on top, and her voice was thin and reedy, barely audible.

The students leaned in to hear her.

"I got very sick after the new baby came, but that had happened before," she said. "There was the rest of the family to care for, so I thought I would just mind it until it got better.

"The fever went away but then I started getting spells. I was working at the factory again and I'd have to stop to catch my breath. The boss didn't like that.

"I was winded at night, too. I couldn't lie down without feeling the weight on my chest; even walking a few steps brought it on." She paused to catch her breath.

The hall had no windows. There were pockets of darkness between the pools of flickering light from the gas lamps.

"I had to stop work at the factory. My legs were so swollen I could hardly move. I was staying home all day, not even getting up to mind the children."

Lydia stepped forward to speak. She squeezed the patient's shoulder encouragingly.

"So when Mrs. Porter first came to the Dispensary as a patient, she presented with progressive shortness of breath and leg swelling. Knowing what you do of her history, what questions do you have?"

There was an uncomfortable silence. The students were not yet used to a dialogue. They expected to be lectured to, but Lydia preferred not to drone on at them. She wanted them to ask questions.

At last, a bold hand was raised in the back of the hall. "What kind of illness did you have after the baby was born?" It was a simple question.

"I had a terrible fever, like my eyes were going to burn out of my head. My hands and feet ached. Then the cough, so hard that bits of blood would come up on my handkerchief," Mrs. Porter said.

As the students warmed up to the format, the pertinent questions surfaced: how did the shortness of breath progress, was it associated with exertion, was she taking any other medications/tonics that might have affected the condition, how soon after the fever/cough resolved did the new symptoms start? Lydia guided them through a physical examination: noting the patient's legs swollen to the midcalf, brawny and edematous; the distended neck veins; the slow, labored breaths. She asked a few students to come to the front to listen with their stethoscopes, noting the extra heart sound and murmur.

Lydia returned to the lectern.

"Very well, how do we draw the threads together? Without a diagnosis, we cannot begin to treat the patient."

The students, emboldened by the question-and-answer period, posed possible diagnoses: myocarditis, cirrhosis, renal failure, dropsy. Lydia wrote the possibilities on the blackboard, impressed with the students' initial efforts.

She had coached Mrs. Porter on what would happen during the clinic, that this exercise was only to further educate the students, that no answers were to be unearthed for her today. It was always the most difficult moment for Lydia, not being able to offer anything more to help. Mrs. Porter had been given the only available treatment. She had been dosed with mercury regularly since her diagnosis, the diuretic effect of the compound helping with fluid retention. Now she had progressed to the dreaded symptoms of toxicity from the very medicine that was meant to help her: numbness and tingling in the feet, headaches, gait abnormalities. Mrs. Porter searched Lydia's face as if to say, If there is nothing to help me, then what was this show for? The flicker of hope deadened into a slack stare, a defeated acceptance. No matter how Lydia prepared the patients, the reaction was always the same. It would not be long before the young woman succumbed to heart failure.

She helped Mrs. Porter stand and guided her to the door. An attendant was waiting to put her in a hansom for home.

An image of Anna at their last meeting surfaced, unbidden. The girl had been so fearful.

"That is all for today," Lydia told the students. "Please review your notes carefully. I can guarantee this case will appear on the final exam in some form."

There were good-natured groans at the mention of exams. Lydia smiled and collected her notes.

The passage was teeming with students hurrying to their lunch break before afternoon clinics commenced. Usually she stopped to chat, but Lydia was troubled by too many thoughts, among them the dull anger in Mrs. Porter's eyes.

Lydia descended the wide staircase, running her fingers along the groove of the banister. She entered the main lobby on the first floor, leading to the warren of faculty offices. There she stopped short.

At the end of the hallway stood Anna, restored to the bloom of health. Lydia was so disoriented, she nearly gasped in shock.

"Anna!"

She breathed in, feeling incalculable relief, and rushed forward. But she was mistaken. It was not Anna at all.

"I am sorry, Doctor, I had to come see you," the woman spoke. "I did not know what else to do."

"It is no trouble, Miss—" Lydia stumbled.

"Ward. Sarah Ward. I am Anna's sister."

"Of course," Lydia said, poorly concealing her discomfort. "You look so much like her from a distance."

Sarah gave a small smile.

"Please come in." Lydia closed the office door behind her, ready to face the terrible news that she expected. Why else would Sarah be here?

At closer view, she could see the difference between the sisters: Sarah's high cheekbones and fair skin dotted with freckles, the light blue eyes.

"Forgive me for coming unannounced," Sarah said. The diffident words did not match the young woman's demeanor. She met Lydia's gaze with confidence.

"I could not wait. I have a friend watching John today, so I cannot stay long. I must be able to catch the afternoon train home."

"Where have you traveled from?" Lydia asked.

"We live near Havertown. We thought it best for John to live outside the city, for his health. Truth be told, we live in cramped rooms in the village. It is all we can afford. But at least I can take in piecework so I needn't leave him. We are close enough that Anna could come home to visit."

Sarah shrugged off her coat, revealing a calico dress radiant with tiny cornflowers. She settled into a chair.

"I know that Anna had been coming to see you in the clinic. I haven't seen her in two weeks. It is so unlike her. She visited us regularly."

As Lydia looked through the frosted glass door, she could see the silhouettes of students walking through the hallway.

"When I last saw Anna, she was very upset. But she was anxious to leave. She didn't want me to examine her further," Lydia said.

Lydia had been so busy with her work, her attention pulled in many directions by her teaching and clinical duties. She had not followed up with Harlan. Had he spoken to Inspector Volcker about Anna?

"Could she have taken time off to rest, perhaps stayed with a friend?" Lydia asked.

Sarah shook her head. "No matter what, she would have sent word to me."

"Was she behaving strangely when you last saw her?"

"No. She was home on a Sunday visit. We had our usual lunch together. We were able to go out for a bit with John in the wheelchair. He is too weak to walk now."

Sarah gave her a halfhearted smile. "She was the one who kept our spirits up."

"Do you know if Anna had any friends in the house?" Lydia asked.

"I know she was liked by the other girls. There were a few names she mentioned in passing," Sarah said.

"What about a young man?" Lydia asked.

"I don't know. You must think it odd, two sisters who are close as we are." Sarah hesitated.

Lydia watched her. The young woman looked down at her lap, her fingers twisting a pleat of her dress.

"Perhaps there was someone." Sarah looked up at Lydia, her face clouded with worry. "But I am not sure."

"What makes you say that?"

"At the last few visits, she seemed more eager to get back. Usually she would linger with us until the last moment. Perhaps she was going to meet someone."

Anna may have wanted to keep it secret, Lydia thought, knowing the news might be upsetting to Sarah. How would a suitor fit into the tenuous balance of their lives?

"Have you tried going to her employer's home to inquire?" Lydia asked.

Sarah shook her head.

Lydia understood: a young woman walking up to the servants' entrance of a grand house asking after the whereabouts of a chambermaid would be dismissed.

"That is why I came. I know it is much to ask, but could you go?" Her voice was rising, the composure cracking. "I am terribly worried about her."

Lydia had no authority to present herself to Anna's employer. But surely it was reasonable to inquire after her welfare, especially since it was clear the girl had been missing for over two weeks?

"She considered you a friend. Please. I have no one else to turn to."

Lydia hesitated. She had no idea what lay behind Anna's disappearance. She knew only the cursory details of her life, what Anna had chosen to reveal to her. But there was a sense of urgency now. Sarah had only confirmed what she herself worried about. And hadn't Lydia told Anna she would do anything to help her, that she only needed to send a message and she would come?

"Give me the address, Sarah. I will do what I can."

6

Volcker and Davies awaited the men from the police surgeon's office. They combed the immediate area around the body for almost three hours before Volcker expanded the search outwards. The hillside veered steeply to the water's edge, covered with rocks and the occasional large boulder. The weather had been cold for the past few weeks, but with no snow or rain, the ground was hard packed, with little mud. They found few signs of abnormal markings or footprints. Volcker was hopeful that the girl had left something behind on the bank, a clue to her identity. The river path north of here was a maze of unmarked trails and overgrown foliage.

Volcker sent Davies upriver to search. The sergeant did not mind as he knew this part of the river well. When he was a child, his mother would often ask him to take his younger siblings on an excursion. He had leapt at the chance to escape to the quiet, as the tenement house in which they lived teemed with screaming children and blaring noise from the neighbors' quarrels. His little brothers and sisters would run up the broad path, squealing with delight as he chased them. He was the ogre coming to capture the ladies and knights of the castle, all of them flushed with excitement. It was an urban forest, made even more mysterious by the ruins of the old mills that dotted this edge of the creek. There were covered bridges and dilapidated walls, hidden stone doors leading nowhere, the remnants of estates from Revolutionary War days layered upon one another.

The woods were quiet. It was early afternoon now. Davies took in a deep breath, redolent of moss and damp. From this vantage point on the path, one could look down at the quiet creek as it snaked through the trees, at times hidden by pockets of foliage. He tried to imagine the young girl walking this same path in the last moments of her life.

They found it after a half day of searching. About one mile up the river from the discovery site, the current became much swifter. The distance across was almost a quarter mile, and the black water looked menacing. Davies had abandoned the path entirely and clambered over the rocks, hugging the river's edge. They almost missed the inlet. It was not obvious, obscured as it was by dense brush. Davies pushed through the undergrowth, and suddenly they were standing in a clearing. He turned to the others, giving a triumphant shout.

Volcker joined him, seeming to materialize from the air, almost crowing with excitement. "Aha!"

They had stepped into a hushed chapel in the woods, the trees forming an arch over their heads. They stood shoulder to shoulder in the space, the only sound the lapping of water at the edge of the pool. On the bank, resting on a flat boulder, a folded coat awaited the return of its owner. At the foot of the rock, a pair of leather boots with buttons sat at attention; to one side was a black bag. It looked as though someone had alighted here for a swim and was expected back at any moment. Volcker paced the perimeter, peering into gaps in the foliage. Davies bent down to inspect the clothes.

"Sir, the material of the coat looks very similar to the cloth of the dress."

Volcker crouched down to look. He unfurled the coat to its full length, examining the lining and feeling the pockets.

"No tag from a dressmaker's shop. It is plain, but good quality."

Davies watched as his boss did the same with boots. They looked like they belonged to a child, Davies thought with a pang of sadness. Volcker picked one of the boots up, placing his large hand into the toe. He removed the laces, feeling the stiffness of the leather. He put it aside.

"Here is where we shall find our treasure." Volcker reached for the small velvet bag. By now the two of them were sitting cross-legged on the floor of the clearing.

"A young girl comes here to take her own life. She wants to do it quickly, anonymously. As you say, Sergeant, it is too neat, like a stage set in the theater. The clothes are prominently displayed, not lumped together behind a shrub."

"She wanted it to be found," Davies said.

"Exactly—or someone else wanted it found," Volcker said.

He placed the bag in the circle in front of them and opened it; inside they could glimpse a slim book and a cosmetic case.

"This should keep us busy for some time. Collect these items carefully and let's meet back at the station house."

7

L ydia sat at the circular oak table and reviewed her notes. It was the first meeting of the faculty thesis committee. As a graduation requirement for the degree of Doctor of Medicine, each student was to "write a thesis of her own composition and penmanship on some subject which has direct application to medicine"; with that sentence, vague in its scope, the floodgates to creative inquiry opened.

The meetings would occasionally take an adversarial turn as each faculty adviser defended their own subject. As they took their places, they were ready for a good-natured sparring match: the surgeons versus the physicians and the laboratory scientists versus the clinicians. Anthea and Harlan sat across from Lydia with Victoria Bailey, physiology, at the end of the table. Today there was a new face in their midst, Dr. Richard Harper. Anthea said he was "on loan" from Pennsylvania Hospital, filling in for one of the medicine faculty on leave. One of their colleagues had recommended him, an old classmate from Harvard. He nodded in greeting with an imperious tilt of the head.

"Welcome, Dr. Harper. As you see before you, we have several rough drafts. The senior students have until the end of the term to finish, but we do appreciate the early birds, so to speak. I have also included examples from prior years as a comparison."

Anthea perused the list. "A good mix of surgery and medicine, basic science topics, along with our proselytizers. Where would we be without them?"

She was referring to the few proposed thesis topics each year that seemed less about medical science and more platforms to instruct. Some past notable examples included "Alcohol: Gateway to Immorality" and "Venereal Disease and Its Destruction of Society." The students were gently steered back to the more scientific aspects of their subjects.

"Here we are, our preliminary group of drafts: 'Granulomatous Diseases of the Lung,' 'Syphilis,' 'Sequelae of Rheumatic Heart Disease,' 'Mercury and Its Toxicity,' 'Appendicitis,' 'Surgical Excision of Ovarian Tumors,' and finally, "The Physician's Duty as Educator.'" Anthea read off the list of titles.

Dr. Harper snorted.

"Is something amusing?" Anthea asked. She peered at him over the top of her reading glasses.

"I would hardly call that last one an example of intellectual rigor. I presume we are not teaching Sunday school but rather educating physicians?"

"Oh dear . . . a serpent in our midst," Victoria Bailey whispered in Lydia's ear.

"I beg your pardon, sir. The range is broad to be sure, but it allows the students choice," Anthea said.

"A pity. Some of the topics are a bit flimsy, wouldn't you say?"

He picked up a thesis on top of the pile from a past year and waved it over his head. It was entitled "The Role of Public Health and Hygiene."

"With my own students, I demand a certain academic standard," he said. "They do not expect to be coddled or study soft subjects."

The room fell silent at the audacity of the speaker, who was behaving like a dinner guest roundly insulting his hosts.

Lydia stared at him. How dare he, she thought. How dare he belittle the work done here. He looked so pleased with himself. His red hair was combed and parted, the looping mustaches groomed to perfection, like the thick fur of a fox. He looked around the table at them, a supercilious curl of a smile on his lips.

She had faced so many men like Harper, those who doubted her intelligence at every turn. Usually she would shrug it off, persuading herself that focusing on insults would detract from the work. But not today. She thought of her students and the devastating hardships so many of them had overcome. She thought of her early days in Philadelphia, filled with self-doubt as to whether she would finish her degree. Even now, after more than ten years of practice, there was the need to prove herself over and over again. There was no denying the personal toll extracted by all the years of struggle. A man like Harper would understand nothing of that. She could feel cold anger rising. No more politeness and reserve today. Lydia, the junior member of the faculty, who rarely spoke, did so now.

"It would do you good to read some of these theses first. Your prejudice prevents you from being objective. It is an unfortunate trait for a scientist."

Harper blushed, ugly red blotches traveling up his neck.

"With what do you take issue? Do you disagree that it is a physician's duty to educate the public?" Lydia asked. "Think of Ignasz Semmelweis and puerperal fever. Joseph Lister and antisepsis for the surgical patient. Their work will change the course of public health. How can that not be relevant?"

"I do not take issue with that, er . . . " Harper paused, clearly not knowing her name.

"Dr. Weston," said Lydia, emphasizing the honorific.

"I merely suggest that the topic choice illustrates the concerns that we in the medical community have against colleges such as this one. There is little depth of thinking."

Then why was the bloody fool here? Lydia thought furiously. To report to the medical society on their inadequacy?

"Our students have proved their skill time and again," she said tersely.

"Now, Dr. Weston." Harper gave them an oily smile. "You misunderstand me. My comment was intended for debate. But you have laid bare another criticism. There is no need to become overly emotional at mere discussion. It is moments like this that prove women don't have the even temper to handle life-and-death crises."

"That is foolish of you, Dr. Harper. It reflects poorly for a man of science to make assumptions without evidence. I imagine you would be taught that in medical school, no?"

Harper looked around the table for support, but the others sat in stone-faced silence.

"Are you quite through now, Dr. Harper?" Anthea was seething. "If we are making rash judgments about women, then allow me to add another: we know how to get the job done. Shall we?"

They settled to work discussing the thesis drafts. The time passed quickly, even more so after Harper excused himself for a prior engagement.

"It is a good start," Anthea said. "Let us adjourn for now. What a horror was unleashed on us. But not to worry, I shall take care of Dr. Harper myself."

They left the room in a cluster.

Lydia leaned against the wall, taking a deep breath. She waited until the others had passed and motioned to Harlan.

"Well done, Lydia. I think Harper would do well to hear more people speak the truth," he said.

"Thank you. No doubt Anthea will finish him off as only she can do," she replied. "But I must speak to you about a visit I had this morning."

She told him of her meeting with Sarah Ward and the disturbing news that Anna had not been seen by her family for a fortnight.

Harlan looked worried. "I spoke to Volcker, but he has not sent me any news. We can go see him in the morning after the anatomy lab."

Lydia nodded.

"Would you like to come dine with us tonight? Anthea and I would love to have your company," he said.

Lydia sensed his concern, but she declined the invitation. She felt an unusual weariness, drained from the meeting but more unsettled about Anna's disappearance. She needed an evening's respite at home.

SHE LEFT THE COLLEGE BUILDING as the afternoon was drawing to a close. The street was full of people, factory workers and clerks, mechanics and students mingling together. She hailed a hansom at the corner of Ridge Avenue to take her home. She sat down, the perch giving her a prime vantage point for the theater on display as the city moved past her. The hansom joined the throng of carriages and omnibuses, livery vans carting goods, jostling for position down the avenue. The smell of woodsmoke was in the air. The tall gas lamps were being lit, like a graceful necklace of lights being strung together.

Lydia had arrived in Philadelphia as a medical student, fresh from the confines of home and the women's seminary, her worldview colored by those sheltered experiences. The vigor of the city had loosened her natural reticence, and she thrived on her newfound independence. It was a place still forging its identity in the years after the war, the boldness of an industrial city tempered by its decorous Quaker influence. Commerce thrived; every imaginable manufacturing concern was here in some form, the products ready to be shipped to the rest of the country by the juggernaut of railroads that fanned out like spikes. The city was burgeoning with people but retained its small-town flavor, the ubiquitous row houses interspersed among the factories and shops.

The layout of the city hewed closely to William Penn's original vision, stretching between the Delaware and Schuylkill rivers and divided by the vast expanse of Broad Street, the numbered streets running from north to south and the gracefully named streets like Spruce, Pine, and Chestnut going east to west. The hansom passed down Broad and into the center of the city. Lydia looked up at the ornate public buildings under construction that would eventually house City Hall and other municipal offices. The edifice surrounded an interior courtyard with tower entrances on four fronts, allowing carriage and pedestrian thoroughfare. Everywhere there was expansion, a buoyant sense of optimism as the city prepared to host the Centennial Exposition, the World's Fair, in Fairmount Park next year.

She called to the driver to turn onto Chestnut Street, her favorite. The Broadway of Philadelphia contained multitudes, revealing its own sophistication against the inevitable comparison to New York. Over the years she had discovered many pleasures: theaters and the music hall, the gracious hotels Girard House and the Continental, the grand emporiums that were purveyors of every imaginable need and luxury, the stately mansions to be admired from afar.

But Lydia would always see the city intertwined with her own journey, through the lens of medicine. Few places in the country could offer the depth and breadth of institutions related to Philadelphia's distinguished medical schools. She marveled at the robust scientific community that had developed in tandem: the publishers of medical textbooks, the makers of surgical tools and implements, the specialty hospitals for orthopedics and ophthalmology. It was the world she moved in, the life that had given her a purpose.

The driver stopped near Washington Square and she paid the fare. She followed the familiar lanes towards home, fatigue settling in. She walked up the three flights of stairs to her flat. It was an aerie perched atop an old mansion. At the door she removed her coat and shoes and cast an appreciative glance around her sanctuary. The drawing room was reminiscent of a ship's stateroom, lined floor to ceiling with bookshelves. Lydia had laid down the ancient dhurries that had graced the floors of Father's study; even after all these years, the gold and blue threads woven into the rugs cast warmth. The walls were adorned with framed prints: sketches of the woods near her childhood home and the faded watercolors of the Darjeeling tea estate where Mother had grown up.

The windows in this room overlooked the trees in the square across the street. The late afternoon light was giving way to dusk. But instead of the treetops in the park square, Lydia saw the light playing shadows on the recesses of her childhood garden where the forest edged the field. She could feel a familiar sadness enveloping her like a cloak. The images would come unbidden, portals into her life of the past. She could hear Father's voice—"At last, time to put your lessons away!"—and see herself lying on the worn rugs before the roaring fire. At the word from Father, she would leap up with excitement. Lydia delighted in their excursions, preparing since morning in the hope that she would get to go, gathering a satchel of food. The mist of twilight lay atop the garden path. Lydia looked over at Father, his eyes closed and hat off, taking in the night air like a restorative drink.

One of Father's favorite exercises was the search for patterns: pebbles in a brook or striations in a pane of glass. "It is all waiting to be seen," he would say, "the mosaic reveals itself." He encouraged his children to write in their journals, putting down their thoughts. His favored advice was "Train your mind to think methodically. Even though it may yearn to pull away, then it will not deceive you."

On these special evenings, Mother would wrap Lydia up in a shawl, grumbling, "Utter mischief, this—all for looking at a few stars." But she smiled indulgently. Father led the way down the path, their figures silhouetted against inky trees. Lydia would follow the bobbing lantern through the woods. They listened to the soft coos of owls in the trees and the rustle of small animals in the short grass, momentarily silenced as they walked nearby. When they reached the forest clearing, Father would lay out the thick blanket, and the two of them would lie side by side in silence, their eyes adjusting to the deepening night. The jeweled stars emerged slowly, revealing their glory one by one until the sky was awash with pinpoint dots. She could feel it even now: the dampness of the grass below the blanket, the comforting bulk of Father's shoulder at her side, the night closing in around them.

Now, outside her windows, darkness encroached, but inside all was light: a fire burned in the hearth and the teakettle hummed in the background. She closed her eyes and listened to the fire crackling. But she couldn't settle her thoughts. Her neck ached with strain. Rest would not come now.

Lydia went to her desk. It was a draftsman's table, the wood procured from the Maine woods. The large surface gave her space to spread all her papers and stack the overflowing books: botanical treatises, materia medica and anatomy texts, novels and poetry, tattered English translations of the Gita and Ramayana. She took up a pile of case histories to mark. Her clinic students met once a week during the term to see patients; these were the written records of that study: a history of present illness, physical examination, social history, details about habit or dress, anything that may be relevant to the patients' treatment. Lydia was ruthless about the importance of keeping meticulous records, telling her students, "Someday, you will be caring for a patient alone, perhaps in the middle of the night, in a log cabin on a windswept prairie. Who will you have to rely on? Only yourself!" Her students would smile at the dramatic example, but they did what she asked.

She reached for her own journal and turned to the creased pages on Anna Ward. The introductory page of Anna's history, where she listed general details about the patient, was as bland as ever.

- Anna Ward, age 20
- Family history: father dead at age 55 respiratory failure, questionable tuberculosis; mother died of cancer of the breast, age 50
- Sister age 24 living, brother age 10 neuromuscular disease
- She has no prior serious illnesses known
- History of measles in childhood, radius fracture at age 15, ovarian cyst, iron deficiency anemia
- Unmarried
- Employed as chambermaid
- Began menses at age 14, irregular pattern worsening for last year

Lydia despised what she considered an irrelevant part of the history, but she included it as part of convention. She noted her thorough physical exam, her usual practice for the first meeting with a patient. She read her notes:

A appears well, normal gait and pleasant bearing, no pallor noted, sclera anicteric, neck supple, no thyroid hypertrophy. Her heart rate is normal with no murmurs/rubs/gallops noted on auscultation, lungs clear; abdomen is soft, no hepatomegaly; musculature normal in tone and development.

Anna had returned two months later for a visit at the Spruce Street Clinic.

20th April 1874: Anna was in good health until the last 2 years since employment commenced, now with periods of overwhelming fatigue, easy bruising/bleeding, feels short of breath with minimal exertion, no shortness of breath at rest. No signs of overt bleeding.

Lydia read on: "Nutrition consists of one regular evening meal per day, mostly starch, eats only intermittently during the day, little water consumption. She is unable to take regular exercise but has long periods of physical work."

Lydia could alter the details slightly and this description would fit any number of patients. She had suspected anemia. On exam she had noted pale conjunctiva, elevated pulse and respiratory rates. She had done a urinalysis and blood count, which revealed iron deficiency. Simple enough, she thought. She prescribed a supplement and advised better nutrition, which seemed to alleviate the problem.

On another visit, a few months later, she had noted: "Intermittent abdominal pain, primarily in the epigastrium, worse after meals, has tried ipecac to no avail, no change in bowel pattern or weight loss." The exam had been equivocal, and the complaint had resolved on its own. And yet another, "A is plagued by persistent headaches, brought on by overwork; no seizures or loss of consciousness, no visual changes, wakes with the headache, usually present through the day." She had spent much time with Anna advising on sleep, exercise, fresh air, occasional dosing with mercury to alleviate pain. How useless it all seemed, she thought. Her advice seemed both preposterous and patronizing.

Lydia continued reading. She turned up the oil lamp on the desk as the embers of the fire burned low.

A pattern revealed itself.

The visits were based on psychosomatic complaints: headaches, myalgias, abdominal pain. Each time the symptoms resolved with little treatment, never progressing to the need for more intense intervention or hospitalization. Anna had been coming to see her regularly almost every eight weeks; Lydia had not seen this before. How right was Father's dictum, the individual parts revealing the whole. It was not uncommon for many of her patients' homesickness or grief to manifest in vague aches and pains. Anna had been coming to her for comfort.

It was a year into the visits that the focus of Lydia's notes moved away from medical problems. She read an entry from late December last year, near Christmas:

19th December 1874: No reason for A's visit today, she can report no specific complaint. Upon further questioning, becomes tearful, emotionally labile, difficult to speak in full sentences. She describes her mother's death from breast cancer, almost seven years to the day.

Lydia put the book down. It was extraordinary how her notes could call to life a vivid memory. The December visit had been a bleak moment in the usually cheering days before the holidays. They had sat in her exam room watching the snow fall outside the windows.

"Do you want to tell me what happened?" Lydia asked.

"It was a terrible time, Doctor." Anna's eyes filled with tears. Her grief was still fresh.

"She was so ill, wasting away before us. But the worst was the pain." Anna had closed her eyes. "The agony she endured from that wound. The doctor said it couldn't close. There was nothing to do except to bear it."

Breast cancer was difficult to treat; many patients presented to their physicians too late to act. Even then, the treatment offered little hope. Lydia knew what Anna's mother had faced: excision of the tumor followed by searing chest wall pain and an open wound with purulent drainage, all only to endure months of agony before succumbing to the final infection. Many accomplished surgeons refused to do the surgeries for these reasons. It was not because of cruel neglect but to spare their patients this inevitable suffering before death.

Anna shuddered as the tears fell. It was a catharsis, as if years of anguish had been released within her.

"Mother did not want morphine. She said it would take her away

47

from us too soon. But how she suffered. I would sit by her side while she slept. She was so restless, always moving in her sleep."

"How old were you?"

"Twelve," Anna said.

She looked down at the soaked handkerchief, knotting the edges.

"Father was lost in grief. Sarah and I had to take charge. Sarah took in embroidery work. I helped with errands at a local shop and looked after the neighbor's children for some money."

"Had you and Sarah been in school?"

"Just in the village. Father thought we should learn to read and write but nothing more. But Mother insisted. She was determined for us to be educated."

Lydia could see a gleam of happiness appear on Anna's face, as if a light was piercing the dark memories.

"She would read to us constantly. She would save money to buy books for us to have at home. We learned the poems by heart and recited them as if it were a theater. Silly, wasn't it?"

"No. I don't think so at all."

"I suppose others thought we had airs. But she always encouraged us. She wanted Sarah to be a schoolteacher." Anna put her face in her hands, overcome again.

"I miss her terribly. She would have liked you so much, Doctor. You are just what she believed to be possible."

Lydia was touched by the quiet emotion in those words.

"But then Mother died and it was a struggle to survive. Father died soon after, of pneumonia. It made sense for me to go into service. I don't regret it. I did what I had to do. But I miss my learning."

Anna's struggle was in many ways her own, Lydia thought. It was an image of what her own family had endured after her father's death. They had been reduced to penury, a cruel blow after the idyll of her childhood. The house was taken by the bank. Lydia and her mother began living in rooms at a boardinghouse, their lives fractured. But in the depths of loss, a fierce tenacity had grown in Lydia. She had continued her schooling and earned a scholarship to a women's seminary.

"We have this in common, Anna," she said. "I lost my father at a young age as well. Our lives were changed. I lived in poverty for many years."

Anna looked up in disbelief.

"Your schooling might have ended, but your education can continue. Just as your dear mother said, so much is possible. I know it to be true."

Lydia pulled down several volumes from the bookshelves that lined her clinic office.

"My father was also a great believer in reading." She handed over Whitman's *Leaves of Grass*. "This was a favorite of ours. After Father died, I often felt closest to him when I read these books that he left me. It was like a part of him was with me still."

Lydia was surprised at herself. She rarely confided in anyone the grief of her father's death.

"There was so little I felt I could control after his death, but the books transported me. I could be in a place far outside myself." Lydia smiled as she watched Anna hold the book. "There are many more where that came from, I assure you."

Her clinic notes thereafter included short lists of titles as the book sharing continued. Lydia would add little addenda: "Enjoyed *Wuthering Heights* and *Jane Eyre*, not surprising, *Villette* and perhaps Mrs. Gaskell's *Cranford* next time?" Lydia would make notes of lectures, library hours, bookshops for Anna to try. It had been a strange schism: on the one hand, Lydia dispensing medical treatment to her patient and, on the other, a burgeoning understanding between them. Anna's reading over the year improved vastly, as she asked for more ambitious works; the last few entries had included *Middlemarch*, *The Small House at Allington*, *Great Expectations*.

Lydia's gaze drifted to the wall above the mantelpiece. She had hung three watercolors commissioned from a Concord artist there. This was memory's long view, the portrait of a special place. Her favorite was the center painting, a view of the pond through the dark woods that had been her swimming hole. She walked over to her bookshelf and touched the spine of *Leaves of Grass*. On the front page of the book was written: "To Miss Lydia Narayani Weston, on her birthday. Dismiss whatever insults your own soul." She smiled at her father's inscription, the ink faded after so many years. She had marked the page of one of her favorite passages.

I believe a leaf of grass is no less than the journey-work of the stars, . . .
And the tree-toad is a chef-d'oeuvre for the highest,
And the running blackberry would adorn the parlors of heaven,

Was there a better paean to nature's beauty than this? Lydia thought. She knelt at the hearth and stoked the dying embers of the fire. She thought of the pleasure she had taken in decorating this private space. The art and books were carefully chosen and paid for on her own. Her independence shielded her, but was the protective carapace hardening around her, setting her apart from her emotions? At the core was the need to protect herself from the disruption of her childhood. What had started as a promise to her mother had become the guiding force of her life.

There was little comfort in the memory, the long nights sitting with her mother in their cramped rooms as the candlelight died down. Lydia could still feel the exhaustion of those days, as she drifted without purpose, untethered from the familiarity of her past life. She had found work at a factory. Their need for money was dire and she was ready to succumb, ground down by the difficulty of survival. Lydia told her mother that she was going to give up her studies. In the near darkness, her mother's profile looked like a statue. She seemed barely capable of taking breath, as if the toll of grief had made her physically weak. But they argued terribly.

"This moment in your life will not determine all the others. You must not act out of fear." The vehemence behind her words was unmistakable.

Lydia knew so little of her mother's life as a young woman, of what hopes she'd had. In the naïveté of childhood, she had never asked that question. But it was in the depths of loss that her mother's confidence emerged. They had taken in bookkeeping work, ostensibly to be done by her brother. But it was Mother who proved herself to be the shrewd accountant; slowly, the money accrued and they were able to pay off their debtors.

Lydia closed the casebook. She placed it on top of her dissection kit. The small wooden case was filled with her tools. Her sheaf of notes was ready. Tomorrow she and Harlan would be teaching the first gross anatomy lab of the term to the new students. She vividly remembered that day in her own education, the mixture of apprehension and excitement she had felt. It had been a private moment of celebration fraught with meaning, as she thought of her mother's example of self-reliance, how the determination to transcend circumstances had given her the opportunity to study medicine. Had Anna felt the same in the aftermath of her mother's death, that strengthening of her resolve?

Lydia watched as the fire settled down, casting its flickering shadows on the wall. The oblivion of sleep finally took her.

8

L ydia could see the students nervously exchange glances. They were standing together in the smaller room off the main anatomy labora-tory, awaiting instruction. The space had the dank feel of a subterranean chamber, buffered by thick walls, the sharp tang of preservative in the air. There were four young women, their aprons covering the length of their dresses. One student visibly blanched and another placed her finger in the tight space between her neck and starched white collar as if to loosen it, to provide more air.

For most of the students, this was their first experience of seeing a dead body. But Lydia suspected it was not the sight of the cadaver laid out before them that was frightening. It was the eerie silence of being observed, by a macabre audience that sat in wordless judgment. Against the wall, on shelves that ran the length of the room, sat row after row of skulls, the dark hollows of their sightless eyes leering and watchful. It was a gruesome li-brary of memento mori: the skulls were of every imaginable shape and size. Some were smooth and untouched, others ravaged by disease, their sur-face riddled with porous depressions, parts of the bone eroded into jagged shards. Below the skulls, there were more bones, long separated from their owners: radius and ulna, tibia and fibula, the ball joint and shaft of the humerus and femur, clavicle and ribs. Each was neatly tagged and labeled, ready to be examined. Many were perforated with circular bullet holes and others sawed off midshaft in amputation. Time had mitigated the violence of death, giving many of the bones a smooth white sheen.

Anthea, ever the unofficial majordomo of the college, was mortified at the sight. "Surely we have enough detractors as it is, without you terrorizing the students further. Couldn't the specimens at least be stored in a cabinet, out of view?" she implored her husband.

But Harlan had resisted her entreaties. There is nothing to fear, he told the students. The body is your teacher. He had started collecting the bones during the war, in his work as a regimental surgeon. Lydia knew he followed the example of his own mentor, the pioneering surgeon Dr. Thomas Mütter at Jefferson Medical College, who had donated his vast collection of specimens to the College of Physicians for education. None of it was used to shock. Harlan's reverence for the bodies and what they could teach was paramount. Lydia heard occasional stories from other medical schools, the jocular attitude towards cadavers, staged humorously with a cigar in the mouth or a hat jauntily poised on the head, photographed with the students. Harlan would not tolerate that behavior from either students or faculty.

"Come closer to the table. You will see nothing standing so far away," Lydia said to the students. Her voice was not unkind.

Lydia had been teaching this class for many years, though its subject lay far outside her chosen specialty. Since her first days at Woman's Med, she had spent countless hours in the lab, and Harlan had noticed her skill early on, the steadiness of her hand and the calm state she inhabited when doing the work. He offered her a job as assistant, preparing the dissection models. It was the systematic approach that her orderly mind craved, dispelling ambiguity.

There was still great public distrust of the so-called body snatchers and resurrectionists using ruthless means to coerce grieving families, rumors of stealing corpses from cemeteries under cover of night. Worse still was the memory of "burking," the ghastly moniker attributed to William Burke and his accomplice, William Hare, the Edinburgh murderers who sold the corpses of their victims to an anatomist. There was little understanding of the scientific research that went into the study of cadavers, how vital it was to give medical students the proper training to treat patients and to operate on them.

But it was true that Philadelphia's abundance of medical schools had given rise to a scarcity of cadavers, with colleges vying for bodies. A shadowy trade had sprung up around this shortage. Wealthier neighborhoods installed guards to protect cemeteries, but poorer districts had no such option. Bodies were procured from the potter's fields of almshouses at Old Blockley or the mental asylum; some were obtained from prisons after executions and others came from the police: unknown corpses of those who had succumbed to disease or neglect, or victims of suicide. Often the cause of death was not known, but sometimes the body would reveal itself: blackened lungs wasted by emphysema and a lifetime of factory work; a bulbous, enlarged liver covered with diffuse nodules from cirrhosis; a necrotic tumor of the colon eroding the smooth lumen.

The cadaver was lying facedown on the table with the back exposed. The head was covered by a white cloth. The students opened their dissection kits, the metal instruments pristine. Lydia had them take out each tool: the rounded and pointed scalpels for cutting and incision, forceps to manipulate tissues, curved scissors, and the heavier cartilage knife. There were less obvious implements, like the hook and chain: three chains connected in the center by a circular loop; at the end of each chain was a sharp curved hook. It looked like an instrument of torture that could garrote a man. It was used to retract larger parts of the body during dissection.

Dissection began with the back as its structures were simpler and it built the foundation for technique. Harlan joined them. He watched as

Lydia palpated the bony landmarks: the wings and ridge of the scapulae, the prominent vertebral bodies starting at the occipital protuberance and proceeding down the spinous processes of the thoracic and lumbar vertebrae, protruding through the skin on this thin person.

Lydia made the first incision in the midline. She had the students try it, putting her hand over each of theirs to show how to apply the correct amount of pressure. The consistency of the skin was different from living tissue, with a slick and unnatural feel. She demonstrated how to make a small incision in the skin flap, to dissect into the plane and gently pull away, preserving the subcutaneous tissue and fascia underneath. It was like an excavation: soon they could see the superficial muscles of the back, the trapezius and latissimus dorsi, then the rhomboid major and minor connecting the scapula to the spinal column, serratus posterior, levator scapulae. All your tedious lessons in Greek and Latin will at last come to good use, she told them. They laughed at the tired joke, but she could see that they were relaxing into the work.

She showed them how the spinal accessory nerve ran along the border of the trapezius and where the thoracodorsal nerve and artery nestled into the deep muscle within the fat. The process was slow and laborious, requiring intense concentration to properly dissect, each layer building upon the next.

They worked steadily until the wooden door to the lab creaked open.

"Sir?" A student appeared on the threshold. "There is a policeman here. He says he must speak with you."

"Yes, of course." Harlan put his scalpel down and wiped his hands on a cloth. He instructed the students to continue with their work. Lydia looked up at him in question.

Harlan stepped out into the main room, what the students called the sky parlor.

Volcker stood in the center of the room, holding his hat in his hands. A younger man was at his side.

"Good morning, Thomas. Please come through," Harlan said.

Harlan Stanley had first met Volcker on a murder case involving a complicated gunshot wound. The inspector had scoured surgical field manuals to piece together the crime. His dogged pursuit had led him to Harlan's seminal work on battlefield wounds and to the man himself. Over the years, Harlan had worked on many more cases with the police, relishing the intellectual challenge. His relationship with Volcker could be tense when they disagreed, but it had respect at its core.

Volcker walked through the long room, past the numbered lockers where the students kept personal items. The walls were adorned with anatomical diagrams pinned up by the students.

They made introductions. Lydia had come to stand at Harlan's side, her features clouded with worry.

Sergeant Davies looked uncomfortable as he walked gingerly between the rows of tables. Several of the cadavers were lying exposed, wooden blocks propped underneath the torsos to properly angle the bodies for dissection. The decimated forms were faint echoes of their human selves. Davies kept his eyes on the ground.

Hanging above each table was an angular metal structure that jutted its arms out; it looked ready for a circus acrobat to take hold and start swinging through the air. The metal arms served as the tributaries of gas pipes and lamp sconces had been affixed to the outlets to provide light.

"It is the young woman you asked me about, the patient of Dr. Weston's." Volcker bowed to her slightly. "I sent a constable round to check on her a few days ago, to the address in Winfield Place. He was told she had gone away. No one knew if she was expected back to work."

"I know very well of whom you are speaking." Harlan drew in his breath sharply. He privately seethed at Volcker for laying bare this terrible surprise in front of Lydia.

"I needed to speak with you right away," Volcker said. "A woman's body was discovered in Wissahickon Creek yesterday. There is no other way to say this, except to show you."

"Are you sure it is her?" Lydia was ashen.

The detective removed a small diary from his pocket; written in black letters in the bottom right corner was the name: "ANNA WARD." An address was noted under it.

Lydia leaned forward, pressing her hands to her face.

"Identification based on a preliminary exam is difficult. The facial features of the corpse are distorted from water retention, but we found all of this," Volcker said.

He emptied the contents of a velvet bag onto the table, removing the folded clothing and shoes.

It was the ephemera of a life. On the table before them were linen handkerchiefs, gray with age; a fountain pen, a stack of blank note cards, a necklace, and a diary.

"What do you make of this?" Volcker held up the necklace, a small locket at the end of a thin gold chain.

Harlan took it out of his hand. He opened the clasp, revealing a two-sided locket with an indentation for a portrait to be placed.

"My sister had one of these given to her when she was married, one likeness of her and one of her husband," he said. This one was empty save for a few strands of light brown hair curled into the groove.

They turned to the clothing. The fabric of the dress was plain, with a thick tulle-covered petticoat sewn underneath. It had survived the water nearly intact. They spread the items against the black lacquer of the table.

How pathetic it all looked, Harlan thought. It reminded him of the soldiers' kits that they would discover on corpses from the battlefields, the precious mementos that were meaningless to others. The young woman had had no idea that these cherished items would be picked over by strangers.

"Suppose the girl was intent on suicide. She chooses a secluded space where she will not be interrupted. She takes off her coat and folds it and descends into the river. It is the personal items that are troubling. If she was so intent on killing herself in a hidden spot, why not just walk into the river and be done with it? Why were her belongings found so easily?" Volcker asked.

"Because her identity would be established. Yet you say there is no note," Harlan said.

"What if she was dead before she went into the water?" Volcker said.

"You mean she was murdered first and then a scene created to suggest suicide?" Harlan asked. "Perhaps. Drowning is notoriously difficult to prove as a cause of death. It is an easy camouflage for murderers to hide their work."

Volcker nodded. "The police surgeon did a cursory exam of the body and has determined death by drowning. He doesn't think there is enough evidence to warrant an autopsy, but I do. You told me that the girl appeared agitated at the clinic visit with Dr. Weston and then disappeared. Now, two weeks later, her body is found in the river. The circumstances are suspicious."

"Yes," Harlan said. "We will need to examine the body as soon as possible."

"I know her sister," Lydia spoke. "She was worried about Anna's disappearance. She will agree to us doing a postmortem. I am sure of it."

Volcker nodded and the policemen stood to leave. The students were gathering in the anteroom. They spoke quietly as they drifted back towards the worktables.

Harlan guided Lydia to the smaller chamber and shut the door behind them.

"It is too late. I waited too long to act. I told her sister I would check on her. I could have done more." Lydia's eyes filled with tears, her voice shaking.

Harlan felt culpable as well. He should have followed through with Volcker.

"You cannot blame yourself." But he knew she did, that she would excoriate herself.

Lydia shook her head. "If you knew this young woman, Harlan. Suicide . . . it is impossible."

"Volcker agrees with you."

"But how will he prove it is murder?"

"That is why he needs us," Harlan said.

He felt tired, suddenly aged. He had dismissed Lydia's concern as needless worry and now the young woman was dead. He rose and walked to the glass cabinet mounted on the wall. It was here he kept his surgical tools; in a drawer were the medals he had been awarded for valor on the battlefield, as a surgeon attached to the 81st Pennsylvania. He brought out the battered case that he had carried with him through the bloody years of war. On the pebbled leather there was a bullet hole like a gaping wound. The case now held his dissection and surgical tools, polished and ready for work. It was his reminder to honor the dead, those he had been unable to save, by taking care of the living.

The thrumming mass of destruction wrought by Fredericksburg was with him always but he never spoke of it. Death followed him and permeated his life, but it was the war that had been the crucible of his character. Harlan's renown had been built upon his skill on the battlefield, but his humility was singular. It touched him now. He felt sorrow at the loss of this young life, but more so the sense that he had failed Lydia.

She stared ahead, unseeing. "I will speak with Sarah. I owe her that much."

"There is no need to do that. Volcker and his men can take this on."

"No, I would prefer to be the one to tell her. And I would like to assist with the autopsy, Harlan."

This time he knew he could not dissuade her.

"That you will, Dr. Weston."

Part Two

HOUSE CALLS

9

Volcker and Davies stood on the front step. It was half past ten in the morning. Davies rapped on the door knocker with the edge of his club. A bitter wind from the river wended its way through the streets. Volcker's thin frame was swaddled in layers of wool, the mulberry-colored scarf a gift from a sister in Munich.

Davies leaned over the side of the railing. In the back courtyard, he could see a horse-drawn black van stopped on the flagstones, making morning deliveries.

"No matter," Volcker said. "We shall wait."

Davies looked up. The house was three stories high, the brick façade a burnished copper with shutters that adjoined the tall windows. None of the grime of the city seemed to penetrate this fortress.

"Knock again," Volcker said. Davies dutifully lifted his club to do so. At that moment, the double-sided door opened on one side.

"May I help you?" A voice heavy with disdain greeted them. A man showed himself through the aperture, his hand held firmly to the door.

"We are here to see the gentleman of the house," Volcker said.

"He is not expecting any visitors."

Volcker produced his card with a flourish.

"Certainly, we could remain here. I am sure the neighbors will be stirring soon. We could speak to them first if you prefer," Volcker said.

The man stood aside reluctantly.

"It would be preferable if you came through the rear door," he began.

"No, that is quite all right. We are not here on servants' business," Volcker said.

They stepped onto a marble floor, rivulets of gray streaked beneath their feet. It was only the entryway of the house, but a huge crystal chandelier was suspended from the ceiling, already ablaze at this hour of the morning. In the center of the room, a giant mahogany table sat with a floral centerpiece: roses, lilies, begonias flowing out of a porcelain urn.

"Please come through."

"Thank you, Mr.—" Volcker said.

"Healy."

They followed Mr. Healy down the hall, stepping onto a plush carpet. The depth of the rug concealed the sounds of their footsteps. They passed the dining room. Davies glimpsed a table perfectly laid out with silver and china, surrounded by twelve chairs and an unlit chandelier, a smaller version of the one in the foyer. Lush ferns draped out of standing planters around the room; the smell of furniture polish lingered in the air. And the quiet, Davies marveled. They might have been the only three people in the house.

"In the library, please," Mr. Healy said. He directed them into a large room that ran the width of the rear of the house.

"That will do. You may finish later," Mr. Healy said. A young girl knelt at the fireplace grate, sweeping ashes at the hearth. At his words, she scurried out of the room with her small shovel and pail.

Mr. Healy closed the door behind him as he left with no further instruction. Volcker sat on the sofa, folding his arms behind his head. His legs were outstretched, resting on the coffee table.

"Quite grand, eh?" Volcker winked at Davies. He was anticipating the pleasure of making himself disagreeable. Davies knew Volcker was capable of great sensitivity when questioning suspects. He had seen it time and again. But fair or not, the inspector had a deep suspicion of the wealthy and his contrarian nature reveled in the goading aspect of these interviews.

Above the mantel, a pair of wooden oars were affixed to the wall, as one would place a painting. Bookcases ran the length of two sides of the long room. The marble-topped end tables adjacent to the sofa were stacked with more books and also held statues and decorative boxes. Davies picked up a small ivory tiger. He could see the etched black stripes on the figurine's back, its tiny mouth open in a menacing snarl.

It was silent save for the chime of the grandfather clock they had passed in the hall. A desk dominated the opposite side of the room. It was covered with ledgers neatly stacked. The porcelain oil lamp was set low and two chairs faced the desk. This was a gentleman's study, the smell of pipe smoke lingering.

"Edward Samson Curtis, age forty-five, heir to an iron foundry fortune," Volcker said aloud. They had traced the name from the address in Anna's diary. Last evening, Davies had rushed to the office of records, scouring the city archives for title deeds to homes in the Old City, birth and marriage records.

Curtis had owned this house for fifteen years. The newspapers described his frequent society and charitable activities. In the older papers predating the war, there were large advertisements for the Curtis foundry, "incorporated and family-owned since 1830, purveyors of fine ironwork for home and industry."

The door opened. Volcker stood. Curtis entered, dressed in a gray suit with a silk cravat knotted at the neck. His face was narrow, an angular jaw clenched in disapproval. But his eyes were distinctive, a curious pale brown color. They gave a feline quality to his gaze, alighting on Davies before settling on Volcker.

"Mr. Healy informs me that you are from the police." He did not introduce himself.

"I am Inspector Volcker of the Philadelphia police, and this is Sergeant Davies," Volcker said. "We are here to inquire after the whereabouts of a maid in your employ, Miss Anna Ward. Her family says she has been missing for two weeks."

Curtis pushed out a short laugh.

"Is this what the police squander their time with these days, errant housemaids?"

"Could you please confirm whether you know the name and if the young woman is employed in this household?" Volcker said.

"I am afraid I can do neither, Inspector. I have little time to concern myself with the staff," Curtis said.

"Perhaps you should, sir. Her body was dredged out of the river yesterday," Volcker said.

At least the man appeared ashamed at this revelation, Davies thought. Curtis went to the fireplace and rested his elbow against the mantel. He was not tall and the encroaching heaviness of middle age was stretching the silk of his waistcoat.

"I beg your pardon." Curtis walked towards the desk, gesturing to them to take the seats opposite.

"We found a diary among her belongings; her name is written in it with this address. Her sister confirms that she was employed as a chambermaid," Davies said.

"There is suspicion as to the cause of death, whether or not she ended her life," Volcker said.

Curtis looked surprised. "What do you suspect happened to the girl?"

"Her body was found in the river. It is unclear how she died, but likely she drowned." Volcker was not about to reveal more than necessary.

"A suicide then?"

"As I said, it is not clear, sir."

"A watery grave. How dreadful."

"We would like to interview your staff members to learn more about Anna's final days in particular."

Curtis sighed. "I can't see how anyone here would be involved, but if you must."

"We will not trouble you for a moment longer than necessary."

Volcker opened the front of his coat and removed a sheaf of papers.

"Here you will find the legal documents that you require, the magistrate's approval for your review."

Curtis sat down and made a show of reading through the papers.

"It seems I have little choice. What will you need?" Curtis asked.

"I need to know about Miss Ward's duties here, who she spent time with both in and out of the house."

Curtis nodded. He lifted the brass bell at the corner of the desk and rang it, the cheerful peal reverberating through the room. Healy appeared at the door.

"Sir?"

"Please take the Inspector and his sergeant to Mrs. Burt," Curtis said. "She is the housekeeper. I take it you will conduct your interviews discreetly?"

The sod could care less that the poor girl was dead, Davies thought.

"Of course, sir," Volcker said.

They followed Healy out of the room. He set a swift pace down the hallway that led away from the magnificent atrium. They crossed onto black and white parquet squares like clumsy pawns on a giant chessboard.

Healy led them down a staircase in the rear of the house where the ceiling sloped precipitously. The two policemen held on to the railings to balance, crouching as they stepped down the abruptly steep stairs. Healy pushed a swing door and they stepped into the kitchen.

Davies nodded to the servants as the men walked into the hallway off the main room.

Healy knocked on a narrow door and turned to them. "Allow me a moment to prepare Mrs. Burt," he said, but his caution was not needed.

"Good morning, Inspector." A clear voice emerged from behind the door. Healy stood aside to reveal a petite woman dressed all in black. She did not seem resentful at their presence.

"Please come in," she said. They sat in two chairs next to the fireplace. The room was a miniature version of the study upstairs, adorned with beautiful items. Mrs. Burt sat opposite in a green damask armchair. On a side table was a lacquer tray laden with a tea set and delicate china teacups.

She gestured toward the teapot in inquiry.

"Yes, please," Volcker said.

She pulled back her sleeves with practiced flicks of the wrist. She removed the cozy, lifting the pot high so that the amber liquid poured out in a graceful arc into each cup.

"There you are," She handed the two cups across to the men. "Sugar?"

They shook their heads in polite decline.

"I doubt that you have been apprised of the reason for our visit," Volcker began.

Mrs. Burt folded her hands in her lap. She was trained to listen. She did not flinch when Volcker described the discovery of the body. If she was surprised, she did not show it. He had left out the bit about questionable suicide.

"Are you sure it is Anna?" Mrs. Burt said.

"Yes, all evidence at this moment indicates it is."

Mrs. Burt opened the drawer of her desk. She removed a stack of folios and selected one. She returned to the chair opposite them, opening the folder.

"I have been with the Curtis family for many years. As such, I have been in contact with many people of different stripes, as I call it." Her voice had a pleasant burr to it, perhaps the remnant of an accent.

"And it takes a deft hand to manage them all," Volcker said.

Mrs. Burt nodded at this compliment. "I keep detailed notes on everyone who has worked in my charge."

The file looked like one of the dossiers they kept for the petty criminals down at the station, Davies thought.

"The work is demanding, so I can ferret out the idle. Anna was an exceptional worker," Mrs. Burt said.

"When were you aware she was missing?" Volcker asked.

"I last saw Anna on her leave day. She said she was going to take care of her brother. I wasn't surprised. It happens frequently."

"How long had she been employed here?"

"Three years. She came to us at age seventeen. Many of the girls start at that age, perhaps even younger. If they are fortunate, they can leave to get married or return to their families."

"Perhaps you can read us some of the information you have there."

She turned through the pages of the file. Mrs. Burt read off the dry details of Anna's existence, date and place of birth, years of service, the positions she had filled around the house. Mrs. Burt was revealing nothing they did not already know.

Davies looked at the wall above the fireplace where a fine pair of black-and-white etchings of a cathedral were hung. A few small figures stood in front of the cathedral pen.

"How many people are on the staff here?" Volcker shifted tack for a moment.

"Fifteen, including Mr. Healy and myself."

Fit for a king, Davies thought.

"I see," Volcker said. "I will ask you to prepare a list of those individuals. We need to speak to all of them."

"Did she get on well with the other servants?" Davies asked.

"There was a bit of the usual resentment, only because she was willing to do more than was asked," Mrs. Burt said.

In the far corner of the room, a row of bells was mounted on the wall; a peal like the ring of a tiny church bell pierced the quiet.

Mrs. Burt looked up. "That will be Mrs. Curtis. I must go now."

Volcker nodded. As they rose to leave, she spoke abruptly, as if to stop them.

"I saw you admiring the etching, " Mrs. Burt said.

Davies nodded.

"Indeed. The detail is remarkable, " Volcker said. "Is it Chichester? Coventry?"

"Very good, Inspector. Yes, it is Coventry."

"What a lovely memento," Volcker murmured.

"For some perhaps. I keep the picture there as a reminder, my hometown as it were. I spent many days playing in the cathedral close with my brothers while our parents sold goods at market day. Through a series of bad loans, my father lost quite a bit of money. He squandered our meager savings on alcohol."

The policemen were silent, waiting for this grim tale to unfold.

"There was no recourse. I had two older brothers, who could at least be useful to the family by working. But what to do with a little girl of eight?"

She gave them a bitter smile.

"One day they brought me to the close. There they left me, never to return. I was too much of an encumbrance."

The men instinctively looked at the etching, now menacing, the peaceful scene transformed.

"Do not think me callous, Inspector. I am sorry to hear of Anna's death. But self-pity is a useless indulgence for people like us. Anna would have understood that."

VOLCKER AND DAVIES SAT ON the low brick wall that edged the garden, having completed an initial round of questioning. In front of them, the box stalls of the stables formed a straight line. A pair of horses absorbed in their meal paused to look at them curiously.

The brief interviews done thus far had been useless. It was unclear whether Sally the chambermaid was more frightened of Volcker's stern demeanor or whether she had done something wrong. She dissolved in tears before a single question could be asked. One of the cook's assistants was eager to be questioned and volunteered information that was blatantly untrue. She was convinced that she had seen Anna at the open-air market just yesterday when she was sent to buy onions.

Davies stared at the far wall of the garden, where a small building stood. It looked like a ruin. Volcker followed his gaze.

"They call that a folly in the English garden," Volcker said with a smile. "It is a fanciful building serving no useful purpose. It is merely for decoration. I have seen Egyptian pyramids, turreted castles, Roman ruins."

"I can't imagine, sir," Davies said.

"Someone in this household has romantic notions, and I will wager it is not Mr. Curtis," Volcker said.

Davies looked back at the high windows of the house. He saw the slight movement of a curtain, a pale hand withdrawing suddenly. The curtain was still again.

"Are you all right?" Volcker asked.

"Yes, sir." Davies felt embarrassed, brushing off his mild unease.

The midday sun was mellow and cast a pleasing warmth over the courtyard. There was a strange peace about the scene as the quiet hum of work went on around them. They watched as two young men clad in long aprons scrubbed the flagstones. A kitchen maid sat on the step peeling potatoes, collecting the thin ribbons of skin in a bowl. Davies and Volcker sat in almost companionable silence, partaking of the refreshments that had been foisted upon them by the cook.

Volcker grimaced at the dregs of his cup.

"How many bloody cups of tea do you think we will have to endure before this investigation is over?"

Davies smiled. Their presence was obviously irritating, but they had been shown the obligatory courtesy, perhaps in the hope of driving them away with hospitality. Not a chance with Volcker, Davies thought.

"I'll take these back to the kitchen, lest they think we have nicked the china," Volcker said, gathering the cups and plates. "Then we can return to the station."

"Yes, sir."

Davies stood. As he waited, he walked over to one of the horse stalls.

"There now," he said, extending his hand to the chestnut mare who peered over the railing.

The horse nuzzled her nose against his hand and shook her mane, the glossy sheen of her coat glowing in the sun. The stall was swept clean and hay was neatly stacked in the corner. A small bucket on the floor held vegetables, a pile of carrots, celery, and lettuce.

"You can give her one if you wish. She likes the carrots best."

Davies turned to see a young man regarding him. He was shorter than Davies, and he had a saddle slung over his shoulder. His thick brown hair fell over a wide brow and his dark eyes were watchful.

Davies obliged.

"Just admiring the horse. She is beautiful."

"Wasn't always so. She was worn out from overwork. Mr. Curtis was going to have her put down. But he said I could keep her if I looked after her."

"He obviously found the right person for the job."

"We suit each other." The young man put the saddle on the floor of

72

the stall. He placed his hand on the bridge of the horse's nose and rubbed softly. It was a tender gesture and the horse bent her head in response.

"You are a policeman?"

"Yes."

"I heard you were asking questions about Anna."

"Did you know her?" Davies asked.

The young man nodded. "She was a friend."

He took a bristle brush off a peg on the wall. Davies watched as he brushed the mare's coat, the broad strokes careful and unhurried, the attention to detail deliberate. It reminded Davies of how he used to help his father polish his boots, kneading oil into the leather to soften it. The work may have seemed inconsequential, unnoticed by others, but he had taken great pride in it.

"How long have you worked at the house?" Davies asked.

But they were not able to speak further. Mr. Healy came down the steps from the kitchen followed by Volcker.

"Paul! No more dallying with the horses. You are wanted in the house!" Mr. Healy called.

"I must go," Paul said.

Volcker raised his hand to Davies, signaling for him to come.

"That makes two of us then," Davies said.

He joined the inspector and they walked down the long driveway, their boots clicking smartly on the pavement.

10

Lydia climbed into the hansom cab. As she stood on the short stair she came face-to-face with the driver.

"Twenty-second and North College Avenue, please," she said.

"Yes, ma'am." He was an older man; his clipped white beard lay against the lapels of his coat. She could see him give her a surreptitious glance of measure. He took his seat behind her on his perch and tightened the reins. The horse started off at a trot.

The police surgeon had dallied in releasing the body to them. It was late in the evening but Harlan did not want to delay the autopsy for a moment longer. Lydia was going to join him at the college.

Now she sank into the seat, wrapping her cloak around her like a blanket. A light rain was beginning to fall, giving an ethereal quality to the deserted street.

She thought back to the wrenching meeting she had left, with Sarah Ward.

Sarah had confirmed that the diaries and clothing found on the riverbank belonged to her sister. The young woman had arrived alone. Had she no one who could have come with her on this grim errand? Lydia thought.

The policemen had waited in the anteroom and Lydia and Harlan had taken her in to view the body. Sarah had insisted on seeing the face.

She had stopped short at the edge of the table and closed her eyes. Lydia thought she might faint. Anna's face was engorged, the skin so distended from fluid that it was difficult to make out features. But Sarah knelt by her sister's side, reaching out to touch the thick hair, holding the strands against her cheek. Volcker had shown her the gold necklace found with the body. Sarah told them it was a gift from their mother as a remembrance, a few strands of her hair nestled inside the locket. She nodded her assent that this was Anna as tears streamed down her face. Sarah had agreed to the autopsy; with that permission, they were able to proceed.

"Here we are, miss."

The driver pulled to a stop in front of the college building. The huge windows were imposing in the darkness, like those of a Gothic mansion haunted by unseen spirits. The driver stepped down and offered Lydia a gloved hand for support.

He glanced up at the building. "Are you sure you will be all right? Is someone expecting you?"

He had determined that she was respectable, not on some illicit errand at this hour.

"Yes, thank you. I am a doctor. I work here."

She paid the fare and he tipped his hat to her. She walked up the stairs and rapped on the great door. The porter came to the window, his sallow face visible through the pane.

"Good evening, Mr. Wilson."

"Good evening, Doctor. Dr. Stanley has already arrived."

Mr. Wilson returned to the small anteroom off the main hall. Lydia could see a folded newspaper and a steaming cup of coffee through the open door, companions to pass the lonely night.

The lobby was cast in shadow. Lydia walked along the polished floor, the sound of her footsteps reverberating like the beat of a drum in the silence. She reached the top floor and walked through the sky parlor, past the tables with misshapen lumps hidden beneath their shrouds. The room was dark save for the light coming from Harlan's back room.

She placed her bag on the desk and removed an apron. She cinched it at her waist, her canvas gloves used for dissection folded in the front pocket.

The side bench was set up with a series of scales used to weigh the organs as they were removed. Next to these were metal basins of varying sizes. They were stacked in a precarious tower: these would hold the organs after they were dissected away from the body. The squat reagent bottles were lined up like bulbous soldiers in an army. The liquids inside were murky, jewel tones of ocher and amber. Lydia washed her hands and scrubbed under the nails with the brush kept at the stone sink.

"Ready to begin," Harlan said as he stooped slightly to get through the doorframe. "The porters have brought the body up through the carriage entrance." He motioned to the table in the center of the room.

They stepped in closer. The body had been removed from the muslin bag that had encased it, and now Anna's remains lay under a white sheet. Harlan expertly folded over the top edge of the sheet to reveal the upper torso. He creased the sheet into thirds, leaving the body completely bare.

Lydia had seen all manner of death in this room, bodies that had succumbed to neglect, flesh rotting from exposure to heat, maggots infesting the skin; corpses ecchymotic and bloated from stab wounds, beatings, falls. It was the full range of human misery. But this was fresh horror, the body of someone she had cared for intimately as a patient. Since the news of Anna's death, she had veered between shock and utter disbelief that this vibrant young woman had met such an end. What had happened in those terrifying last minutes of her life? She must have been so afraid. Anna's body was exposed, the skin a pallid gray. They could see the faint edges of putrefaction, a pea green smudging of the skin, edging the lower part of the abdomen. The process was arrested now that copious preservative had been applied to the body. There was more than a single compound used. Harlan was constantly experimenting with embalming techniques he had learned during the war, mixtures of arsenic, mercury, alcohol, and other substances that could slow the process of decomposition.

Lydia gripped the edge of the table for support. In the stillness of this somber room, the pain of grief was like a pressure on her chest. She drew in a breath, feeling a sorrow so palpable she feared she might be overcome. Here lay a friend, her young life prematurely ended. She thought of her conversations with Anna, encouraging her to read and explore, to seek an education. How little she had really done for the girl. Lydia had it all effortlessly at her disposal: the connections and the means. How easy it would have been for her to intervene and advance Anna's education, as she had done for countless others.

The oil lamps were turned up to their brightest exposure. Harlan was watching her. She said nothing but nodded at him to signal her readiness.

He handed her a pointer. It had a wooden handle attached to a long thin metal spike. He had one in his hand as well and would use it to point out marks and abrasions, and to test the tensile strength of skin and tissue while preventing further contamination.

Harlan used another pointer to pull the layers of matted hair away from the scalp. He tugged at the roots of the gruesome wig of thick black hair attached to the bloated face. He prodded the layer of tissue just under the skin. As he pressed with the tip of the instrument, clear fluid seeped out in a tiny rivulet.

"There is a fair amount of waterlogging in the tissue remnants," he said. He leaned in to look closer at the mouth. There was a subtle covering of frothiness.

"There are faint scratches on the face," Lydia said.

Harlan walked around the table, observing the body. The skin was unmarked on the hands and legs, and the exposed part of the neck above the dress. There was little debris under the fingernails. Curious, Lydia thought; if there had been the natural struggle when drowning, Anna would have been clutching at branches and the mud banks of the river.

They stood on either side of the table to turn the body. Harlan placed his hands under the low back and pushed as Lydia pulled the body towards her. The corpse was slick and heavy. Harlan put two wooden blocks on the table and they shifted the weight of the body onto the right, propping it up. It looked as if the corpse was curled up in bed, clutching a wooden pillow to the breast.

The back of the body was a rich purple, the tissues saturated with the wine-dark color of denatured blood. Lydia pressed her finger deeply into the skin of the lower back. As she withdrew, the color did not blanch.

"It is not bruising, and it certainly appeared after death," Harlan said. "It is lividity."

"But this is an unusual pattern for a drowning victim," Lydia said.

Harlan crouched down to look closer.

"Agreed. Lividity might appear around the face, neck and chest, as a body turned in the water," he said. "Or if the current was turbulent enough, it may not be visible at all."

But if the body had been lying supine after death, Lydia thought, blood would pool in areas of dependent gravity, the back, buttocks, and thighs, as they saw here. The pattern would occur first as patches and eventually become confluent, with the purplish discoloration reaching its full intensity between eight to twelve hours. The impression would then be fixed.

Lydia stood at Anna's right hand and moved to lift the arm. The dense resistance of the muscle had given way.

Lydia moved up to the head and observed the neck muscles. When she had first done autopsies, she had been horrified by the ghoulish grimaces corpses presented. Rigor mortis set in soon after death and would be visible first in the smaller muscles of the face, the eyelids and the mouth. The march of rigor would progress to the larger muscles of the upper and lower limbs. After approximately twenty-four hours, the process would reverse. The muscles would return to flaccidity: the small muscles of the neck and face would relax first, the lower jaw would fall. It had happened now, as the body reverted to its natural state.

"Let us sit for a moment," Harlan said.

They pulled stools up to the bench.

"The body has been moved after death. The lividity pattern suggests that she lay on her back for some time," Lydia said. "It refutes the idea that she died by drowning."

"So she was killed before going into the water. Her body was submerged in the river after the fact," Harlan said.

"Yes. Rigor mortis has resolved," Lydia said. "The process could have been affected by the cold temperature of the water, but we can estimate she has been dead for at least forty-eight hours, if not longer."

"But if she was alive only a few days ago, where was she?" Harlan asked. "She has been missing from her employer's house for two weeks."

It was true, Lydia thought. Even if Anna had been desperately ill or cast out in disgrace, surely she would have gone to Sarah for help. Unless someone or something prevented her from coming forward.

"Let us begin the internal exam," Harlan said.

Behind him stood the tray of instruments. Lydia could see the scissors of varying sizes and the toothed forceps, thin but strong, used to pick up heavy organs. The names of the tools were distinctive: the bone cutter, a rectangular tool with serrated edges, reminiscent of a carpenter's saw; the enterotome, blunt-nosed scissors that would gently open the planes of the intestine; the bread knife, the blade long and unwieldy.

The table had holes bored through to allow drainage of fluids. Lydia used a block to prop up the midback, causing the chest to thrust forward and the arms to fall to the sides, as if the torso raised itself in supplication to the heavens.

Harlan made the Y incision from the front of each shoulder to the bottom of the sternum and on to the pubic bone. They retracted the skin, dissecting down through the layers to get to the visceral organs.

"There are no obvious injuries to the chest wall. Her ribs are intact and there is no sign of internal bleeding," he said.

He used the bone cutter, making a cut up each side of the front of the rib cage to remove it, separating the sternum from the rest of the chest plate. He lifted up and out. A grainy film of bone fell from the force of the saw, particles swirling like dust motes in the light. It was like opening a door, revealing the inner sanctum of the chest.

Harlan motioned to Lydia to lean in.

"Before we continue, I would like to make an incision in the lower trachea and look at a section of the lungs."

Though it was a denuded shell of a human being, Lydia marveled nonetheless at the artistry before her: the intricate path of the great blood vessels, the sheath of the pericardial sac like a second skin over the heart. It was Galen's hearthstone, the source of innate heat in the body from which all flowed, shrouded in mystery. She took the scalpel and cut into the membranous sac of the pericardium. She sheared into the thin plane and placed her finger in the hole, swept it to and fro, feeling for any blood clots. There were none.

Harlan selected a scalpel from the instrument tray, the tip glinting in the light. He leaned into the chest cavity and made a cut at the base of the trachea and another into the dense spongy matter of the lung. As he pushed the scalpel in deep, water seeped out immediately, as if from a sponge that had been soaked through. There was an immediate frothiness. Lydia could see the same pattern at the hard ring of the trachea.

Harlan nodded. "This is the vexing problem with waterlogging; the lungs and the upper respiratory passages will reveal this fine froth."

"But it does not confirm that drowning was the cause of death. Any body submerged into water would show signs like this," Lydia said.

The final cuts were made. In one motion, Harlan removed the organs en bloc, freed from their ligamentous attachments. All that remained was the bulbous dome of the diaphragm and the abdominal organs, covered in the muscular sheath of the peritoneum.

At the side bench, Harlan worked to separate the giant mass of organs coiled together, slippery and inelegant. Each organ would be weighed, awaiting further dissection if needed, the contents examined for any lesions or hemorrhages.

Lydia continued her dissection into the abdomen, unaware of time passing. Everything she saw was rich in color, the organs full of vitality, ready for years of life that would not come to be. She tied thin ligatures, clamping off the section of intestine above and below the bile duct.

She used the sharp tip of the scalpel to open along the greater curvature of the stomach. As she did this, a pungent smell met her nostrils, the rank odor of the digestive juices and food in putrefaction, halted for eternity in a stage of incomplete digestion. She carefully moved the tiny brush over the rugae, the ridged folds of the stomach, a world in miniature of mountainous peaks and valleys. The tissue was a healthy color throughout, deep hues of pink. She used the scalpel to fully reveal the inside lining. The pattern was consistent. Lydia prodded with the tip of the pointer.

"Hand me the scissors, please, Harlan," she said, taking a length of intestine attached to the stomach in her hand. She lifted it like a rope and used the scissors to make a swift incision, opening the tube along the outer muscular band. It was again the same pattern inside.

"There is nothing unusual here. We must look further," she said.

They worked silently, scouring every inch of the body for signs of injury. No words were needed between them, they had done this painstaking work so many times. Together they shifted the corpse onto its side again. Harlan lifted the hair as Lydia examined the skull and base of the neck. She drew in a sharp breath.

"Look, Harlan."

She could see a deep purple contusion rising from the pale skin of the neck. It was spongy to the touch, its lacy, ecchymotic tendrils extending down the posterior neck. It had been concealed by the dark mass of hair.

"This localized bruising must be from blunt trauma. She could have a fracture of one of the cervical vertebral bodies. There could be extensive cerebral hemorrhage as well," Lydia said.

"It was likely a swift blow, not from contact with rocks or other heavy matter in the river." Harlan peered closely. "We can give this preliminary information to Volcker in the morning."

"Yes. I am to meet him at the Curtis house," Lydia replied. "He wants me to assist in questioning."

"Then I will complete the autopsy over the next day or two. Volcker will need the confirmatory evidence as soon as possible, to establish cause of death."

Lydia nodded.

But something else was troubling her. It was what they hadn't found. Something was missing and she couldn't quite place it.

11

Lydia sat as Inspector Volcker pushed a piece of paper across the table to her.

"Here is a list of the household staff, as well as the family members who live here," he said. Harlan had informed him of the initial results of the autopsy. Volcker had gone back to the magistrate and obtained a search warrant on grounds of suspicious death.

"Thank you," Lydia said. "Divide and conquer, shall we? I can speak with the young women."

They were sitting in a pantry off the main kitchen at the Curtis house. Just outside the door they could hear a steady thrum of activity.

There were four names on the list: Emily, Joan, Sally, Agnes.

"Your insights will be valuable given your relationship with the victim," Volcker said. "Isn't that right, Sergeant?"

Davies gave a curt nod. He had barely spoken to her. He was likely deeply suspicious of her motives, as someone interfering with the investigation. She doubted he had ever worked with a woman in any professional capacity. She did not need his approval. But it bothered her that he assumed she was not capable.

"Dr. Weston?" Volcker asked.

"Yes, I am ready," Lydia said. She was apprehensive about how she would be able to contribute. But she had been insistent that she be a part of the investigation, first with Harlan and then having him apply pressure on Volcker. To her surprise, Volcker had agreed.

She had never been directly involved in this way before. Since her student days she had worked with Harlan on autopsies, thanks to the generous offer he'd made knowing she needed to earn extra money. But that was a scientific exercise, detached from the victims. Still Lydia was glad to be set into action, freed from the paralyzing shock of Anna's death. If she had failed Anna in life, she would do everything she could to help her now.

Volcker held the door open. "Shall we?"

He smiled at her kindly, sensing her hesitation. She knew Harlan trusted him and so would she. She relished a challenge and this was no different than any other. Was that not what she told her students?

"Yes, Inspector."

THE STAFF WAS ARRAYED IN the kitchen.

"This is everyone, Mrs. Burt?" Volcker asked. Mrs. Burt and Mr. Healy were seated at the head of the table, like the stern parents of an unruly brood.

Healy nodded.

"Very well. We have had the opportunity to speak with many of you. For those who don't know, I am Inspector Volcker of the Philadelphia police. This is Sergeant Davies and Dr. Weston, my colleagues on the investigation."

As he spoke, Lydia watched the faces of those assembled. Davies had identified each of the maids for her. At the end of the table, they sat in a cluster. Sally's ruddy face was pinched with worry, and next to her sat the impassive Joan, her hands folded over an ample belly. Agnes was clearly the youngest. She looked pale and bewildered. Sitting apart was the lady's maid, Emily, elegant and aloof.

"As you may know, the body of Anna Ward was found on a bank of the Schuylkill River two days ago. It was assumed that she had killed herself, a suicide by drowning. Identification was made through the personal belongings found nearby, and a diary in which she had inscribed her name."

The cook gasped and one of the young maids gave a nervous giggle, quickly silenced by Mr. Healy.

"To everyone who knew her, this is a shock. Anna was happy with her position in this house. What would drive her to such a desperate act?" Volcker continued. "Yet based on our preliminary investigation, her death appears to be suspicious. An autopsy is under way to determine the exact cause of death."

The faces in the room were watchful. Lydia could see glances exchanged, many of the servants unsure of what this news meant.

"We will be questioning each of you. I have a search warrant here"—Volcker waved a pamphlet in front of him—"as well as Mr. Curtis's permission to go over the house."

Another flutter of protests.

"Please wait for further instruction," Volcker said.

At this, the room dissipated into chaos. A few groups clustered around the urns of tea set up on the dining table. There was voluble energy as people accustomed to doing hard work found themselves in a moment of forced idleness.

Volcker drew Davies and Lydia to a corner.

"Charlie, you get started upstairs. Curtis is nervous, so very willing to cooperate."

"All right, sir." Davies nodded. He disappeared into the stairwell, his footsteps echoing up the stairs.

"Dr. Weston, see what you can find out from the maids. Allow them to unburden themselves." He gave her a knowing smile.

Lydia had practiced medicine for more than ten years. She knew how to elicit a confidence. By now, it was a practiced art.

"I will tell you all I learn, Inspector."

LYDIA RETURNED TO THE KITCHEN with a cup of tea. She discreetly took a seat next to Emily, the lady's maid.

"I can't say I am surprised, what happened to Anna," Emily said.

"How can you say that?" Sally was on the verge of tears. "What could she have done to come to this end?"

"Come off it, Sally. We were all fed up with her, you as well," Joan said.

"Always carrying on with such airs," Emily said. "That's the trouble with not knowing your place."

Emily was a pretty girl, her auburn hair tied with a ribbon. Lydia could see the others clustered around her, wanting to curry favor.

"But why would she want to kill herself, or worse, someone want to hurt her?" Sally's eyes were wide.

"Maybe we should ask her special *friend*, Paul." Emily's lips curled in a lupine snarl.

"Were they more than friends?" Lydia asked.

They all turned to look at her.

"Paul is handsome. We aren't the only ones to take notice," Emily said.

"But can you imagine, our fine lady Anna? With the stable boy?" Joan snickered.

"Paul had other interests besides Anna," Emily said.

"Oh, you don't know that. A bit jealous yourself, perhaps?" Joan said.

Emily blushed.

At the back of the room a dark-haired young man stood beside Mrs. Burt, helping to rearrange the chairs used for the meeting.

"Is that him?" Lydia asked.

Emily nodded.

The young man paused in his work. He looked over at Emily and smiled. She turned her head away.

"You are just angry because she took your place with Mrs. Curtis," Joan said.

"And what of it? I was getting tired of it anyway. It is not an easy job," Emily said. There was a sharp intake of breath at this revelation.

Lydia said quietly, "It is best to be honest. Anna is dead. Nothing you say can hurt her."

"So you were her doctor?" Agnes asked. "Anna told us she went to see a lady doctor."

"Yes, I took care of her in my clinic. That is why I am here, to help the police find out what happened to her."

Emily regarded her imperiously. "Are you a real doctor? Not one of those homeopaths who dole out pills and tonics?"

"Yes." Lydia was used to this dismissal. "I earned a medical degree after years of study just as the gentlemen do. I also teach students at Woman's Medical College."

This statement was met with silence. It was a life so removed from their daily existence, she might as well have been a visitor from a far-off land.

"Well, it is just my opinion, of course, but when the mistress gets into her moods . . . her melancholy takes hold over everyone," Emily said.

"We have to tiptoe around and keep quiet," Agnes said.

"It drives Mr. Curtis mad," Joan added.

"She takes to her room and won't talk to anyone. If she does, she gets short and angry with them. Mr. Curtis tries to avoid her, just like the rest of us," Emily said.

"How so?" Lydia asked.

"He spends more time at his club or off at the house in the country. If you ask me, it's no good to have your husband far off like he is," Joan said.

"What about the children? There are two sons, yes?"

"The boys are at school most of the time. When they are here, it is Mrs. Burt who cares for them."

"Fair blows me away. What could Mrs. Curtis have to worry about? Pots of money and us at her beck and call," Agnes said.

"Even the saintly Anna was tiring of the madam's moods. Mrs. Curtis had her fussing with her wardrobe, dressing her hair, going on missions in the tenements. It can be exhausting when the madam gets herself in a state," Joan said.

Lydia stirred a lump of sugar into her tea. She set the spoon down on the table.

"Tell me more about Paul. Was he courting Anna?" she asked.

"Who knows?" Emily said. "Do something nice for Paul and next thing you know, he is sweet on you. Besides, she was always off after that crippled brother of hers. She couldn't say no to anyone."

"And what about that diary Anna had? How she would go on, scribbling day and night," Joan said.

"Did she ever show you what she wrote?" Lydia asked.

"No. But what did she have to write about? Endless work, that's what. Don't make for interesting reading, does it?" Joan said.

But no one answered her.

The young women all stood immediately, at attention, as a group of soldiers would at a barracks review.

"So now I see where you all have disappeared to."

Lydia could hear a cultured voice behind her, the hint of irritation unmistakable.

"I beg your pardon, Mrs. Curtis," Emily said.

Mrs. Burt rushed over, ready to appease.

"It is my doing, ma'am. I am sorry you had to come to the kitchen to find us. The police asked us to gather for their announcement."

"I understand. But I won't be late for my appointment," Mrs. Curtis said.

Lest anyone forget who was truly in charge, Lydia thought.

Lydia stood and faced Mrs. Curtis. They were the same height. Her blond hair was swept into a neat chignon and she wore a burgundy wool dress. Her finely chiseled features were clouded by displeasure.

"This is Dr. Weston. She is working with the police investigators," Mrs. Burt said.

Mrs. Curtis gave a nod of acknowledgment but said nothing.

"Come along, Emily. And if you all are finished with the meeting, it is time to return to work."

Mrs. Curtis left the room, followed by a chastened Emily.

There was a palpable sense of relief after their exit, the mood visibly relaxed. Mrs. Burt oversaw the clearing of the room as the staff prepared to return to work. The other maids stood and cleared the cups and plates off the table.

Lydia drew Sally aside.

"Could you please show me Anna's room?"

"Of course, Doctor."

Sally led her into the hallway and the stairwell. Lydia looked up the spiral staircase, a space reminiscent of a church belfry.

They climbed slowly and reached the top, emerging under the eaves. The runner carpet was thin and Lydia could feel the floorboards beneath the soles of her boots. The walls were covered with nondescript wallpaper, as if the opulence of the rest of the house had come to an abrupt halt. Along the hallway a door was ajar. She could see a single bed, covered in a plain duvet, not unlike a monastic cell in its sparseness. The bedside table held only a pitcher and bowl.

"All of these rooms, Sally, they are for the servants?"

"Yes, ma'am, this is the ladies' side. The men are on the other side of the house."

"Do all the servants live in?" Lydia asked.

"The important ones do."

"And where are you from, Sally?"

"Gettysburg. It was my sister that helped me get the job here. She is in service in the city as well." Sally chatted on. Her cheerful nature no doubt craved company.

They passed into an anteroom. Lydia suspected that beyond this was the central staircase dividing the house.

"Anna's room is at the end of the hall here." The girl stepped aside to let Lydia pass.

The roof sloped and she had to bend to walk through the narrow doorway. The room had an iridescent glow from the whitewashed walls and it gave the impression of brilliant light. It was empty save for two iron-frame beds and a steamer trunk. Lydia sat on the edge of the bed and felt the sharp jab of the bedspring cut into her thigh, pushing up through the matting.

"If you need me, ma'am, I will be in the alcove at the end of the hall," Sally said.

It was good to be alone in the room that had been Anna's only retreat. Lydia was drawn to the dormer window. She sat on the wide sill and opened the pane. A gust of bracing air came in. Far below she could see the activity of the back courtyard.

She turned back to face the room. If Anna had needed to hide something, where would she do it? Lydia pushed the mattresses up and looked for openings in the seams. In the corner was a dresser topped with a chipped basin for morning ablutions. The drawers were empty and unlined. Lydia pulled each drawer out all the way, running her hand along the frame of the box.

She set her reticule on the floor beside her and opened her writing case. She ran her hand over the burnished wood, remembering when her mother had chosen it for her at the central bazaar in Darjeeling. The top of the box propped up and formed a writing easel, a desk that could be set on a flat surface.

Lydia made quick notes of the people she had met and the conversations she had been privy to.

Then her gaze alighted on the tin trunk beneath the bed. She crouched down and slid it out. The latch was undone. She opened the battered lid. The trunk was empty save for a notebook. Lydia slipped the book into her bag and quickly shut the trunk. She went to the door and called into the hallway.

"Sally? Would you please join me?"

Sally returned to the threshold. Lydia gestured to the bare bed opposite. The girl sat obediently.

"Have you been told anything?"

Sally shook her head.

"But I heard others talking. So it is true then? Anna has been murdered?" she asked.

"Yes. It appears she drowned herself in the river. But the police have reason to believe that her death is not so simple."

Sally gasped, her eyes widening in fear.

"I got the impression in the kitchen that you were her friend. You seem genuinely sorry she is gone."

Sally nodded. Her hand was clamped against her mouth.

"Anything you tell me will only help."

"Yes, of course—of course," Sally's voice shook slightly. "When I first came here, I missed home. I had never been apart from my people. Anna was so lovely to me. Mrs. Burt and the mistress liked her. I could see that. Mrs. Curtis would often call for her to do something special."

"Did Anna confide in you?"

"To be sure! She knew so much, had so many stories to tell. If it hadn't been for her parents dying, she never would have come to be a servant."

"Did she speak of anyone from childhood she kept in touch with?"

"No. Mostly we talked about her brother. It isn't fair, seeing as some have so little to worry about and Anna had so much," Sally said. "But she would carry on. It was just her way."

"When did you last see her?"

"Same as Mrs. Burt, going on two weeks now. She never said anything. If she had only told me what was troubling her, perhaps I could have helped . . ." Sally started to cry.

"Do you have any idea what could have driven her away?"

"I don't know, ma'am." Sally shook her head. "But I was always worried about Anna, that something like this might happen to her."

"Something like this?"

"It was just she had to be particular, too much so." Sally struggled to find the right words. "She didn't mean it unkindly. One time Agnes took a bit of extra ribbon from the missus to make a new dress, without asking. What business was it of ours? But Anna marched straight to Mrs. Burt and made a fuss. Agnes was furious."

"So you think she may have angered people?" Lydia asked

"A lot of gossip. But it had to be something terrible, for her to come to this end? I think that was why she was writing in her book."

"Did she ever show it to you?"

Sally shook her head. "She kept it locked in a trunk. But no matter how worn out we were at the end of the day, she would write. She told me so."

The space was so close that their knees touched. A dull light streamed through the window, shifting to dark as clouds moved across the face of the sun.

"Did she buy them for herself?"

Sally nodded. "Except for that last one of course. Have you seen it? It was her young man that gave her that beauty."

"Paul?"

"*No!* That horrid Emily—eaten up with jealousy she is!" The girl's face flushed with anger. "Anna was nice to him, but nothing more."

"If it wasn't Paul, then who?"

"She never said. I knew she had met someone in the last few months. On her day out, she dressed up so special. I said, Are you going to see your little brother looking like that! She just gave a laugh and didn't say anything."

Sally smiled at Lydia knowingly.

"She started to bring home little gifts. I noticed. A silk handkerchief or a pair of gloves. I knew she hadn't bought them herself. Then she brought home the beautiful little book. So fancy, almost too rich to write in. Maybe she wrote about him in there?"

"So she would see this young man on her days out," Lydia said. "Not in the house?"

Sally shook her head.

"I am sure of it; I would have known. If it had been one of our lads, she would have said so."

"Perhaps she met him on one of her outings with Mrs. Curtis, a servant in another house?"

"Oh no, ma'am. I can tell you he was not like us, not a servant at all. That's why she was so secretive about it. He was a toff all right, a gentleman."

LYDIA WALKED BRISKLY BESIDE DAVIES and Volcker. They had left the Curtis house and were heading towards Rittenhouse Square, where she could catch the omnibus across town.

She told them of her conversations with the maids: the gossip about Paul O'Meara.

"Seems like a few of the young women were sweet on him," Davies said.

"But there is more," Lydia said. "One of the maids, Sally, told me that Anna was meeting with someone outside the house."

"Did Sally ever see the man? Does she know his name?" Volcker asked.

"No," Lydia said.

Davies snorted. "How can she be sure then? She could have made it up. It sounds like a hunch, nothing more."

"Anna was a keen diarist," Lydia said. "According to Sally, she would make entries every night without fail. She kept the books in a tin trunk under the bed. I found this one in her room."

She held up the dun-colored notebook; it looked like an account book one could buy in any shop. "But Sally said Anna's suitor had given her gifts, among them a diary she treasured. It was very different from this one."

Davies glanced at Volcker.

"As you know, we found a journal with her belongings by the riverside. I have it with me. Let me show you." Volcker stopped walking and removed a small book from his case.

He held it up. It was a vivid royal blue and thin layers of gold filament woven into the cover glinted in the light.

"Aah, yes," Lydia said.

"Sir, this is the flimsiest of connections," Davies said incredulously. "From this, we assume her suitor was a gentleman?"

"Do you have another suggestion?" Volcker asked.

"No, but this is hardly solid evidence—"Davies began.

"It is not," Volcker said. "But let us give Dr. Weston an opportunity to work and not tear down her efforts completely. I once did the same for you, Charlie."

Davies flushed. Volcker's words stung, hitting the mark with accuracy. In his early days on the force, Davies had been relegated to patrol the beat in the tenement he had grown up in. He had chafed at the drudgery, longing to be part of a detective's team. But it was clear there was little hope of advancement; he lacked education and his only qualification was an eagerness to learn. It didn't help that he was ill at ease in the convivial atmosphere of the force, misunderstanding the social cues that came so easily to the others. None of the inspectors had been willing to take him on except Volcker. Volcker could be critical and demanding, but he was never condescending.

"This is useful information, Dr. Weston," Volcker said. "So Anna was behaving differently in the last few months. Her manner was changed. She was taking care with her appearance on her day out, receiving mysterious gifts."

Lydia took the book from him. The thick vellum pages were covered, dense handwriting crowding every inch of the space. She read a few lines.

"What does it mean?"

"It is gibberish to me, just words on a page," said Davies.

"It's poetry, Sergeant," Lydia said. "But only fragments, broken up phrases."

"Perhaps you could take it and try to make sense of it?" Volcker asked.

12

Lydia settled into the comfort of her window seat, restored after a warm supper. She tucked her bare feet under the blankets. It was good to be home. It had been a long day but the impressions from the Curtis house had stayed with her. She looked outside into a sheet of gray as rain thrummed against the windowpanes. A fire burned merrily in the grate.

Inspector Volcker had given her the diary found at the river with Anna's belongings. She placed the two books on the table in front of her. The one she had found in Anna's trunk was a ledger, the kind of cheap notebook that could be bought at any stationer. The other was a peacock amidst geese: royal blue pebbled leather, the pages edged with gold leaf.

Lydia hesitated before opening the first book. She had been afraid of what she might discover in these pages, delving into intimacies. But the beginning pages were mundane accounts of daily life: things to buy, a record of the weather, notes about work.

2nd September 1873, light fog in the morning, cool; spool of red thread for S; last oranges at the market

And another:

> 5th January 1874: bitterly cold, wind under the eaves, little sleep, worked in scullery today, mended petticoat

Lydia could feel the misery of that day in those few words. One could imagine the frigid cold of the attic bedroom, the exhaustion that prevented sleep. There was much, in terse form, about Anna's brother, John's illness.

> 15th March 1874, at the doctor's, more expensive salve for John's legs, spasms terrible at night, Barton's pharmacy fee

The number next to this entry was crossed out. There were a series of numbers written beside it. Perhaps they were desperate calculations, to see how she could possibly afford the physician's fees.

And another: "home on a half day, John crying terribly, Sarah spent, ask Mrs. Burt about piecework."

Had she tried to earn more money or asked for help to supplement the family's income?

Lydia continued reading through the entries, until one for an early autumn date caught her eye.

> 10th October 1874: fine autumn day, walked at Wissahickon, birds on the river, leaves changing, found stones for John

Lydia made note of this. Anna had been familiar with the walking path at Wissahickon, where her body had been found.

As the diary progressed in time, the short, circumspect notes were replaced by dense pages of writing, not one inch of the paper free of ink.

> Library hours, lecture at the Franklin Institute, Dr. Harding—new consultation for John? send money for Sarah, purchase iron tonic

Many of the entries made little sense, streams of phrases that seemed disconnected. But there was a sense of urgency, the words spilling onto the paper in a jumble. Anna continued to mark the date and a brief note about the weather.

Lydia was touched to see her own name appear several times. Anna had recorded the titles of books she recommended. There was a list of addresses of libraries in the city, a schedule of free lectures offered at their own Spruce Street Clinic, a note "encouraged by Dr. Weston to attend, free" or "Doctor W. recommends Mrs. Gaskell, similar to Middlemarch and the Brontës." Yet another: "Dr. W says there may be a chance for an apprenticeship!!" There was nothing more written, the exclamation points expressing the excitement of that possibility.

Lydia opened the blue diary. On the first page Anna had written in her neat hand:

> *The Soul that rises with us, our life's Star,*
> *Hath had elsewhere its setting*
> *And cometh from afar; . . .*
>
> *Shades of the prison-house begin to close*
> *Upon the growing Boy,*
> *But he beholds the light, and whence it flows,*
> *He sees it in his joy;*

It was incomplete, but Lydia recognized the lovely passage: Wordsworth, "Intimations of Immortality." She paged through the rest of the book. It was filled with similar fragments of poems, each entry dated. There was no mention of places or names of friends, no thoughts of her day. Anna had been collecting verse, as in a commonplace book.

The joy of intellectual exploration permeated these pages. Anna was reading for pleasure; what a comfort that must have been to her in the unwelcoming Curtis house. Lydia looked across the room at her own bookshelves, groaning from the weight of her treasured volumes. Reading was her solace, literature the sustaining force of her life. She thought of the countless times she had sought refuge in her books, when literature had provided the ballast and strength of an old friend.

Lydia made notations in the margins of Anna's book, folding over the pages to mark passages. She was grateful for the proximity of her library to consult. There were many excerpts she recognized, the fragments of Rossetti, Tennyson, Blake jumbled together in no order. With others that were unfamiliar, it was like a pleasurable game as a phrase would prompt her to search in one of her anthologies.

There was a glimmer of hope too. But could it all be attributed to Anna's newly discovered passion for knowledge? Perhaps there was something else to be hopeful for? Or someone?

Lydia read:

> *How say you? Let us, O my dove,*
> *Let us be unashamed of soul,*
> *As earth lies bare to heaven above! . . .*

> *No. I yearn upward, touch you close,*
> *Then stand away. I kiss your cheek,*
> *Catch your soul's warmth,—I pluck the rose*
> *And love it more than tongue can speak—*
> *Then the good minute goes.*

It was a passage from Browning's "Two in the Campagna," an unabashed declaration of love. Surely Anna would have written her most intimate thoughts in a diary. Why not reveal a suitor's name in this most private of places?

Lydia read on. The pages were filled with romantic poetry. Anna was in love and expressed her happiness through verse.

Lydia opened the plain diary. She looked at the month of May 1875: there were gaps in the notes detailing mundane activities, dates missing. She laid the blue diary next to it and could see entries that coincided with the missing dates: at first, the imagery was joyful, of verdant spring and blooming flowers, fulsome brooks. Had Anna met her lover on those days or received a gift? Perhaps these entries were a secret way of marking her days with him, a code only she would understand.

But then something changed.

> *Murmuring how she loved me—she*
> *Too weak, for all her heart's endeavour,*
> *To set its struggling passion free*
> *From pride, and vainer ties dissever,*
> *And give herself to me forever.*
> *But passion sometimes would prevail,*
> *Nor could to-night's gay feast restrain*
> *A sudden thought of one so pale*
> *For love of her, and all in vain:*

It was Browning again, the lines a fragment of "Porphyria's Lover." It was a strange choice, Lydia thought. The poem spoke of love but its meaning was disturbing, suggesting madness and obsession. Was Anna being coerced into something she didn't want to do?

Lydia paused. It was a layered puzzle. She felt a strange connection to Anna through these words. Those closest to her knew nothing of her most private thoughts, but perhaps the answer was here. Why had she been so careful to hide her lover's identity?

Lydia had to find out where the diary had come from. And she knew exactly who to ask.

13

It was easy to miss the sliver of a bookshop hidden on a side street off Pine. Lydia pushed open the door. It was early morning and the sign perched in the window read CLOSED. But she knew Mr. Kohler would be in the back. A discreet wooden sign hung over the door, reading KOHLER'S RARE AND ANTIQUARIAN BOOKS. Lydia had discovered the shop years before. She had been on an errand for a birthday gift, an edition of Hardy's poems to ease the homesickness of an English friend. The shop was designed as an intimate library, vertiginous shelves reaching to the ceiling. The only natural light came through the front windows, the rest of the space was plunged into a delicious mustiness. None of the books seemed to be arranged in sensible order, by author or subject. Yet a keen reader could detect the alliances: Ruskin's *Seven Lamps of Architecture* and *Unto This Last* edged next to a slim folio of Christina Rossetti's *Goblin Market*. Lydia had been distracted from her errand and was soon perusing a stack of books, deeply content.

A gentleman bearing a strong resemblance to Father Christmas had approached her. Rolf Kohler was stout, with snowy hair and beard, impeccably dressed in a pin-striped suit. "Excellent choices, madam," he said, a hint of Old World formality piercing through his fastidious English. He had given a short bow, a bibliophile's salute of sorts. That had been five years ago. He had been delighted to learn she was a physician. He lived in a flat above the shop, his curated collection suggesting private means. Lydia stopped in once a week to shop but also for conversation.

On this morning, he came immediately at the ring of the bell.

"Dr. Weston, what a pleasure," he said. "You are just in time."

He nodded over his shoulder to a plate piled with sliced pieces of Sacher torte. On the table behind the desk sat a steaming pot of tea.

"I am afraid I have come on business, Mr. Kohler."

"Of course, of course." He gestured for her to sit down. She placed her bag on the counter and took out the diaries.

"May I?" Mr. Kohler asked. As he turned the pages, she could see the faded ink in Anna's hand.

"These belong to a young woman who has died," Lydia said.

She delivered only the barest details of Anna's life, that she had been a servant. But she told him the truth of everything else: her murder and the suspicion of a love affair gone awry. She shared what Sally had told her, that the beautiful diary had been given to Anna by a suitor. She could count on his discretion.

"A tragedy." Mr. Kohler shook his head sadly. "But how can I help, Doctor?"

"I need you to help me trace this," she said. She held up the second diary, the blue a vivid smear of color, like the runny azure on a painter's palette.

"How lovely. Do you know if she purchased this one for herself?" he asked.

He squinted to look at the binding. "The quality is exquisite. May I?"

He took the book, running his hand over the soft cover.

"I will inquire with a friend who is a stationer. It is Italian paper—see the Florentine pattern on the flyleaf?" Mr. Kohler said admiringly.

Lydia could see the floral inlay, multicolored flowers in an arabesque pattern, with gold filigree etched in.

She watched as Mr. Kohler paged through the diary.

In the last half of the book, the handwriting was a cramped scrawl.

> *The grave's a fine and private place,*
> *But none, I think, do there embrace.*
> *Now therefore, while the youthful hue*
> *Sits on thy skin like morning dew,*
> *And while thy willing soul transpires*
> *At every pore with instant fires,*
> *Now let us sport while we may.*

"Andrew Marvell's exhortation to love before inevitable death comes for us all," Mr. Kohler said. "'To His Coy Mistress.' A carpe diem poem of the first order. There can be no mistaking the meaning. But the tone—it is sly and a bit menacing."

Again, that worrying hint of coercion, Lydia thought.

And then the next page:

> *A happy lover who has come*
> *To look on her that loves him well,*
> *Who 'lights and rings the gateway bell,*
> *And learns her gone and far from home;*
>
> *He saddens, all the magic light*
> *Dies off at once from bower and hall,*
> *And all the place is dark, and all*
> *The chambers emptied of delight:*

"One of my favorites, I must say. A most beautiful poem about devastating loss. Tennyson wrote it in memory of his dear friend and fellow poet Arthur Hallam, after the young man's sudden death," he said.

Lydia was unsettled by the passages. Anna couldn't have known the stories behind the poems but the haunting feeling of loss was prescient.

"She was too afraid to write in plain language, that someone might read it. But she would know its meaning in an instant."

"As would a discerning reader like you, perhaps?" Mr. Kohler asked.

In the last pages of the book, the light, charming romantic images were gone. The entries were dated but the poetry excerpts were darker, more disjointed, their meaning unclear.

Anna had written:

> *A child's a plaything for an hour;*
> *Its pretty tricks we try*
> *For that or for a longer space; . . .*

> *Thou, straggler into loving arms,*
> *Young climber up of knees,*
> *When I forget thy thousand ways,*
> *Then life and all shall cease.*

It was a poignant remembrance of a child, lost and gone. Could Anna be speaking of her brother and her realization that he would one day die prematurely? Lydia wondered.

"I don't know that poem at first glance. These last few entries are puzzling as well," Mr. Kohler said. He pointed a stout finger at the page:

> *A mute remembrancer of crime*
> *Long lost, concealed, forgot for years,*
> *It comes at last to cancel time,*
> *And waken unavailing tears.*

Mr. Kohler was quiet. He held the blue book, reading intently.

"She may not be speaking of herself but describing another. A love affair tainted, the lost child. Please be careful, Doctor," he said.

He held the last page of the book up for her to see. There was only one thing written.

I tell my secret? No indeed, not I;
Perhaps some day, who knows?
But not today; it froze, and blows and snows,
And you're too curious: fie!
You want to hear it? well:
Only, my secret's mine, and I won't tell.

He looked up at her with concern. Lydia knew the Rossetti poem, like a child's riddle. But it was deceptively innocent, a taunt with a hint of spite. Anna had discovered something, concealing it under the veil of poetry, so only she could decipher its meaning. Was it a dangerous game she had played, confident of the upper hand, until it was too late?

14

Volcker loved chess. Davies could see the deep wrinkles furrowed in concentration as the boss perched on a stool. Davies moved his queen into position for checkmate. Volcker had taught him to play years ago as a term of employment. They had played outside courtrooms waiting to testify and in the cells at the station house before questioning suspects. Davies's skill now surpassed Volcker's. He had a surprising gift for executing attacks.

"Ruthless, my boy, ruthless," Volcker said as he took down the king.

They were sitting in a room off the kitchen, waiting for Dr. Weston. She was coming from the medical college after teaching her class. Volcker had asked her to be present for the interview with Mr. and Mrs. Curtis.

Davies said nothing. He resented being at her beck and call. If Volcker insisted on her help, then it was she who needed to adjust her schedule to theirs instead of the reverse. It was a criminal investigation that they were conducting yet the boss seemed almost smitten. What made her presence so necessary? Davies thought. She hadn't unearthed any information they couldn't have found themselves.

Volcker rose to his feet as she approached.

"Dr. Weston."

"I am sorry I am late. I have just come from a morning lecture. But I wanted to show you this as soon as possible."

She removed her gloves and opened her bag. She brought out the blue diary and told them of her meeting with Mr. Kohler.

"The diary is very expensive. It is something that she couldn't have bought for herself. It must have been a treasured item. There are only the passages of poetry in it. Look at this entry for June third," she said.

Davies and Volcker dutifully read:

> *Shall I compare thee to a summer's day?*
> *Thou art more lovely and more temperate.*
> *Rough winds do shake the darling buds of May,*
> *And summer's lease hath all too short a date.*

"This one is from a sonnet by Shakespeare. Do you see?"

Volcker looked at her blankly.

"It is a summer's day," he said.

"That's right." She nodded in encouragement. "The beloved is even more beautiful than a summer's day and will long outlast its ephemeral nature. There are many passages like this one, describing romantic love."

Volcker held the book up, squinting to see the print. He read aloud:

> *How do I love thee? Let me count the ways.*
> *I love thee to the depth and breadth and height*
> *My soul can reach . . .*

"Sir, please," Davies said. He sensed that they were on the perilous cusp of one of Volcker's tangents. If word of this nonsense got round at the station house, they would be subjected to pitiless ridicule. He could almost hear it now.

"It is her way of expressing her feelings, in a code only she would understand," Dr. Weston said.

"I can't see the connection," Davies said. This was a murder inquiry, not a lesson for a pair of daft schoolboys.

"But who could question the meaning of this? 'I love thee with the breath, smiles, tears, of all my life,'" Dr. Weston read.

She looked from one to the other. "Come now, gentlemen. Surely one of you has written a love letter before?"

There was an awkward silence. Volcker cleared his throat.

"Well, perhaps you can continue to delve into it and keep us apprised. Now let us go meet with the Curtises themselves," he said.

IT WAS THE MOST EXQUISITE room Lydia had ever been in. How she coveted a space like this, she thought, but she suppressed this unwelcome feeling. The sunlight streamed in through the windows, warming the wood floors. The room was appointed for all manner of leisure: a dainty pianoforte in the corner; a wooden easel propped up, pots of glistening watercolors crowded at the edge of the palette; a reed basket containing embroidery hoops and thread. On the walls were two watercolors from the latest Paris exhibition done in the new Impressionist style. Lydia had read of these painters, their work so different from the staid realism of the past. In one, she could see the broad strokes of a sunrise casting light on an expanse of water and in another, a woman standing sentinel at the crest of a hill. She longed to see one of the paintings up close.

Mrs. Burt indicated three chairs facing the love seat. The grandfather clock chimed.

A side door in the wall paneling opened. Mr. and Mrs. Curtis entered. Mrs. Curtis held on to her husband's extended arm, as a queen would with a courtier.

Beatrice Curtis looked luminous in a simple dress, a gray silk cut on the bias, with an amber brooch affixed at the throat, trailing the scent of lilies of the valley.

The policemen seemed immune to the vision of loveliness that had appeared before them. Volcker made the requisite introductions.

"Thank you, please sit down." She gestured to the chairs.

"All right, Volcker. You asked to speak with my wife and we have acquiesced. Now keep your questions brief," Edward Curtis said.

"It is a tragic business," Mrs. Curtis murmured. "I am saddened to hear of Anna's death, of course. But regrets are useless now. How can I be of help?"

She seemed softer and more pliant today, in the solicitous presence of her husband. There was no hint of the steely competence that had been on display for the staff, Lydia thought.

"When did Anna start working here?" Volcker asked.

"A few years ago. It was her first job, I understand. But it was soon obvious that her talents lay far above scrubbing the floors."

"Why did you choose her to work with you?"

"I trusted her," Mrs. Curtis said. "There is always a sense of keeping one's guard up with the servants. I never felt that way with Anna. I would have dismissed Emily straight off as a lady's maid and intended to do so."

"Did Emily know that?" Lydia asked.

Mrs. Curtis's gaze turned to her.

"I imagine she did. And she would be none too happy about it, I am sure."

A loss of position would be a blow to Emily, a disruption in the hierarchy of the staff, Lydia thought.

"Mrs. Burt tells me you teach at the Woman's Medical College," Mrs. Curtis said.

"Yes. I also attend in the clinics, and that is how Anna came to be my patient."

"Most impressive, Dr. Weston. I can only imagine the fuss that would ensue if we cast off dear old Dr. Musgrove, but I must say I would like to have a lady physician. Yet you also help the police with investigations?"

"No. This is the first time I have been involved like this."

"Of course, it makes sense as you had a personal connection with Anna."

"She had been in my care for the last two years," Lydia replied.

"You would be quite an example for her to look up to. A doctor and professor." Mrs. Curtis nodded in approval. "Do you meet much opposition to your work?"

It was odd, Lydia thought. It was as if they were having a private conversation, one that might have occurred between two friends. It was shrewd of Mrs. Curtis to make an alliance of equals with her and invite confidences. The men watched in silence.

"There are many who feel women doctors are unequal to men, despite similar training. But the work continues," Lydia said.

"Leading by example. It is ever thus, I think, the need to prove one's worth."

Lydia nodded. Surely she had not been called in to discuss the merits of medical education for women.

"It may not seem so"—Mrs. Curtis gestured around the room, the wave of her hand encompassing its luxuriance—"but I was not born into this life. My father owned a small pharmacy. I would often help him, compounding and preparing medicines. But he wanted me to have an education. To him that meant teaching. It was the most grandiose thing he could imagine. I did attend Mount Holyoke Seminary, as a scholarship student."

"Did you complete your degree?"

"Oh no. It was the usual story. I met Edward at a regatta party on the Charles. He was there with friends from university. I don't think I was quite the prize my mother-in-law hoped for."

"Nonsense, my dear," Curtis said, smiling indulgently at her.

"But we were in love and soon married. But you didn't come here to speak about me," Mrs. Curtis said.

"No, we did not," Volcker said impatiently. "You say that you knew Anna well. Did she ever confide in you about personal matters?"

"She told me of the tragic situation with her brother. I offered to help with money for a consultation. But she refused."

"Did you not think it odd when she disappeared without explanation?" Volcker asked.

"Of course, I was sorry she chose to leave. But I am not a keeper of these young women."

Volcker persisted. "But when a well-loved servant vanishes, is no effort made to find her? You knew how much she stood to lose if she left. Did that not concern you?"

"She was a servant, Inspector, not my daughter," Mrs. Curtis said coldly.

"In the days prior to her disappearance, did you notice any change in her behavior?" Lydia asked. "She was quite agitated when she came to see me in the clinic. No one here was aware of that?"

"It is not unusual for the servants to come down with ague and the like, Doctor. She insisted on doing her work," Mrs. Burt said.

"Are you through now, Volcker?" Curtis asked.

"Not quite. I have another question for the both of you. Please tell me what you know of Paul O'Meara," Volcker said.

"I said before, I can't be expected to know the names of all the servants." Curtis was exasperated.

"According to some, he was close with Anna and that may have upset others," Davies said.

"That is preposterous! Who has said this?" Mrs. Curtis looked genuinely surprised.

Mrs. Burt interrupted. "You must be mistaken, Inspector. I can assure you I would be aware of these goings-on."

"So what if there was a connection between these two?" Curtis said. "Her suicide is tragic. Of course we are sorry, but I cannot see how it involves any of us."

"She did not die by suicide. She was murdered," Volcker said.

"What?" Curtis asked. For the first time, his bravado was gone; real worry appeared about his features.

"Then it must be an unfortunate attack of some sort," Mrs. Curtis said.

"No," Lydia said firmly. "It was planned. Based on the autopsy results, she was first killed and then moved. The body was put into the river to suggest suicide."

"But you can't think someone here was involved in her death?" Curtis asked.

Curtis stood and walked over to a small table, where a pitcher of water and two crystal glasses stood. He lifted the pitcher and began to pour. Lydia could see his hand tremble, the tremor gaining momentum as he held the movement. He used his other hand to try to suppress it. He took the filled glass and raised it to his lips. His hand shook uncontrollably as he did so. The glass dropped to the floor, shattering into pieces.

"Edward!" Mrs. Curtis cried out at the jarring sound.

"I beg your pardon. My hand slipped," Curtis said.

Mrs. Burt moved quickly to pick up the shards of glass on the floor.

"You see how this news has upset us," Mrs. Curtis said. "All of this is such a terrible shock." She put a pale hand up to her brow, covering her face. "I feel quite faint."

"Enough, Volcker. Now look what you have done," Curtis said angrily.

Volcker and Davies stood.

"Allow me, Mrs. Curtis." Lydia stepped forward and knelt at her side. "Are you all right?"

"Please leave us for a moment, Edward," Mrs. Curtis said. Her husband nodded and led the others out.

Lydia remained in the room. She put her hand on Mrs. Curtis's wrist. The radial pulse was slow and steady, the skin cool to the touch. There was no hint of distress.

"Do you feel light-headed?" Lydia asked. "I have a stethoscope in my bag and can examine you further."

"No. I am all right. May I have my blanket?"

Lydia dutifully brought over a cashmere throw and draped it onto Mrs. Curtis's legs.

"Much better."

It was a strange show: the delicate beauty, the exquisite clothing, the feigned distress. Edward Curtis was the blustering protector, but his wife hardly seemed to need it.

"I am afraid you caught us unawares by this news. Do not think me unfeeling."

Lydia was surprised at this honesty. She decided to probe further.

"There is another possible suitor. A gentleman."

"That doesn't surprise me. Anna was a lovely girl, noticed by many."

"Do you have any idea who it could be?"

"No, and she would never have confided in me."

Mrs. Curtis was right; there had to be privacy, something held close and dear.

"I would often send Anna alone to the dressmaker or the milliner. There is a shop on Chestnut where I buy silk for all the trim on my clothing. She chose the most exquisite items. It was almost better than going myself."

Mrs. Curtis stood up, casting off the blanket. She walked to the small rolltop desk next to the window. There was no sign of unsteadiness.

She consulted a book that lay open on the desk. "I have written the addresses in my diary. Perhaps she met someone while out on an errand."

A shopkeeper or merchant would certainly seem a gentleman to the likes of Sally and Anna.

"I had forgotten." Mrs. Curtis smiled. She handed Lydia a piece of paper that was pressed into the book. It was a printed program for a concert at the Academy of Music, an evening of Schubert lieder based on the poems of Goethe.

"It was a few months ago, a benefit recital held by the hospital auxiliary board. Anna had helped me dress and I asked her if she would like to join me. There are often spaces in the stalls to stand," Mrs. Curtis said. "I thought she might find the music tiresome. But she was transported, so quiet in the carriage ride home."

It was like the poetry volumes she had loaned Anna. Did one need wealth and education to enjoy beauty? Lydia thought not.

She could see a row of photographs on the desk. They were the typical photos of charity events, the participants looking stilted and formal. But one was a striking tableau: Mr. and Mrs. Curtis stood with another couple, the men flanking the women. Even in the stark black-and-white image, Lydia could almost see the ruddy, boisterous expressions of the men, arrested in midlaugh. Between them stood the two women, one dark haired and the other flaxen. Their expressions were solemn and quiet, with eyes fixed on the camera. Their shoulders touched but they looked to be standing a world apart from their husbands.

Mrs. Curtis followed her gaze.

"That is Robert and Ida Thornton. Robert is Edward's great friend from university days. They can't seem but to have a good time in each other's presence. The Thorntons founded a charity in South Philadelphia. Anna and I would often go to help."

Lydia knew the area well. The "South Pole," as it was called by her students, the hinterlands to those on the campus at Twenty-second and North College.

"People from the neighborhood come to get assistance. Many are young women, abandoned by their families. In recent months, I have been busier with my children and other charity work. I often sent Anna in my stead."

"So she would go alone?"

"Yes. I was afraid she might find it overwhelming," Mrs. Curtis said. "But Anna seemed invigorated by it. She kept asking to go back."

Mrs. Curtis wrote on a piece of paper and handed it to Lydia.

"Ida is such a fiend for good works that the rest of us can hardly keep up. But there is a sense of being united in common purpose. I could see that would be exciting to someone like Anna. There are many young people working together, from all walks of life. Anna could have met someone there as well."

"Thank you, this is very helpful," Lydia said.

Mrs. Curtis nodded.

"I never told Anna that I came from modest means, that we had that in common. I know what it is like to have very little and want more."

DAVIES AND VOLCKER NOW SAT in a narrow stall off the main stables. They were waiting to interview Paul O'Meara. Dr. Weston had returned to the medical college and Davies was glad to be alone again with Volcker. Davies felt uncomfortable around her. She was so confident and assured.

The smell in the room was pleasing, of oil and wood shavings, discreetly covering any unpleasant odors from the stable. The implements of horse care were affixed like art on the walls: bridles, thin leather leads and whips, strange metal loops attached to a handle.

There was a rap on the door as it opened. Mr. Healy stood on the threshold. He led them through the door into the back courtyard. Davies looked up at the ominous clouds overhead. They made it to the stable door as fat pelts of rain started to fall onto the sleeve of his peacoat.

Healy gestured to a door embedded in the stone arch. Davies and Volcker ducked into the warmth of the stable.

The room was cast in darkness from the storm. In the corner stood a cot covered in a cheap blanket. A lantern sat at the edge of a table. Its light flickered at intervals as the wind screamed through the bars of the windows. A young man sat at the table.

"Paul?" Volcker asked.

It was the same young man who had been tending the chestnut mare on the first day the policemen had been at the house. But now he looked gaunt, his face drained of color. His eyes were swollen and red-rimmed.

"Yes, sir, that's me."

"You know why we are here?"

Paul nodded.

"No one in this house seems to want to volunteer anything about your connection with Anna. You had best tell us the truth," Volcker said.

"When did you last see her?" Davies asked.

"About three weeks ago."

"Anything odd about how she was behaving?"

"No, sir. But she was always worried about her brother."

"What is your job here? Working with the horses?"

"Yes, sir. Else I am in the garden."

"So you got to know Anna. Where did you meet with her?" Davies asked. They had walked through the warren of rooms that were the servants' quarters, the men firmly separated from the women.

"There is a shed at the end of the garden. I drink my tea there and Anna would join me. She was always going on about the books she was reading. Told me I should try it." He smiled, his features lighting up at the memory.

"How did you come to be hired here, Paul?" Volcker asked.

"Mrs. Curtis did it as a favor," Paul said. "Didn't have anywhere else to go. But my dad worked at the foundry a long time ago, so I came here to see if they would give me a job."

"Did you ever meet Anna outside the house?"

"Sometimes. She would walk with me by the river."

"Paul, isn't it strange that she told no one about your connection?"

"She said it was just for the two of us," Paul said.

"But a young girl walking out with her young man, that is a matter of pride. Yet she told no one, not even her sister?"

Paul said nothing.

"Did that make you angry?" Volcker probed.

"No, sir." The young man looked up at them, the dark eyes welling with tears that fell freely. He pressed his lips together, struggling to maintain his composure. His voice broke with emotion.

"She was kind to me."

Davies felt a rush of pity. Here at last was an honest expression of grief, so different from the shrewd and calculated responses of others they had questioned.

Volcker nodded. "We are done here for now."

Part Three

STASIS

15

Lydia grasped the child's hand in her own.

"Hold it steady, just like that. Keep it flat in the palm of your hand."

The little boy looked to his companion for guidance. His brother shrugged unhelpfully. Neither one knew what to say to the well-dressed lady who had taken an interest in them.

"There you are, now feel the weight of the disk in your hand," Lydia said. She took the boy's wrist and moved it back and forth to show him the movement.

He released the disk. The quoit flew in a triumphant arc and landed with a clang on the metal post a few yards away.

"Good on you, Billy!" his brother cried. Billy flushed with pleasure at the unaccustomed success.

"Well done." She shook hands with him in mock formality. "Now remember what I have taught you for next time."

"Yes, madam." Billy broke into a pleasing gap-toothed grin. She watched him run into the alley at the edge of the street.

Lydia stood, her knees aching from the strain of crouching. The edges of her cape dragged along the dust of the makeshift playing court, a patch of earth marked off by the neighborhood children.

"You're a dab hand, Doctor. I wouldn't have expected that."

She turned to see Sergeant Davies standing behind her.

"Really, Sergeant?" she said. "I loved this game as a child. I vied endlessly with my brother to be first." She dusted off her hands using her gloves. "I should challenge you to a match."

"Perhaps I will have to take you up on that." He gave her a small smile.

They were in the heart of South Philadelphia, the swath of the city below South Street stretching from the Delaware to the Schuylkill River. The vast area had been consolidated into the city limits in 1854, a diverse collection of districts like Moyamensing and Passyunk, Grays Ferry and Southwark. Each was like a village with its own distinctive feel, some with newcomers and others entrenched for generations, ready to supply labor to the city's textile mills and railroad depots, docks and shipyards. Each group, Irish, Italian, Black, put its own distinctive stamp on the neighborhood, carving out space to preserve culture and tradition. There was a sense of community and vivid life on every street: in the churches and parochial schools, the thriving open-air markets, the shops selling Italian pastries and Irish linen, the pubs and fraternal societies. And woven through it all were the ward bosses and gangs, who drew fierce allegiance and stoked territorial animosities. At times, the uneasy alliances in close quarters broke down, erupting into lawlessness.

Lydia had been in these neighborhoods since her student days. Woman's Med had gladly joined the fray, alongside the temperance workers and sanitary inspectors, to provide medical care to those who desperately needed it. Her first memory was of being engulfed by a crowd as she struggled to keep up with the intrepid Anthea on obstetrics rounds. It was a raucous assault on the senses as they navigated the labyrinthine alleys, a cacophony of voices surrounding them, the smell of frying food mixing with the pungent odor of rotting garbage. It had been a training like no other, far from the comparatively sedate wards of Woman's Hospital. She recalled stepping into the windowless flats, the oppressive warmth of being crowded into a small space, the large families watching in solemn silence. She had learned to think quickly and be adaptable, to work with very little. It was difficult work, compounded by a feeling of powerlessness, tending to those with the diseases that flourished in unsanitary conditions, like dysentery and typhoid. But like Anthea, she had developed an abiding affection for these communities, those who gave the city its striving heart.

Today the footpath teemed with people. There were children everywhere, trailing behind their harried mothers, racing joyously, bursting through clutches of people. A group of old men sat on the front stoop of a building, watching the unfolding drama of the street. The square was ringed by narrow brick buildings, many with open windows allowing a watchful gaze on the activity below.

"Careful now!" Davies sidestepped two young boys chasing each other, their thin frames a blur.

"It is a few blocks down, closer to the river," Lydia said, looking at the address Beatrice Curtis had given her.

They turned in to an alley. Lydia looked above their heads at the teetering stairways, like spiders with spindly legs clinging to the side of the building. A boy crouched on one of the landings and watched them through the bars of the grate.

"Here it is," Lydia said. They stopped at a door that looked like the façade of a shop; to the right was a bay window. A brass plaque on the door read: BLAKE TRUST.

Davies opened the door slowly. They stepped into a room with high ceilings and the back wall an expanse of windows. It must have been the floor of a countinghouse, an ideal location near the river where goods were brought off the barges and inventoried.

From across the room, a woman saw them.

"I am Ida Thornton," she said. She was slim and petite, her brow creased with worry. "Beatrice sent me a note about what has happened to Anna."

They followed her into an office, sitting across from her as she gestured to the two chairs. They made brief introductions.

"So you knew Anna?" Lydia asked.

"Oh yes. She was a great help to us. I will miss her," Ida said.

Her voice trailed off as if she realized the finality of her words. "What a tragedy this is, I can't imagine how her family must feel . . ."

"Mrs. Curtis said Anna often came here on her own . . . ," Lydia began, but she was quickly interrupted. Ida Thornton stood, looking expectantly towards the door.

"That is Robert, my husband. He was out in the neighborhood on a delivery."

Robert Thornton strode into the cramped room, filling the space and looming over his wife. He was tall and broad-shouldered. Lydia recognized him immediately from the photograph. His cheeks were flushed, but not just from the cold. Lydia could see the spider veins, the splintered blood vessels, telltale signs of heavy alcohol use. His skin was bloated and puffy over heavily lidded eyes.

He spoke loudly despite the close quarters of the room.

"How do you do, aaah . . . ?" He paused.

"This is Dr. Weston and Sergeant Davies. They have come about Anna."

"Doctor? A lady doctor?" he asked, a brow arched in amusement. "My goodness, what will the modern world serve up next?"

He looked from one to the other as he removed his gloves.

"What is your specialty, if I may ask, Dr. Weston?"

"Medicine" came the terse reply.

Thornton nodded, as if he knew exactly what that entailed.

"To each his own, I suppose. I find it a travesty when a woman needs to seek employment. After all, she is the keeper of all that is good in the home and hearth." He smiled at his wife and patted her on the head as one would a child.

What an insufferable speech, Lydia thought. It had no doubt been delivered on many occasions.

"So Beatrice Curtis is involved in your work?" Lydia asked.

"Oh yes, we have been friends for a long time," Ida said. "Robert rowed an eight with Edward at Penn. Bea is a great supporter, helping with whatever is needed. Anna started coming with her about a year ago."

"Did Anna have any friendships here that you noticed?" Lydia asked.

"Ida could say better. The volunteers mix with one another. There is an informality that many appreciate," Thornton said.

"You make it sound like a bad thing, Robert," Ida said. "I did not look at her as a servant, someone beneath us."

"Was there anyone in particular she seemed close to?" Lydia probed.

"No, I can't really recall," Ida said. "There are some university students who volunteer here, and I can introduce you to them."

"Yes, that would be helpful," Lydia replied.

"So you are a police investigator as well?" Thornton said. "You must keep very busy, Doctor."

Lydia met his gaze.

"It is hardly a job for a lady. You should tread carefully. Not everyone is as receptive to questions as we are."

It was not a friendly admonition.

"Well, you are welcome to speak with anyone here," Ida said firmly. "We want to be of help in this terrible business."

"Yes, of course," Thornton said. "I am afraid I am due back out on an errand, but Ida can show you about."

They followed her into the larger space. The room had the orderly hum of a well-run school. A few women sat together, putting careful stitches into swatches of fabric, their heads bent in concentration. In the corner, a group of girls with slates perched on their laps watched as an earnest young man patiently explain sums written on a blackboard.

"Please, we can talk more freely here," Ida said. She gestured to a low table. Lydia and Davies sat on stools across from her.

"When Bea sent me the note, I could scarcely believe the news," she said. "But you must be honest with me. Why are you here, really? It cannot be so simple as trying to trace Anna's friends."

"We know that Anna had a suitor but he has not come forward."

"And you think she might have met him here?"

"We don't know. From the entries in her diary, it seemed she was having an affair," Lydia said.

"I see," Ida said. "I wish she had confided in me. It is young women like her that we are seeking to help. Was she in any trouble?"

"I don't know, but the last time she saw me, she was very upset. Soon after that she disappeared altogether," Lydia said.

Ida nodded. "I liked Anna tremendously. In the beginning, she followed Bea's lead. But I could see she was capable. I don't know that Bea would encourage that kind of intelligence. She does not feel the same urgency to uplift her fellow sisters."

An interesting observation, Lydia thought.

"How did you get started in this neighborhood?" Davies asked.

"It is my family money that allows us to do this work," she said. "I had the good fortune to have a mother with the zeal of a missionary. Little did my father know how she filled my head with what it was possible for a woman to do. When Mother died, she left me her own considerable fortune. Father was furious, but he was powerless against the terms of her will. I think she would have approved of what I have done."

Lydia could hear the pride in her voice. Ida Thornton was like so many of her students, who had thrown off the constraints of society to pursue the work they deeply believed in. But how did Robert Thornton see this work, or fit into it? It seemed to be clearly hers.

"Do the participants come from this neighborhood?" Davies asked.

"Mostly it is word of mouth, occasional referrals from the sanitary inspector. Many are young women, often with a child or two, cast off from their families. They need much more than a job."

"How many are on staff now?" Lydia asked.

Ida nodded to the two men at the blackboard.

"Andrew and Lewis are students at Penn. Andy's mother is a dear friend of mine. She wants him to understand how the poor live, to temper the riches of Croesus as it were. He brought a few friends and now we have a fresh crop of teachers."

Ida stood up. She led them back towards the front of the room.

"But to understand this place, you must speak with Paul O'Meara. Perhaps you have met him already? Even after ten years, we are still outsiders. He has become our general factotum, overseer of all. Isn't that right?"

She smiled warmly as she spoke to a young man sitting on a stool. He sat with his legs splayed out, a casual guard at the front door. He did not stand to greet them.

"Paul." Ida Thornton's voice was stern. "Please introduce yourself to Dr. Weston and the sergeant."

He obediently stood.

So this was Paul, Lydia thought. She had not observed him closely at the Curtis house. He was young, not more than a boy himself. He was of medium height with thick chestnut hair and large dark eyes. There was a sullen charm about him, the way he seemed indifferent to Ida's authority.

"I didn't expect to see you here, Paul," Davies said.

Paul nodded. "Mrs. Curtis lets me come. Mr. Thornton needed help as they were having trouble getting people to come in. No one trusted them, thought they were religious cranks."

"So you know how to get things done. Always a useful man in a place like this," Davies said.

"I lived in the neighborhood for a time. I do what the Thorntons need me to," Paul said. "Most who want to do good come in and leave us where we started. Not Mr. Thornton. He takes care of people."

There was an interesting fluidity between the two households, but Ida Thornton's relaxed attitude towards social mores must have been a relief.

"I do my own rounds in the morning, rather like you doctors," he said. "I find out who needs what, medicines or food. If someone misses a day, I check on 'em."

A young woman passed them, carrying a tray laden with bowls of soup. She wore a starched pinafore over her dress. Her face was scrubbed and shiny, with pockmarks marring her complexion. Her skin was so deeply pitted it looked as though dark holes had been punctured in the surface. She set the tray down solemnly.

The other women came to the long table. A few nodded shyly to Lydia and Davies.

Ida sat at the head and offered grace for the meal. Lydia and Davies approached the two young men Ida had identified as teachers. They sat next to one another on a narrow bench.

"Andrew Cole." A sandy-haired young man with a broad face offered his hand in greeting. "This is Lewis Euston."

"It is unbelievable what has happened to Anna," Andrew said.

"Ida said her body was found in the Schuylkill," Lewis said. He had a milky complexion with fine features. A lock of dark hair fell over his forehead and he brushed it away.

"Yes."

"God, how terrible," Lewis said. "Do you have any idea who could have done it?"

"Not yet," Lydia replied. The conversation stopped at the far end of the table. The young woman who had served them soup stared, her mouth slightly open.

"How did you all come to work here?" Davies asked.

"The two of us have been here the last six months," Andrew said. "My mother is a real bluestocking. She heard Ida speak at her club, so that was the end of it for me. But I am glad I came."

He grinned at Lewis. "I dragged this fellow into it. He is a medical student. It was time for him to see the light of day."

"Did you both know Anna?" Lydia asked.

"Yes. I thought she was a friend of Mrs. Curtis's. I couldn't believe she was a servant," Andrew said.

"What a wretched thing to say," Lewis said. "The poor girl is dead."

Andrew blushed. "She carried herself differently. It was obvious she had been educated."

"We invited her to help the younger children with their letters and sums. She was quite adept. She brought her own books, good volumes of poetry and literature. I would mark ones she should read," Lewis said.

"Did you spend time together outside of work?" Lydia asked.

"Yes. It gets a bit lonely hanging about with this lot," Andrew said, cocking his thumb towards his friend. "Ida has connections at some of the women's colleges, so others come in, do short-term tutoring and the like. Certainly, we all go for coffee or have a meal at the pub after our work is done. Anna was always welcome to come with us."

"I asked her to join us for picnics at the river or walks in Wissahickon on Sunday; loads of Penn students go. She would usually refuse," Lewis said.

Andrew Cole gave Lydia a shrewd look.

"You seem surprised, Dr. Weston. We have cast off the ways of the older generation. My father thinks he will get a communicable disease just by setting foot in the tenement. That is not how I choose to live," he said.

"Was there anyone she was particularly close to?" Lydia asked.

The young men exchanged glances at this question but did not speak.

"Perhaps you could give me the names of some of the others that came to these gatherings," Davies said.

"Of course, Sergeant, I would be happy to. It was just a bit of fun, you know?" Andrew said.

But would it have been that for Anna? To these young men, a romance would be a casual diversion. But was it here that she had met the young man she had fallen in love with?

Ida Thornton came to them.

"I hope we have been of help. Please, if we can do anything more, do not hesitate to call on us." She pressed her calling card into Lydia's hand. Her home address was written on the back.

LYDIA STEPPED INTO THE ALLEY with Davies. The sky was tinged a brilliant pink as dusk set in.

"What do you think?" she asked.

"It seems the place, if any, she could have met someone. Perhaps one of these young men took advantage of that." Davies shook his head. "It's a shame, what's happened to her. If only she had kept to herself."

"Do you suggest she did not know her place, and that is why she was killed?" Lydia asked.

Davies pressed his lips together.

"No. It just seems too good to be true. The servants mix with heiresses and all are considered equal. There is nothing wrong with bettering yourself but best to keep to your own."

"They are gentlemen. Anna would see them as such," Lydia said. "To them, it might be mild flirtation. To Anna, it would represent much more, a means of escape."

"Come now," Davies scoffed. "What would happen if one of those young men brought Anna home to meet the family? It is well and good to have high-minded sentiments, but it's not acceptable to marry the help."

"That may not be true. Perhaps one of these young men truly loved her," Lydia said.

"With all due respect, Doctor, what would you know of this?"

"I know what it is like to have to work hard to prove yourself."

"Oh yes, the revolutionary lady doctors of the medical college, forging a new path," Davies said snidely. "You remind us of that at every turn. But it is not the same. Most here don't have enough money to buy food or pay the week's rent."

"Don't lecture me, Sergeant," Lydia said, her temper flaring. "It is no concern of yours, but I worked all through medical school to pay my tuition. I have more in common with the people here than you think."

"I doubt that very much," he said.

She stopped walking and turned to face him. She could feel her anger rising. He was so sure of himself.

"You see me as insensitive to Anna's plight. But you know nothing of the poverty I experienced after my father's death. You have no right to judge what you don't understand."

She remembered how it had felt like a triumph when she arrived at the women's seminary for college after diligently scraping together the tuition from menial jobs. She had stood out amidst the sophistication of her classmates, many of them the products of expensive girls' schools, her unfashionable clothes earning their disapproval. Would Davies understand the careful accounting she had done each month to afford food, the quiet forgoing of socials to save money, and the dawning humiliation that her home study had been wholly inadequate preparation? To many of the other girls, those years were a finishing school before marriage. But to Lydia, her education was a path to independence. She focused on her studies with an intensity that bewildered her classmates and left her isolated.

Davies was quiet. He rubbed his hands together from the cold. They walked down the deserted alleyway towards the street.

"Suppose Anna had fallen in love." Lydia stopped again. "She equates flirtation with love and naïvely hopes this may result in marriage. The young man realizes what began as harmless fun has grown serious. His family will disapprove, perhaps cut him off in disgrace. So he decides to break it off."

"But how did Anna take that betrayal? Did she do something she came to regret?" Davies said.

Lydia considered that prospect uneasily. It was what the poetry in the diary had suggested. Perhaps Anna wanted to reveal the affair. If a wealthy young man felt threatened by a very public reprisal, what had he been driven to do?

They parted ways at the corner, Davies giving her a brusque nod goodbye. She could sense his irritation with her.

It was getting dark and the crowd was thinning. Lydia was not naïve about her safety. A turn into an isolated lane could quickly become dangerous for a woman walking alone. She headed towards the larger cross street to catch the omnibus. A couple passed her, their dark heads bent together. Their faces were not visible. How easy it was to move freely in the city, cloaked in anonymity. She thought of Anna and Paul and the young men at the trust. The casual atmosphere that Ida Thornton had created was a direct rebuke to the rigidity of the Curtis household. Anna had more freedom to do as she pleased at the trust, to carry on an affair without being discovered.

That was an honest appraisal, as her mother would say. It was their code from childhood, asking the other's opinion on a situation, from the most mundane matters to those of the greatest importance. How Lydia longed to hear that voice. She could always rely on Mother to give advice in her forthright way. It had started the day her brother goaded her, teasing that she was too small to climb the oak tree at the edge of the forest. She was determined to show him up, though she was forbidden to go into the woods alone. She had almost reached the top branch when a careless slip of the foot sent her falling. She hit the rocky ground and sustained a painful fracture of the wrist. That evening she lay in bed nursing her arm, sobbing in fury at her brother's treachery. Mother had come to her. But she was not angry.

"An honest appraisal, Lydia," she said. She sat at the edge of the bed and rewound the stiff fabric that the doctor had used to bind the splint, tucking the corners neat and tight.

"You shouldn't have gone into the woods alone. But a little disobedience can be acceptable, to show others what you are capable of."

She smiled. "I have something for you."

Mother brought out a small pouch, the luscious pink silk edged with a gold border. It was one of her treasures from India.

"When I was a girl, I loved to explore the hillsides on the tea estate. My father let me do it, but only if I carried this with me."

Lydia opened the bag and emptied it onto the bedcovers. There was a penknife with a smooth handle and a small flat stone.

"I carved the stone myself, to use as an arrow tip for archery. But it can be used as a weight or flint to start a fire."

Lydia looked up at her with wide eyes, as if seeing her anew. What marvels was Mother capable of?

"Now it is yours. So you can look after yourself someday."

Her mother could never have imagined where that little pouch would go. Lydia could feel the comforting weight of it against her side, nestled into her larger bag, as she stood on the corner of South Ninth Street. At times it seemed childish and ridiculous to keep it. Over the years, she had added items, a box of matches and a thin length of silk rope to use as a tourniquet, and the contents had been put to surprisingly good use. But most of all, its presence gave her strength as she carried it, a feeling of the protection of someone who was long gone.

The omnibus approached. The driver nodded to her and the horse slowed to a halt. She took a seat in the lower carriage as others boarded. An honest appraisal then, Lydia thought. Someone at the Blake Trust knew more about what happened to Anna, she was sure of it.

16

Lydia entered the hospital ward, the heavy door yielding with a push. The room was a study in symmetry, row after row of wrought-iron bedsteads, linen sheets crisply folded into the corners. The smell of carbolic soap mixed with the stuffiness of unwashed bodies. There were windows on each side of the room, covered to the halfway mark with cotton drapes that allowed light to seep through. It was the beginning of morning rounds and staff thronged at the bedside. She could hear the faint moans of pain and rustling of sheets as patients moved in their beds, the sounds amplified in the large hall.

The Woman's Hospital had been founded in 1861. From modest beginnings caring for a handful of patients, the general ward now contained over thirty beds. As she passed through, small clutches of students would look up at her. Lydia could see her group of three in the small alcove at the end of the ward.

"Good morning, Dr. Weston." Eleanor Petrie stepped forward from among the students. "We are ready. I have the patient list for rounds."

"Let's begin." They had a busy day ahead, first with rounds in the hospital and then on to the clinic to see patients.

Each of the students had already done an examination of her patient, noting any overnight events. They had carefully reviewed the vital signs, a particular demand of Lydia's, from a clipboard at the foot of the bed. On it was written the heart rate, pulse, and temperature in four-hour increments for the past twenty-four hours. Each student gave a clear and concise presentation. Lydia asked a few questions as the group made notes.

"Well done! And on the first day, too," Lydia said. There was great pleasure in being with this group of senior students. The arc of their education was almost complete and their clinical acumen showed.

"We have taken to heart Weston's rules of the wards," one of them said.

"Oh yes? And what are they?" Lydia smiled.

"Preparation is everything." Eleanor held up her stethoscope and pointed to the small scalpel, scissors, and length of suture in her apron pocket.

"Never ignore a fever."

"An abscess must be drained."

"Examine the eyes. Pale conjunctiva can be a sign of anemia."

"And when all else fails, decamp to the Continental for lunch," Eleanor said.

They all laughed, Lydia included. They had worked long hours together through the spring term, with complicated patients. On a particularly arduous day, they had finished rounds early and crowded together in a hansom. Lydia had treated them to lunch at the elegant hotel, in gratitude for their work.

"Excellent. Now I know that I have taught you well," she said.

The light mood dissipated quickly as they set to work. The first patient, Miss Carter, was a young woman who had presented with severe low back pain. She had grown weak, eating little in the days prior to admission. Her urine had taken on a dark rust color and she had marked swelling in her face as well as her hands and feet. A closer history revealed that she had had scarlatina a few weeks prior, with a fever and painful sore throat. Her skin had been covered with a diffuse red rash. A urinalysis revealed large amounts of the protein albumin, a sign of Bright's disease. The infection had caused nephritis, an inflammation of the kidneys.

Lydia pulled aside the bedsheets to expose the patient's legs. She pressed her index finger into the lower part of one calf. The skin rebounded. The edema was improving. She listened to the lungs and noted slightly decreased breath sounds at the bases. She put the stethoscope down and used her two fingers to percuss, tapping them against the lower part of the back as the patient sat up straight. The sound was dense and flat, not the usual hollow echo. There was residual fluid in the lungs. Eleanor read aloud the values for urine output. It had improved overnight, a good sign that injury to the kidneys was beginning to recede.

Lydia put little stock in many of the treatments for Bright's disease, ostensibly focused on increasing blood flow to the kidneys. Some used purgatives or emetics, with the idea that clearing the intestines of fluid lessened the strain on systemic circulation. Another remedy called for dry cupping with rounded glass vials over afflicted areas; this would draw blood into the capillaries, ensuring a brisk return of blood to the heart. She had read of hot air and water baths and the so-called imperial drink, cream of tartar and lemon, or, worse yet, bloodletting with leeches. Most of these had little beneficial effect or basis in scientific evidence. Miss Carter would likely continue to recover, with rest and careful monitoring of salt and fluid intake.

The patient had been terrified at the sight of them. Lydia gently reassured her that she would soon go home.

The next case was not so hopeful. Lydia feared Mrs. Dale would not survive much longer despite their best efforts. She was in the throes of late-stage liver disease. She was propped up in bed and visibly struggling to breathe. She was somnolent and confused. Her swollen belly was barely covered by the bedsheets. She was severely jaundiced, every inch of her sallow skin glowing a vivid, fluorescent yellow.

Mrs. Dale had been admitted with a large abscess of the thigh. It had required immediate surgical attention with incision and drainage, the wound expressing copious amounts of foul-smelling pus. Even two days later, purulent fluid continued to soak the dressings. And now there was a new ominous sign: the edges of the incision looked jagged and angry, the surrounding skin bright red.

Both Lydia and Harlan were avid proponents of Joseph Lister's work on antisepsis, from his initial case series in *The Lancet* in 1867, when he applied Pasteur's germ theory to surgical wound infections. Dr. Lister had done his first work on compound fractures, where bone broke through the surface of the skin, giving rise to infection. He demonstrated that dressings soaked in a solution of carbolic acid mixed with boiled linseed oil reduced the incidence of abscess formation and its dreaded sequelae, gangrene and pyemia. Surgeons could sterilize their instruments by soaking them in carbolic acid and use a diluted solution to wash their hands prior to procedures. Dr. Lister had even devised a spray atomizer to purify the air. Lydia remembered the comical sight of Harlan walking solemnly through the operating theater using the small steam vaporizer, the metal apparatus like a lantern attached to the glass vial. He looked like a master perfumer plying his wares, enveloped in a cloud of sweet-smelling carbolic acid spray.

But as with any advance there were the inevitable failures, the trial and error, the need to constantly refine technique. In the wards, Lydia advocated vigorous handwashing, good ventilation, and careful monitoring of respiratory symptoms to prevent the spread of illness among patients. Yet all their efforts at prevention were futile when infection was entrenched.

But for Mrs. Dale there was a more urgent problem. The excess fluid from liver failure was saturating her body, seeping from the cracked lesions on her edematous legs and filling her abdomen and lungs, putting pressure on her heart.

"We will have to do a large-volume paracentesis to ease her breathing," Lydia said. It was a Sisyphean task done only a few days prior, but the fluid had quickly reaccumulated. Lydia gave the patient an injection of morphine for pain. She prepared the syringe with the long glass vial; the large-bore needle attached was thick. At the bedside, Eleanor lined up the large glass jugs that would soon be filled with peritoneal fluid. Lydia showed the students how to palpate the tense lower abdomen to find the ideal entry spot. She advanced the needle into the skin firmly and felt the puncture, the release of pressure as she went through the muscle layer and subcutaneous fat, into the peritoneal cavity. The viscous yellow fluid passed into the syringe, tinged with blood.

Eleanor took her place to continue the arduous task of drawing off several liters. It would take time to do the procedure. She removed the syringe attached to the needle and replaced it with thicker catheter tubing, hanging down towards the floor; copious fluid, aided by gravity, flowed briskly through into the larger glass jars. If too much fluid was removed, it could cause a precipitous drop in blood pressure, but there was little choice at this point.

Afterwards, they discussed the cases in a small alcove off the ward. Lydia reviewed the pathophysiology of cirrhosis. Mrs. Dale had spiked a fever every six hours, from either the suppurating wound or peritonitis, an infection of the abdominal fluid. It was a sign of impending pyemia. The students wrote careful instructions for the nurses and noted when they should be called by messenger for urgent issues.

Lydia sat while the students completed their notes. She used the brief respite to look at her correspondence, rereading the message Harlan had sent that morning. He had completed the autopsy, confirming cerebral hemorrhage as the cause of death. He had found nothing else unusual.

Lydia folded the thin letter. Since the initial exam on Anna's body,

Lydia had been consumed by the police investigation. Harlan's work was thorough and painstaking; it was rare for him to miss anything significant. But she had brought Anna's casebook with her. She intended to go to the anatomy lab this evening and go over everything one final time.

"We are finished, Dr. Weston," Eleanor said, interrupting her thoughts.

Lydia looked up.

"Very well. Let's take a short break for lunch." She consulted her pocket watch. "We don't have long before the afternoon clinic starts."

The students gathered their belongings, clearing the table of their papers.

Dr. Harper, the gadfly of the thesis meeting, peered around the screen that divided the alcove in two.

"Running late, are we?" he said.

Anthea had told the faculty that Harper would have to be endured for a few more weeks, until a suitable replacement could be found. In the meantime, he was precepting students on the medicine ward.

Harper pushed his chair back to better regard Lydia, looking over the top of his pince-nez. He wore an immaculate suitcoat over a white shirt, the edges of the cuffs gleaming in the light. Apparently endless pontification required little hands-on work.

"You see, I do prefer to take my time with the students. It sets a better example of how a doctor should behave." He gestured absently towards the two sitting behind him. "I will admit they are more capable than I thought. But it takes many more hours to instruct than I am used to."

Lydia felt a pang of sympathy for the young women. She could see their papers spread over the small table as they pored over the notes together.

"They are new to clinical work, so that is to be expected," Lydia said.

"Indeed. But still I find a remedial effort must be undertaken," Harper said. He looked up at her group of students curiously. "I must say I find it fascinating here, Dr. . . ."

Lydia could see that again he struggled to remember her name. She was not going to remind him, as she hardly wanted to be drawn further into conversation with this odious man.

"Perhaps we can meet, so I can give you my impressions. There are so many things here that could stand improvement," Harper said.

Lydia gave him a curt nod.

"I doubt that will be possible, as I am very busy," she said. "But I would have to consult my schedule.

"For a day that will never come," she muttered under her breath as she gathered her students together and left the ward.

17

The waiting room was crowded when Lydia and the students arrived after lunch. Patients looked up at them expectantly, sitting close together on wooden benches. It was a free clinic attached to the hospital, so most came with no appointment. There were mostly women and children, with a few men interspersed.

The head nurse approached Lydia. "Bursting at the seams today, we are, Doctor. The first patient would like to see you on your own if you don't mind."

She handed Lydia a slip with brief information: Abraham Griffin, age fifty-two, cough for a fortnight.

Lydia nodded. Many times patients asked for her by name.

She stepped into the dark corridor leading to the exam rooms. A row of windows lined the wall above her head, filtering in the stark light of the gloomy day. She entered the first room.

The patient was thin and tall, his knees bent awkwardly as he perched on the edge of the exam table. His brown hair was speckled with gray, and clear blue eyes peered out at her from under heavy eyebrows. His face was creased with wrinkles, as if he had spent long hours in the sun.

He stood up when she entered. His thick cotton work shirt was untucked, with the suspenders looped off. He was ready to be examined.

"Hello, Mr. Griffin. I understand you have been suffering from a cough."

"Abe, please. Yes, ma'am. It started off dry but last week I brought up the thick stuff, a bit green. Been feeling more breathless the last few days."

"Have you coughed up any blood?"

He shook his head.

"Good. If you can please remove your shirt, I will examine you." She bent to take her stethoscope out of her bag. "Any pain in the chest?"

"I suppose my chest always hurts," he said. Lydia turned back to him and drew in a breath.

His torso was like a hardened shell, etched in a terrible mosaic pattern. From the base of his neck to the lower abdomen, it looked as though his skin was melting, like rivulets of wax dripping from a candle. In some places, it had thickened into ridges of a deep red color and, in others, the complexion took on an unnatural pearlescent sheen, completely devoid of pigment and prone to ulceration.

She had seen severe burns like this before. Her patients had been the victims of brutal chance: the chambermaid caught in the flare of hot oil on an open fire or the factory worker blinded by the abrupt splash of corrosive chemicals. Abe Griffin's wounds could be concealed with clothing. But for many, the cruel aftermath of their injuries only deepened their poverty and isolation. They were deemed unfit for work and shunned because of their visible deformities.

"Didn't mean to startle you," he said. "But you see. My chest always feels tight."

Lydia understood. The hardened skin would act like a vise, causing a restrictive pattern in the lungs. It would be like breathing out against a tight shell, difficult to take in deep breaths. He would be more prone to pneumonia as poor aeration would create a nidus for infection.

She placed her stethoscope on his chest. She heard the slight crackles at the bases, the slight wheeze with forced expiration. The sound was even but faint, as if transmitted through many layers of wool.

"I am not worried about an infection at the moment, so that is good news," she said. "How did the burns occur?"

"Unlucky, I suppose. All I remember is the roar of the explosion then a wall of fire. I woke up in the worst pain I had ever been in. It happened about twelve years ago. I was on a crew at the Curtis foundry, near the river."

So this was not a chance meeting, Lydia thought. He had sought her out.

"I saw you at the house, asking questions with the police. I am a servant there."

Lydia felt uneasy. He was watching her. The room felt quiet, the space between them close.

"I suppose I made it worse for myself. I stayed behind too long, trying to help my men get out."

It was miraculous he had survived, Lydia thought. Patients with extensive burns like his often died from profound hypovolemia, their organs shutting down in rapid succession. If they survived the initial assault, there was the horrific pain and risk of infection to contend with.

"The Curtises don't like to talk about the fire. The family put on a good show, giving money to us survivors, jobs at the house. Maybe it is a penance, to keep us quiet."

"How did you find me?" Lydia asked.

"It was Anna. She told me I should come see you, long before she disappeared. That you might help me with treatment."

"Were you close to her?"

He looked down at his hands.

"She was my friend."

Lydia was touched by his simple statement. Anna was becoming a ghost, hovering at the periphery of the case. The real person had become calcified in a pristine image, her true self obscured by the narratives of those around her. To each of them she was someone different. To Mrs. Burt and Mrs. Curtis, she was the model servant, dutiful and compliant. To Ida Thornton, she was a selfless do-gooder, caring for others amidst her own struggles. Lydia herself saw Anna as a noble striver, pulling herself out of poverty. The images seemed hollow, treacherously one-dimensional.

"Do you know something that might help the police?" Lydia asked.

"I am not sure. But I must tell someone." He looked up at her. "Anna didn't deserve what happened to her. She was a nice young lady, always ready to give without asking in return. No one else in that house would."

"What kind of work do you do?"

He took a short breath.

"I am a valet for Mr. Curtis. His hands are unsteady, tremble something awful at times. The doctors aren't sure what is wrong, but he can't even button a shirt or lace his own shoes. It embarrasses him to no end. But I am hardly one to talk, am I?"

Griffin gestured broadly to the wounds on his chest.

"The work is all I am fit for. I help him dress. Anna did the same for Mrs. Curtis. She was a favorite of the madam's, never a good thing in my opinion. But Anna and I would talk often, have a good laugh.

"One night we were getting them ready for an evening out. I was shining shoes and Anna was pressing a gown. We were in the dressing room next to their bedroom. They were having a terrible quarrel."

"Could you hear what they were saying?" Lydia asked.

"It was about a letter Mr. Curtis had received. The madam is usually a cool one, but she was furious. She asked why he hadn't told her about this before and said that he was hiding something from her. It wasn't the first one he had gotten."

"Did you see the letter?"

He nodded.

"We went into the room after they left. Mrs. Curtis was in tears and he had been trying to console her. He had left it on the desk. Anna and I both saw it. It didn't make sense, no address or name. It just said, 'You will pay for the sins of the past. You have the blood of innocents on your hands.'"

"Do you have any idea what it referred to?"

"It could only be the fire. What else? Many thought at the time that it hadn't been an accident, and those are the kinds of words you don't forget."

"Did Anna know this?"

"She must have. And I worry that she may have told someone."

"You must tell the police. It could be important."

"I can't," he said. For the first time he seemed fearful. "I can't lose my job. I must earn for my children. I am all they have."

But he had come to her. He had been willing to risk that as a testament to his friendship with Anna.

"I took her kindness for granted. I have become like all of them at that house, living meanly and only for myself," he said bitterly. "But the police will listen to you. And perhaps that will help find her killer."

He stood up to leave. She watched him put on his coat, wincing in pain as he extended his arms into the sleeves.

"Abe, it is not too late for you. There are new procedures that can be done to release the skin contractures," Lydia said. "It won't correct the scarring, but it could ease the pain. I can arrange for you to see a good surgeon. It would cost you nothing."

He smiled at her. "Anna was right about you. She said that you would do whatever you could to help. But you would always be honest, no matter how difficult the news."

18

Harlan wiped his hands on his apron. The light was turned low, giving the room an eerie cast. The skulls on the shelf sat in half shadow, in silent witness to the work being done. He had replaced each instrument on the tray, cleaned and ready for its next use. It was an old habit from the war, from his days operating under the most difficult conditions imaginable. It had helped to create order in scenes reminiscent of the most gruesome abattoir.

It happened less frequently now and never at obvious times. He would be caught unawares, when feeling the weak sunlight through the parlor window or walking on a cold winter morning. The images appeared with startling clarity and in an instant he would be back to the bleakest days of Fredericksburg, to the makeshift operating theater in an abandoned church. He could see the soldiers lined up on the tables, bleeding profusely from gaping wounds, their screams of agony ringing in his ears. His heart would pound as he relived those moments: the futile efforts to quickly draw up morphine to ease pain, his arms aching from the strain of performing endless amputations, the metallic smell of blood saturating his hair and his clothes. The worst was the vacant stares of the young soldiers, as if death already held them close. Many were no more than boys.

Harlan's father had begged him not to go to the front. Doing so was a repudiation of the deeply held values of his Quaker upbringing. They had a bitter parting, full of recrimination. Harlan was confident that his skill would be put to good use. He had struggled, at times overcome with despair. There was no way to make sense of the sheer scale of carnage; all the work he had done before seemed, by contrast, to be a quaint academic exercise. But he had found the path back to himself, a way to salvage scant meaning in the face of devastating loss. He worked tirelessly, in any free moment he had, often missing sleep. He made detailed notes of every procedure he did: the types of incisions, the instruments used, the method of amputation, even the length of suture and types of knots tied. He would publish it as a manual for other surgeons to use on the battlefield, so that other lives might be spared. And he kept the last promise he made to himself at the front, when he received news of his father's death. They had never made amends. When he returned home, to the shock of Anthea and his colleagues, he had taken the position of professor at Woman's Medical College, resigning all other posts. He would devote the rest of his career to teaching women students. He had never regretted it.

Harlan had completed the autopsy himself, as Lydia had continued with the police investigation. He had used the trephine, the T-shaped instrument that required considerable force to bore into the skull. Once inside the cranium, he had easily found the dark blood clot, stark against the serpiginous folds of the gray matter of the brain. As expected, it confirmed hemorrhage as the cause of death, the aftermath of blunt trauma to the head.

The cause of death was now firmly established and all that remained was to carefully catalog: to measure and weigh each organ, to examine individual tissue sections if needed, noting any abnormalities. The report could be used as evidence to support a conviction; any careless errors or omissions and a case could be dismissed, as he had learned from past experience.

He looked over at Lydia. She had insisted on coming after a long day of work. He knew that she had to satisfy herself that all had been done correctly.

She was pensive. He could see that the case was wearing heavily on her. They were so alike in many ways, rarely revealing distress.

In front of her, on the lab bench, was a metal tray: she was doing a dissection of the pelvic organs, the uterus and ovaries.

She looked up at him. Her face was drawn.

"Something is wrong," she said quietly.

"What is it?"

"The ovaries here are of a normal size. There is no sign of a cyst. The tissue looks healthy," she said.

She continued the dissection as he watched.

"Harlan, look at this." She gasped.

He came to the edge of the table. It was unmistakable.

"She was pregnant when she died," he said.

"That is impossible."

19

They sat around the table, the surface of the lab bench still slick from Harlan's ministrations. The sky parlor was cold. It was seven o'clock in the morning, well before any students would arrive. Lydia was wrapped in her scarf, the policemen in overcoats. They could hear the clanging of the metal pipes of the radiator, like the jackhammer of a miner deep within the earth.

"The autopsy is complete," Harlan said. "As you all now know, we confirmed that she was pregnant at the time of death."

Volcker clapped his hands to his lap. "What an extraordinary turn of events! There we have it, do we not?"

"No." Harlan's tone was forceful. "You must listen, Thomas. There is more."

He nodded to Lydia.

She gripped the armrests of the wooden chair for support. She feared her voice would break.

"There is no possible way that the body we have is that of Anna Ward," she said.

They stared at her. Davies's jaw dropped open. Volcker stopped walking and gaped at her. The room was quiet save for the patter of the rain on the skylight above their heads.

"What can you mean, Doctor?" Volcker asked.

"Anna had a medical condition that prevented her from having a child. She had an ovarian cyst that was very large," Lydia said.

She saw the confusion on Davies's and Volcker's faces and sought to explain.

"Many times these cysts, or fluid-filled sacs, are harmless. They cause no symptoms. But if they grow or are many in number, they can cause pain or rupture. In a case like Anna's, the cysts can interfere with a woman's menstrual cycle. Without a regular pattern of menses, it is very unlikely for a woman to become pregnant. The condition can be treated with surgery, but it can be difficult to correct."

The policemen stared at her in disbelief.

Lydia opened Anna's casebook to the pages marked.

"Here are my notes. You can see for yourself, what I wrote at her last exam."

At a visit six months prior, Lydia had noted the distension of the abdomen. During the pelvic exam, she had easily palpated the large, firm mass. Anna had had no menses for several months. Because of the size of the mass, it was likely causing pain. Lydia had made a note about possible surgery; otherwise the condition would prevent Anna from having children.

"So there is no physical way she could have been carrying a child?" Volcker asked.

"No," Lydia replied. "I would testify in court to that evidence."

"But you did the autopsy yourselves. How did you not see immediately she was pregnant?" Davies asked incredulously.

"In the early stages, it would not be obvious," Lydia said.

A pregnancy of twelve weeks, as they estimated in this case, would cause minimal enlargement of the uterus, Lydia thought. And they had seen nothing initially, as the pelvic organs were lower in the abdominal cavity, obscured by the loops of colon.

"You know that we were focused on establishing the cause of death and finding evidence to support that. We had no reason to suspect she was pregnant, or that it would have any bearing on her death," Harlan said.

"I see," Volcker said. He stared at his hands, still clasped in his lap, as if in deep thought. But a seething anger was about to erupt.

Volcker stood abruptly. His voice was so loud they were all taken aback.

"Why did you not divulge this information before, Dr. Weston? For days you have been probing and dissecting this body! Surely you must have had suspicions. Yet now you tell us it is *not* Anna Ward?" he said.

"I wasn't sure. And it had no relevance to the case prior to this moment. It was a private matter," Lydia said.

Volcker swung around in accusation.

"What in bloody hell are you all playing at? Do you think that this is a game?" he shouted.

Davies rose from his seat and stood between them.

Lydia met Davies's searching gaze. It was if he was trying to determine if she was telling the truth, if her intentions could be trusted. He turned to face Volcker. He put his hand on the older man's shoulder.

"It is an unfortunate turn, sir, but she is right. And without the doctors' help, we would not have this information at all," he said.

Lydia looked at him in surprise. Davies nodded to her in a gesture of support.

Volcker walked over to the wall. For a moment, Lydia thought he would strike it with his fist. Instead, he rested his forehead against the stone. He did not speak for a few moments.

"I would never deceive you, Inspector," she said. "I did not imagine this would be a possibility."

Volcker nodded wearily.

"Forgive me," he said. "How do we proceed now?"

"Her sister, Sarah, identified the body," Harlan said. "She only had a brief look at the face before she was overcome. She made the identification as best she could."

"Then let's have her in to take another look," Volcker said grimly.

SARAH WARD CAME IMMEDIATELY IN response to Volcker's urgent request. The four of them met her in the sky parlor. She lowered herself onto a stool, austere in black mourning dress.

"Why have you brought me here?" she asked.

There was no way to prepare her. So many times Lydia had steeled herself to deliver terrible news to a patient as death was imminent. But now there was nothing to do but say it aloud.

"We have reason to believe that the body is not Anna's," Lydia said.

"What? What can you mean?" Sarah looked up sharply. "I identified her myself."

"Dr. Stanley and I examined the body closely to determine the cause of death. We discovered that this woman was pregnant when she died."

Sarah put her hand to her mouth, her eyes widening in disbelief.

"But I knew Anna's medical history, the private details that she may not have shared with you. She had a condition that prevented her from carrying a child," Lydia said.

"But you!" Sarah pointed at Harlan. "You convinced me that it was her! I saw her clothes, her diary, our mother's locket. It was all hers, I am sure of it."

"It was difficult to see the features of her face. If you recall," Harlan said gently, "you looked at her hair and her hands. The belongings were hers, but we believe they were placed there to confuse the police."

They crowded into Harlan's autopsy room. The body was covered with a white sheet.

Sarah stopped short at the sight.

"Are you ready, Miss Ward?"

She nodded. Harlan pulled back the shroud.

Even the policemen could not hide their instinctive disgust. Davies brought his handkerchief to his face. Volcker stepped back as if physical distance could shield him from the horror. The face was porcine, the features distorted into a monstrous death mask.

But Sarah leaned forward.

"May I see something else?" She turned to Harlan. "I didn't think to look at it before. I was so sure it was her from the locket. Anna had a scar behind her knee. No one would notice it. She got it as a child. We had been making popcorn over an open fire. The oil splattered and burned her."

Harlan pulled the sheet back to expose the leg. He lifted it slightly and turned it so they could all see. The skin was smooth and waxy.

Sarah knelt and ran her finger over the skin.

"Dear God, how can it be true? I knew it from the face, but I had to be sure. No! No, it isn't her."

"Thank you," Lydia said. "I know how difficult that was to do . . ."

Sarah spun around to face Lydia.

"Do you? Do you know how difficult it was? John cannot understand what has happened, why our dear Anna has left us. And me? I have lived with the anguish that she died at the hands of violence, terrified and alone." The last words faded as she wailed piteously.

"Sarah, I know what you have endured these past weeks. But you must calm down," Lydia said.

"Do not tell me how to behave! You think you are such an example to us all," she shrieked. "Oh, Anna had high praise for you, Dr. Weston. You filled her head with false hopes. As if reading poetry was enough to lift her out of destitution! And now another girl is dead and my sister is missing. And who do we have to help us? No one. Our lives are worthless to you."

Lydia could feel her composure cracking. It was too much to bear the brunt of Volcker's censure and Sarah's grief.

"No! You are wrong. Your sister's life meant much to me." Lydia's voice shook. "I only hoped to show her what she was capable of."

"Even now, you are so smug and sure of yourself." Sarah was livid. "I am sorry she ever met you, Doctor. It is you that I hold responsible, more than anyone."

Lydia could feel tears pricking at the corners of her eyes. Her cheeks were burning. She did not deserve this. She had excoriated herself over what had happened to Anna and what she could have done to prevent it.

"That is enough, Miss Ward," Volcker said. "If your sister is alive, we must not waste a moment."

LYDIA WALKED DOWN THE QUIET street. She was almost home. It had been a long and difficult day. The cold air was a balm and she took in deep breaths as she walked. She had left abruptly despite Harlan's protestations. She knew he was worried about her. But she had to be alone, away from all of them.

Sarah's accusation had wounded her deeply. Was this how she appeared to others? A pedant who lectured others on how to live? She had built her life through an unyielding belief in her own abilities. And she believed in that possibility for all women: for the students she taught, for the patients like Anna that she cared for.

But there was a kernel of truth in Sarah's words. Lydia thought of those she tried to help, the many worthy people who needed her. She was often beset by hopelessness at how little she was able to do.

Yet Anna had persevered. She had courage that Lydia doubted she could have mustered in the same circumstances.

She stepped into the lobby of her building. A single lamp cast a small pool of light. The rest of the stairwell was in murky darkness. She walked up the wide steps, her footsteps muffled as her boots sank into the thick carpet. The stained-glass window above the landing was dark, its brilliant colors muted in the gloom.

Lydia's flat was on the top floor. Her key was in her hand as she reached for the doorknob. The handle gave way easily and she stumbled forward. The door had been ajar.

Lydia snapped out of her reverie in an instant. She stepped over the threshold. The blue and white dhurrie rug in the entryway glowed in the moonlight. She could see the familiar outlines of the room: the love seat, the fireplace, the bookcases. Nothing seemed out of order.

Lydia exhaled slowly. Had she left the door open this morning in her haste to leave? The strain of the case was clouding her judgment. A warm drink and sleep would restore her.

She turned on the desk lamp. The case studies she had reviewed this morning were neatly stacked. She looked at the essays on top of the pile. The papers were out of order. She was exacting and precise, almost seeing in her mind's eye how she had left her work. At the edge of the desk was a smooth stone from the garden in Concord. She used it as a paper weight to secure her most important documents. She had left Anna's beige diary just next to it.

It had been moved. The diary sat at the opposite corner. Lydia leafed through it quickly. There were no missing pages. The blue diary was still safely with Mr. Kohler.

But there was a heavy stillness in the room. She could feel her senses on alert. Instinctively she looked into the small mirror above the desk. Her distorted reflection appeared: her dark eyes wide in a pale face. And then a black shadow moved quickly, as if an apparition had passed through her.

An electric jolt of fear surged through her. She whipped around to face the room and heard the soft click of the door. She ran out onto the landing and bent double over the railing, straining to see any movement below. There was no one.

Lydia stepped back inside and secured the dead bolt. She leaned against the wall and closed her eyes. Her heart was pounding in her chest. Someone had been in the flat with her.

Part Four

DO NO HARM

20

Lydia worked through the afternoon in her office. She was preoccupied with the shocking revelation of the autopsy. And she was disturbed by the incident in her flat. In the light of day, she wondered if she had imagined it. Had it been a fevered dream brought on by exhaustion? She was not ready to share it with anyone else.

In the meantime, she could not let her attention to other important work lapse. She met with students, advising one on a course of postgraduate study in Paris and another on interview questions for a position at Blockley Almshouse.

She and Harlan had met with the policemen earlier. Volcker and Davies had come to the medical college, a sort of peace offering after their acrimonious parting.

"The obvious question: who is the dead woman?" Volcker asked. "We are meant to believe it is Anna. Only we know the truth. The murderer and everyone else will continue to act accordingly."

"It is a missing persons case as well," Davies said. "Anna may still be alive."

"And what was Anna's connection to the dead woman?" Harlan asked. "Perhaps she knew her and knew of the child."

"It could be what she refers to in the diary," Lydia said. "The love affair gone wrong and a child lost."

Volcker pressed his lips together in irritation.

"At this point, I think speculation about poetry is useless. We must find Anna's lover."

"There is something else I must tell you." Lydia described her meeting with Abe Griffin in detail.

"Dr. Weston, you astonish me!" Volcker said. "You are not content to bring the investigation to a halt with one revelation. You must give us another."

But Lydia could see Davies was intrigued.

"It is worth pursuing, sir. Griffin approached her. He has nothing to gain by lying."

"And how can you be so sure of his motives? It could be a malicious rumor," Volcker said stubbornly. "Enough. Now we focus on tangible leads."

At half past six, Lydia collected her papers in her leather bag, hurrying to catch a late omnibus across town. It deposited her just in front of Pennsylvania Hospital as the rain started to fall. She turned up the collar of her coat and stepped nimbly through the puddles.

Lydia stepped up onto her porch, grateful for the lamplight her landlady had left on in the portico. She fumbled with the long key as it slipped in her wet fingers. The door yielded with a click in the lock.

She removed her overcoat, shaking off the rain droplets. She did not hear the heavy footsteps under the stairwell. A figure stood in the darkness and approached her.

"Mr. Kohler!" Lydia gasped.

"Forgive me, Dr. Weston. I didn't mean to startle you," he said. "Mrs. Boylston let me in to avoid the rain."

"Not at all," Lydia said, but she could feel her heart pounding at the surprise. "Would you care to come in?"

"No. No, thank you," he said.

Mr. Kohler glanced over his shoulder as if they might be overheard. He took the blue diary out of his bag. The cover glowed in the dull light.

"I made several inquiries, to no avail. Then I spoke with my friend Jacob Lenz. He owns a stationery shop near Girard's."

It was a grand stretch of Chestnut Street: the façades of the buildings represented a Venetian palazzo, a Gothic manor house, the Byzantine turrets and domes of a pasha's palace, each an ode to commerce. Lydia often treated herself to tea in the Girard House hotel, where the atrium was filled with fashionable shoppers. Her favorites were the quaint shops tucked in between these grand structures with their window displays showcasing the perfect silk scarf or lambskin gloves.

"As we thought, the book was handcrafted in Italy. Jacob rarely sells them due to the expense. When he does, he keeps careful records. That is how he remembered the gentleman. He bought two."

Mr. Kohler opened the book and removed a slip of paper.

"I came straightaway when I received this. I don't know if the name means anything to you," he said.

Lydia unfolded the paper. The book had been bought six months prior, the date noted in ink. Underneath the date, a name was printed and signed: "Robert A. M. Thornton." The address matched exactly the one written on the calling card Ida had given her.

21

Volcker's breath swirled in indignant puffs. Davies was standing with him in the square adjacent to the Blake Trust. They had come straight from the station house after Dr. Weston had given them the information about the blue diary.

"What else could it mean?" Volcker asked. "Thornton was her lover. Why else would he give her an expensive gift? Why else would she write passages of romantic poetry, yet omit her lover's name?"

It was a surprising scenario, Davies thought. What hopes could she have had with a married man?

"He has no criminal record," Davies said. He had done brief research on Thornton's background.

"Robert Allston Michael Thornton, aged forty-five, married to Ida Blake Thornton for fifteen years. He was a classmate of Edward Curtis's, a graduate of Penn in the same year. As he told us, his income comes from his wife's family wealth. She is an heiress to a railroad fortune."

"Interesting, isn't it? She has more than enough money to do exactly as she pleases. She hardly needs Thornton's approval," Volcker said.

It was the same with Edward and Beatrice Curtis, Davies thought. Yet with each couple, it was the partner who lacked the financial means who was clearly deferred to, the person who exerted natural authority.

"There are lists of properties and trusts in Ida Thornton's name. Their primary residence is the same as listed on the card given to Dr. Weston."

Davies was not ready to say it aloud, but he had to admit that Dr. Weston's tenacity had proved to be on the mark. He had been fruitlessly interviewing tradesmen and shopkeepers, painstakingly tracing the comings and goings of all the servants in the Curtis household in hopes of finding a lead. Volcker had been skeptical, dismissing the poetry as romantic drivel. Yet Dr. Weston had persisted. And with the help of the bookseller and the instinct of a good investigator, she had now traced the diary to Thornton.

"Thornton meets Anna at the trust," Volcker said. "He is dependent on his wife's money and along comes a lonely young woman. He draws her into an affair."

"Perhaps Anna wanted to marry him. She could have forced him to decide by threatening to expose the affair to his wife," Davies replied.

"We will find out soon enough. I will get a warrant to bring him in if he won't come willingly. I want to do this in full view of his wife, and the lot of them."

They walked together down the alley. The ground was hard with frost, ice forming on the cobblestones.

Davies knocked briefly and they entered. The large room was brightly lit, a bulwark against the dreariness outside.

"Sergeant Davies, what a surprise!" Ida Thornton stood to greet them, wiping her hands on an apron. She looked girlish, an errant hair falling from her bun. "You have caught us on baking day. I did not expect you."

There were fewer people today. A young girl stood at Ida's side kneading a ball of dough into bread. The chatter stopped altogether at the sight of Volcker peering with interest at the projects on the tables.

Ida frowned. "And who have you brought with you?"

"I am Inspector Volcker, leading the investigation into Anna Ward's death. Is your husband here? I would like to speak with him."

"Robert? I don't understand what you would want with him," she said.

"Just a few questions, I assure you," Volcker said.

"He is working in the neighborhood. I have yet to see him this morning. What is this about?" She looked at Davies. "I have told you all I know."

Andrew Cole was teaching a group in the corner. They all turned to look up at the interruption.

At that moment, the back wall of the room moved. It was an ingenious trapdoor, a rolling wall on casters. Paul O'Meara stepped through the opening, laden down with a heavy crate. His face was slick from the mist and his thick hair matted. His gaze locked on Volcker. Without a word he dropped the box. It slipped to the ground as if a dead weight, vegetables spilling out, the glass of the milk bottles shattering on the hard floor.

"Paul!" Ida gasped. "What is the matter with you?"

But he was gone.

Davies lunged towards the door but Paul was too quick. He had pulled it shut behind him.

Davies rattled the door handle. "He has bolted it from the outside!"

Cole leapt to his feet.

"Come with me, there is another way out."

The policemen sidestepped quickly between the tables and ran behind Cole into the back office. He pressed himself against the wall to allow them through, opening a small door. "Through here, you are just a few feet behind."

The policemen burst forth into the alley. Davies felt the ground give way under him, sliding as though he were on the deck of a ship lurching at sea. The ground was slick with water, copious suds being poured out of a pail. Davies came face-to-face with a washerwoman, startled amidst her vigorous scrubbing. Above their heads, a jagged array of clotheslines ran at angles, billowing white sheets that would never dry in the cold.

Davies regained his balance and started to run.

"I can see the light from the street," Volcker shouted behind him. It was late afternoon and the sun had receded completely, leaving the lane in darkness. Ahead through a slim aperture, the glow of gaslight shone like a beacon. The alley narrowed and the brick walls were a vertiginous stone canyon rising on either side of them.

Davies spotted Paul ahead. God only knew where he was leading them, like a nimble predator and his prey.

"I see him, sir!"

"Keep on, then!" Volcker was breathing heavily behind him.

Paul took a sharp turn to the left but Davies kept pace. From above they could hear jeers and hoots of laughter, their observers enjoying the spectacle of impromptu street theater. "Don't want the coppers on your heels, boy!" screeched one woman leaning over her railing, shouting encouragement.

They came to an abrupt stop, Volcker crashing into Davies from behind. The alley had opened into a small square enclosed by buildings. Davies was disoriented. He had no idea how long they had been running or how far they had come from the trust.

"Where did he go?" Volcker said.

Paul was nowhere in sight. It was strangely quiet, only the sound of water dripping from an open spigot. An old man sat on a barrel watching them with rheumy, unseeing eyes. He spat out a stream of murky brown tobacco.

"Bloody hell, how did we lose him?" Volcker took his hat off and threw it to the ground.

Davies looked up. They were in the heart of the tenement, cheap flats for workers rising one on top of the other. It was a warren that Davies had once navigated easily. But now he was an outsider here.

If they lost Paul now, they would never find him, Davies thought. But why had he run?

It was then that the young woman appeared behind them, out of the darkness of the alley, panting from exertion. Davies whipped around at the sound of her breathing. Her head was covered in a patchwork shawl that obscured her face. She wore mittens on her hands and her black boots were scuffed.

"Come, let me show you. I know where he is." She beckoned to them, reaching her hand out to Davies.

Volcker glanced at Davies.

She led them off the square into a narrow lane. She put her fingers to her lips and pointed up. A staircase led to a door on the second story.

The girl turned and ran away. Davies hesitated. Was it a trap? Volcker nodded to him and patted the lapel of his coat, the holster of his pistol nestled under the wool lining. Davies went first. The rickety staircase creaked fearfully under his weight. When he reached the top, he pounded on the door with his fist.

"Open up! Now!"

There was no response.

Volcker nodded. Davies stepped back and thrust his weight against the door like a battering ram. It started to give. He leaned back and went again. The door opened.

They stepped into a small flat. Robert Thornton was sitting at a table, as if he had been interrupted at breakfast, with a cup of coffee in front of him. He was half dressed, with his shirt unbuttoned and suspenders at his sides. In the corner was a bed that looked as though it had been recently slept in, the sheets rumpled.

"What is the meaning of this? How dare you! Who are you?" Thornton shouted, standing up.

"It is Sergeant Davies, and this is Inspector Volcker, of the Philadelphia police," Davies said.

"I would suggest you come with us, Mr. Thornton," Volcker said.

22

Robert Thornton sat at the wooden table with his hands clasped as a penitent might come to prayer. His skin was beefy and mottled, as though he had had far too much to drink the night before.

"Why have you brought me to the station? I have done nothing wrong," Thornton said.

"Oh really?" Volcker said.

"Can we stop this ridiculous game, Inspector? I don't know why you had to make a scene in front of my wife. I already told him." He nodded at Davies. "Ida and I are at your disposal."

"Tell us how well you knew Anna."

"Not very well."

"Your wife said she volunteered at the trust, coming in with Beatrice Curtis. You did not work with her more closely?"

"No," Thornton said. "I saw her in passing when she came in with Bea. My work varies from day to day. I have no set schedule."

Volcker changed tack. "I understand you have known Edward Curtis for a long time?"

"Ed and I have been friends going on twenty years. He is from a more rarefied world than I but he is generous to a fault. I always felt as though I was one of the family."

Thornton shook his head.

"I can only imagine how he is taking all this. To be dragged into this tawdry mess, it can't be easy," he continued.

"I can't imagine it was easy for the victim either. An innocent girl has died," Davies said.

"I don't mean to be cavalier about her death," Thornton said.

"But help me understand, sir," Volcker said. "Anna was with Mrs. Curtis often, not just at the trust. You say you are a close friend of the family. Surely you saw her when you were a guest at the house?"

"What are you getting at?" Thornton's face flushed. "I spoke with her on occasion. That is all. I am sorry she has died."

Thornton pushed back his chair from the table.

"If you are through with me, I would like to go."

"Just a moment," Volcker said.

He removed the blue diary from his jacket pocket and placed it on the table.

"If you did not know Anna very well, can you tell me why you purchased this book for her several months ago?"

The recognition was unmistakable. Thornton sat down heavily. His face was drained of color.

"Where did you get that?" he asked.

"It was found amongst Miss Ward's belongings. Most puzzling, isn't it? Surely it was a gift from an admirer?" Volcker said.

Thornton said nothing. His eyes were fixed on Volcker.

"We were able to trace the purchase to the shop of Mr. Jacob Lenz, a stationer on Chestnut Street," Volcker said. "But I don't need to tell you this, do I? You have seen it before."

Davies opened the diary and removed a slip of paper. He pushed it towards Thornton.

"Mr. Lenz gave us the receipt for the book. It was signed by you. It is your address listed at the bottom," Davies said.

"So what if I gave it to her? I had nothing to do with her death," Thornton said.

Volcker slammed his hand against the edge of the wooden table. Thornton winced as if he had been struck.

"Don't lie to me, Mr. Thornton. First you tell us that you knew Anna only in passing. Now you admit you purchased an expensive gift and gave it to a very young woman who is not your wife," Volcker said.

"Yes, I bought it for her." Thornton's voice was taut with anger. "She was a friend."

"Do you expect us to believe that?"

Thornton seemed to consider his position.

"Will you tell my wife?" he asked quietly.

"I promise nothing in a murder investigation. But it will be easier if you are honest with me," Volcker said.

Thornton slumped back in the chair. He rubbed his hands against his face, his eyes shot through with streaks of red.

"Do you know what it is like, Inspector, to feel as though you are a witness to your own life?" Thornton said. "When Ida chose to marry me against the wishes of her father, it was a triumph. I loved her and still do. Yet I didn't realize how much my pride would be eroded. Ida's father belittles me, as one would a servant. Ida dismisses these feelings."

Volcker and Davies sat impassively, not a whit of sympathy evinced by his words.

"It becomes natural, absorbing the indignities. The trust is Ida's life work, her passion, funded with her money. I am an afterthought to her."

"Yes, that must be so difficult for you, Mr. Thornton," Volcker said coldly. "Your wife's dedication to social reform doesn't translate well to a life of leisure, does it?"

The petulant bastard. He was like a spoiled child, Davies thought.

"When I met Anna, it was intoxicating. She sought my opinion on all things. I admired the way she tried to educate herself. I suppose we had that in common, both of us trapped in a demeaning position."

"How could you think yourself similar, sir? You are a married man of privilege. She was a servant," Davies interjected. He could not help himself.

"Was Anna the first woman towards whom you had behaved in this way? Perhaps Paul O'Meara helped you procure others?"

"No! I do not prey upon young women."

"We know nothing of you, Mr. Thornton, only that you have lied to us repeatedly," Volcker replied.

"Did Paul know about you and Anna?" Davies asked.

"I don't know," Thornton said. "Why would you even ask? He is a harmless young man. His father died in the foundry fire and Ed and Bea took pity on him like they have done for so many others."

"When did you start meeting with Anna?" Davies asked.

"Six months ago. I took her for a coffee after her work was done. Then it became a walk by the river, or a meal in a pub. We would talk about many things: books to read, exhibits or concerts to attend. I marveled at her energy."

"Did you make promises of marriage to her?" Volcker asked.

Thornton bristled. "We had made plans to be together."

"Then why did you not seek her out when she disappeared? Were you not worried?"

"Of course. I was beside myself. She left no note or forwarding address," Thornton said.

"Did you meet with Anna at your secret flat?"

"I sleep at the flat on occasion when I am working in the neighborhood. It is easier than going home late and disturbing my wife."

"Quite a convenient setup for entertaining a young woman," Volcker said.

"You make it sound so vulgar. I loved her, can't you understand?" Thornton's eyes welled with tears.

"Were you lovers?" Volcker asked.

"I don't have to answer that."

"I will find out in time. Whatever else you have done, you have cruelly manipulated a young girl."

"I would never hurt her," Thornton said, beads of sweat forming on his upper lip.

"Perhaps you tried to break off the affair but Anna refused. She threatened to expose you to your wife and then what? The only way to stop it is to kill her. After all, who would really care about the death of this girl, a servant? Disappearances occur all the time." Volcker was relentless.

"No, no, I did not do that!" Now it was Thornton who was angry, his neck veins bulging.

"Then perhaps someone else found out about the affair and decided to kill her, out of jealousy?"

Thornton looked stricken at this possibility. "You can't mean Ida. She would never harm anyone."

"Don't be so sure, Mr. Thornton. What would you do when all you hold dear risks being taken away?" Volcker asked.

"What do you think, sir?" Davies asked.

"He is a selfish fool. But if Anna threatened to reveal the affair, he would lose everything, his position, his wife's money. He could have been pushed to violence," Volcker said.

"I put more stock in the wife. The affair would be a humiliating blow. Thornton hardly seems worth it," Davies said.

"Perhaps Thornton was carrying on with this unknown young

woman, too, and was the father of her child. Anna could have discovered that betrayal," Volcker said.

"Do you think he is responsible for the woman's death?"

"If so, he is a fine actor. He seems genuinely distraught that Anna is gone. But I could be wrong."

"What should I do with him?" Davies asked.

"Let Thornton sit for a bit. I don't think he will be anxious to get home to his wife. Let's get into that flat and turn it over. I want to find evidence of Anna Ward, or any other young woman for that matter."

23

"I suppose this is your stock-in-trade, Inspector," Beatrice Curtis was seething. "You are not content to destroy the life of one person with rumors. You must cast your net as wide as possible, no?"

She gestured angrily towards Edward Curtis and Ida Thornton, who flanked the fireplace. The delicate beauty of the morning room, which had been so impressive in its first view, now seemed an anemic version of itself. It was like a beautiful face drained of blood, replaced by a sickly complexion.

Davies and Volcker stood quietly.

"He is just doing his duty," Ida said. Her face was tearstained.

"Darling Ida. I am sorry. I don't mean to upset you further," Mrs. Curtis said.

"There is nothing more to say," Ida said. "But I cannot return home." She seemed to be withdrawing into herself. "Has Robert been released?"

"No," Volcker said.

"I still can't believe Robert would do such a thing. My husband preying upon a young woman . . ." Her voice trailed off.

"You needn't say any more," Mrs. Curtis said.

"I am not a child, Bea! Let me speak. There must be a mistake. She may have been pregnant," Ida said, wincing as if the words caused pain. "But Robert would not kill her. He is not capable of that."

Beatrice knelt in front of her chair and clasped Ida's hands tightly.

"My dear, Mrs. Burt will bring you tea in your room. You must keep your strength up. If you would excuse us for a moment," she said. "We have another matter to discuss with the police."

Ida Thornton stood slowly, like an old woman. She left the room.

Edward Curtis led them over to a desk by the window.

The letters were arranged in a semicircle on the table, like a Japanese fan laid out.

"This is all of them," Curtis said. "The first one came six months ago."

"I would like to know why you did not think it important to tell us this earlier," Volcker said.

Curtis looked down at his shoes, like a child facing a stern lecture from Father.

"Please read us one," Volcker said.

Curtis obliged.

It would be foolish to hide what happened so long ago. A reckoning will come.

"This letter was the first one," he said. "I ignored it. In a firm of our size, there will always be detractors, those who find fault with any and every last thing, Inspector."

"Of course," Volcker said.

"During the height of the war we employed almost two hundred people at the foundry. So you can imagine the volume of complaints we are accustomed to dealing with. It exasperated my father to no end. But in those instances, the writers identified themselves. They would seek a forum to air grievances, an interview."

"Was the content of the letters the same?"

"Yes, a vague threat about some long-ago event. It was always written in the same hand, in black ink on the same type of paper. I knew it had to be the same person," Curtis replied.

"Yet you have not shown the letters to the police until now. Why?" Volcker asked.

"I thought it was just a troublemaker. We are in the public eye too much for my liking. Bea is regularly written up in the society pages. We are easily identifiable."

"That is nonsense, Edward," Mrs. Curtis said.

"The demands for money were immediate," Curtis continued. "The letters were addressed to both of us. Bea saw one, else I would not have involved her at all."

It must have been the quarrel that Anna and the servant Griffin had witnessed in the dressing room, Davies thought. Mr. and Mrs. Curtis had been arguing about a letter.

Volcker lifted a card from the center of the table. He read it aloud:

There is blood on your hands. Someday you will pay, to atone for what you have done.

The inspector removed his reading glasses and placed them on the table. He stared at Curtis.

"I am shocked that you did not approach the police. Did you not fear a personal attack?"

"If I thought there was any chance of physical harm, I would have."

"Yet you started paying the blackmailer. Surely that would be seen as an admission of guilt," Volcker said.

"I discouraged going to the police, Inspector," Beatrice Curtis said. "And I thought we should not acquiesce to the demands."

"It was my decision to pay," Curtis said. "For a family like ours, the taint of a scandal would be enough."

Volcker held one of the cards up to the light. He could see the faint edge of the line where a cutout piece of paper had been pasted on the card. It was well done. The letters had not been written in the blackmailer's hand, so as not to be recognized.

In the last three months, the letters had been more frequent. The writer's tone was more confident as time progressed.

You think you are very clever, sir. Justice will be had for those harmed by your greed.

And another:

The death of innocents cannot be abided. Soon all will know what you have done.

"To what is the writer referring? The death of innocents?" Volcker asked.

"It could only be related to the foundry fire during the war," Curtis said quietly.

"Not this again, Edward!" Beatrice said. "Edward has an unconscionable fear about this. It is a moment he does not want revisited at any cost."

Curtis bristled in irritation.

"Why do you think this fire is at the root of it all?" Volcker asked.

"It was the worst accident in our company's history, Inspector. There is not a day that goes by that I don't think about it, how we could have protected those who worked for us."

Curtis's face was pale.

"It was at the end of 1863. Gettysburg was a fresh wound with so many lost in battle. Our response was to produce more iron for munitions, swept up in the patriotic moment. Quite frankly, it was too much for my father."

"How so?" Volcker asked.

"He had presided over a family firm. Now we were a behemoth of war production. There were crews of men working double shifts, the furnaces going night and day. There was a large fire in the main furnace. The explosions destroyed the building; about thirty men were trapped inside and died. Many more were . . . maimed, disfigured." Curtis's voice was quiet.

Beatrice Curtis took her husband's hand and held it.

"The fire department investigators made an example of us. My father was never an easy man to do business with. It was an opportunity to be vindictive," Curtis said.

"What was the outcome?"

"It was an accident," Curtis said firmly. "I never doubted that. But in the end, it did not matter. Father was accused of being a profiteer. No matter that my brother had died at Shiloh or the work we had done for the war effort."

"Was compensation given to the victims?" Davies asked.

"The victims' families were paid handsomely. We are generous to a fault," he said bitterly.

Paid handsomely or paid off? Davies thought.

"It is a tragedy to be sure," Volcker said. "But how could you be held accountable now, after so many years?"

"I don't know," Curtis said. "Father and I tried to trace every man involved, to help the families in some way. But perhaps there is someone who wishes to wound us still."

The light in the oil lamp flickered down and they sat in the encroaching darkness.

"I can still see them vividly, the young men whose lives were ruined by horrific burns," Curtis said. "They would never be able to work again."

"Did you try to trace the letters?"

"There was no formal postmark. They had not been sent through the mail."

"Do you think the blackmail is related to Anna's death?" Volcker asked.

"I can't imagine how. But the letters stopped three weeks ago, just about the time Anna left the house."

VOLCKER AND DAVIES EACH RETREATED to one side of the hansom. The cab jostled them along the street, the horse's hooves beating at a steady clip. They were on their way back to the police station.

"Does anything strike you as odd?" Volcker asked.

"Why reveal the blackmail letters now? It seems convenient that it happened just after we questioned Thornton."

"Precisely. I think it is an interesting diversion, intended to direct us away from Thornton."

"Do you think Curtis is trying to protect his friend?"

"Perhaps. Though I doubt he is foolish enough to jeopardize his reputation for a lout like that."

"But, sir," Davies said, "if the fire is at the root of the letters, what is prompting the blackmail after so many years?"

"It is odd. It is also curious to me that Curtis felt it better to pay someone off rather than involve the police."

"Suppose there is a connection to the past," Davies said. "Say Anna discovered the blackmailer. She threatens to come to the police and is targeted for her knowledge."

"I don't believe it, Davies. Thornton is our man. We just need the evidence to prove it."

Davies knew Volcker's moods well enough to see that he wouldn't budge, like an obstinate mule stopped in his tracks. But Davies pressed on.

"The Curtises have been very loyal to the victims' families. Some work for them now," he said. "If the letters came without a postmark, it must be someone with easy entry to the house. Could the blackmailer be a descendant of someone killed in the fire?"

The hansom pulled up in front of the station house.

"Perhaps Anna was the blackmailer," Volcker said. "She discovered something incriminating and decided to use it for personal gain."

"But according to Dr. Weston, she was with Abe Griffin when he saw the letter in the Curtises' bedroom. She was as shocked as he was."

"It could have been a show."

"It seems out of character."

"No one is a saint, Davies. Her brother is desperately ill and medical bills have likely brought her to the brink of penury. Who among us would not take a chance for money?" Volcker asked.

Davies was silent. He would not agree with that cynical view.

24

⌐—————————◡—————————⌐

"Thornton admitted to the affair?" she asked.

Davies had led Dr. Weston into an office just adjacent to the front desk. He was surprised to see her. She had come on her own to the station and asked to speak to him.

He told her what they had learned during Thornton's questioning.

Davies nodded. "He said he bought the diary for her. They had been carrying on for at least six months."

She did not remove her coat and hat. She sank into a wooden chair, her gloved hands clutching a small case.

"Extraordinary."

"Volcker is sure Thornton is behind it all. He will consider no other possibility."

"Aah. The inspector is in dogged pursuit of his man and nothing will deter him, not even evidence to the contrary."

Davies smiled in spite of himself. She was observant. It was Volcker to the mark.

"Of one thing we are certain: Thornton is a rogue who took advantage of her," Davies said.

Dr. Weston nodded. "He is a pompous boor. We saw that ourselves at the trust. He behaves as he wishes, a sense of entitlement without consequences. I have met many a Mr. Thornton in my time, always cloaked in respectability. In my world, they use the medical degree as a shield, to flaunt their power over others."

Her words were blunt, but she did not seem bitter, Davies thought. It was a statement of fact.

The idea of a woman doing hard work was nothing novel to him, his mother and sisters had done so since he was a boy. It was not a matter of choice or fancy. Over the years he had absorbed the stories of demanding employers, the indignities they had to suffer through for their hard-earned wages. But Dr. Weston was an educated lady in a position of respect. He had not thought of how she might face unjust suspicion, that she had to prove her worth repeatedly.

"The diary connects Thornton to Anna," she said. "It is simple. Almost too simple."

"It doesn't explain the unknown body," Davies agreed. "Anna is still missing. And how and why is this young woman connected to it all?"

Dr. Weston nodded. "The body is found by the river, an apparent suicide. Her clothes and belongings are staged. We are meant to believe it is Anna. The murderer must have been aware that this unknown woman was pregnant. It would only enhance the deception: Anna killed herself, distraught over an illicit affair."

"So perhaps someone knew of the affair and was trying to set Thornton up," Davies said.

"Exactly," she said. "To draw attention away from something else."

She removed a card from her case.

"We know that Anna saw the blackmail letter that the Curtises received. Perhaps she saw others."

Dr. Weston handed him the card.

"This is the name of the foreman at the foundry. Abe Griffin says he would be willing to talk. They are friends. He was there the night of the fire and can tell us more."

Davies took the card.

"I would like to go with you," she said.

"No, absolutely not," he said. He stood up, signaling the conversation was over.

He agreed that there could be more to this line of inquiry. But Volcker would be furious if he investigated this on his own, even more so if he had Dr. Weston in tow.

"Please, Sergeant." She looked up at him. "I was as shocked by the autopsy results as you all were. You must believe me. Anna might still live. This could be important."

He hesitated.

"Besides, I am the one who gave you the lead."

She was right. He had to be fair and give her that. He relented.

"All right, we will go."

25

Lydia could see Davies half standing in the cab, searching the crowd on the street for her.

She was at the corner of Eighth and Pine, their designated meeting place. She raised her hand to him and the hansom slowed to a halt.

She could tell he was surprised by her appearance. She was wearing a plain navy wool dress and cape. It was free of adornment save for a few brass buttons down the front. Her dark hair was tucked under a cap, not a stray hair visible.

"I didn't recognize you, Doctor," he said. "I almost mistook you for one of the temperance workers that frequent the neighborhood."

"God forbid," Lydia said.

Davies extended his hand to help her into the seat, but she didn't need it. She nimbly climbed the step and sat next to him.

"You told me we must be discreet, so as to blend in better. So there you are, Sergeant."

The hansom clattered along Eighth Street. In a short span, they turned onto Front Street, running parallel to Delaware Avenue and the eponymous river that served as an eastern border of the city. The neighborhood shifted into a gritty commercial nexus: residences and shops were replaced by gas and steelworks, textile mills and railroad freight yards. Many businesses supported the triumvirate of coal, iron, and steel; these in turn fueled the powerhouse industry of the railroad. Lydia knew the names: Baldwin Locomotive Works, William Cramp and Sons Ship and Engine Building Company, Kensington Iron and Steel Works, some of the storied firms that anchored the city's economy. The area was a shrewd location for the foundry. It was perfectly situated near the freight depots of the Pennsylvania and the Philadelphia and Reading railroads. And it was only a few blocks to the thriving waterfront of the Delaware, to the naval dockyards and wharf landings of the steamship companies whose vessels crossed the Atlantic. It was a stepping-stone to the rest of the country and the world.

Davies asked the driver to drop them off a few blocks from the foundry. Lydia could feel the clammy warmth that hinted at their proximity to the water, even on the cold day. The mournful horn of a steamboat sounded in the distance. The air was a potent mixture of steam and smoke billowing from towers that rose around them like a city unto itself.

They passed groups of men in work clothes, their faces stained with sweat and soot, the sound of rough laughter in the air as they jostled along the footpath. There were no women on the street. Lydia kept her eyes down and walked next to Davies.

"The foreman's name is Matthew Jones. He asked us to come at the change of shift," Lydia said. Abe Griffin had sent a message with instructions. He was adamant that they shouldn't ask for Jones by name.

The foundry occupied almost a full city block. Above the main gate was a simple sign: WILLIAM CURTIS AND SONS IRON FOUNDRY, PHILADELPHIA. At the entrance, she and Davies paused as a stream of men passed, coming off the day shift. The main courtyard was like a bustling town square, the open workshops of blacksmiths and carpenters lining the yard. The huge tower that housed the blast furnace stood in the center. Lydia craned her neck to see the top. A steady stream of smoke from the furnace trailed into the sky.

Davies easily found the shop with the green door, as instructed by Griffin. It was an empty blacksmith's workshop, the massive hearth devoid of fire. Lydia could see the heavy shovels with handles and the long, thin iron rods, implements that could withstand the fiery heat of the furnaces. She and Davies stood together in the near darkness.

The door slid open, allowing through a crack of light. A man stepped in. Lydia could see he was compact and muscular, giving an immediate impression of strength. His black hair was cropped close to his head. He held a small gas lantern aloft and peered at them.

Jones was angry.

"You shouldn't have come here. What the hell were you thinking? Abe said you were a doctor. He didn't tell me you were a woman!"

"Please, Mr. Jones. Abe said you might be able to help us with more information."

Jones shook his head.

"No, someone might see you. You must leave."

"Please. A young woman has been killed and another is missing. She was a servant in the Curtis house. She was a friend of Abe's and mine," Lydia said.

"So he said."

Jones pulled the door closed behind him, his figure illuminated by the light from the lantern. He sat down on a stool in front of them. He was tense and uneasy, shifting in his seat.

"All right then. I owe Abe a lot. He told me that this business is causing the Curtises a lot of trouble."

"Yes," Davies said.

"Good. Time for them to suffer a taste of their own medicine."

Lydia exchanged glances with Davies.

"Some said the fire was not an accident," Lydia said.

Jones regarded them shrewdly, saying nothing.

"Is it true?" Davies asked.

"We all wanted to do our part for the war effort. The foundry was a big producer for the Union. So many of ours had joined up. It was our way of helping them, pulling long shifts and working overtime," Jones said. "But what happened here in 'sixty-three should never happen again."

"How so?" Lydia asked.

"This is dangerous work. Anyone who doesn't understand that is a fool. But safety was lax. Some of the equipment was old and the men were exhausted. Everyone knew it, the Curtises above all. Yet they continued to make money off our backs."

"Did anyone speak up about the problems?" Davies asked.

"Those who tried to were silenced," Jones said bitterly. "After the explosion, they shut down the foundry for a week, then it was business as usual. It was just enough time to clear out the bodies."

"Did they try to put safety measures in place afterwards?" Lydia asked.

"Edward Curtis is a rich man's son." Jones's voice was full of contempt. "He understands nothing of the work, but always makes a show of walking about here, ever the benevolent master. But we are expendable to them."

"Why do you stay?" Lydia asked.

"For my men. There are some who are willing to accept any risk for good pay. But it won't always be like this. Someday soon the union will take hold."

They could hear footsteps outside the door. Jones looked over his shoulder.

He handed Lydia a small piece of paper.

"Here are the names of those who died in the fire. The Curtises gave a lot of support to the victims' families. As if that could make amends for what happened."

He stood up.

"I hope that helps. I am sorry about your friend."

He nodded to them and left.

Davies stood and peered around the door. He motioned for Lydia to follow. There were fewer people in the yard. The evening shift had settled in. As they passed the base of the tower, Lydia could see through the open door. The massive stone walls of the furnace rose from the wide base. She tried to imagine the structure as a searing inferno, engulfed in flames, terrified men trapped inside. But today it looked pristine, with no sign of the destruction wrought so many years before.

They came to the main gate. There was a narrow walkway above their heads, a promontory to view the yard. Edward Curtis stood looking down, his figure silhouetted against the sky. He looked directly at them. But he made no effort to stop them. Lydia pulled the brim of her cap down and hurried behind Davies.

"The Curtises must have suppressed the story. It won't be difficult to trace the reporter who wrote it. I have contacts at the *Inquirer*," Davies said.

They sat across from each other in the coffeehouse. The temperature had dropped precipitously while they were waiting for the omnibus, so they had sought refuge indoors.

Lydia had compared Jones's list of the fire victims to the roster of servants in the Curtis house. She recognized the familiar surnames immediately: Montgomery, Johnson, Briggs, Griffin, Wade, McBride. There were at least eight people whose last names matched those of the dead: chambermaids, gardener, footmen, cook, valet.

"So perhaps a father or grandfather as a relation?" she asked.

Davies nodded. "Hold the victims close and continue to support them. Give them no reason to doubt your innocence."

"Any of the servants could have done it. Griffin didn't say if he saw an envelope with a postmark. It would be easy for someone in the house to deliver the letters."

"Will you tell the inspector?" Lydia asked.

"Of course. He will come around."

Lydia leaned forward.

"Perhaps Anna discovered that the fire was not an accident and this is what she referred to in the diary, when the poetry shifts to the darker passages."

"Enough, Dr. Weston!" Davies said. "Please, enough."

Lydia was taken aback at his anger.

"It means nothing! The poetry is so vague, you could use it to suit any scenario you wish. You must leave it now," he said.

"It is all we have of her voice, Sergeant," she said.

The visit with Jones had been unsettling. She knew Davies regretted bringing her along to question him. And had Edward Curtis recognized them?

Davies laid his hands on the table and took a deep breath.

"You have helped us so much in this investigation. But this is not the same as asking questions at the Curtis house. The ground is shifting beneath us. It is not a game," he said.

His clear blue eyes met hers.

"Promise me you won't investigate any further on your own. It is too dangerous. You could get hurt."

26

The elderly man stared at her defiantly, his protuberant belly pushing through the bedclothes. His face was flushed and the tip of his nose covered with splintered blood vessels. He looked weather-beaten, with white hair that stood on end. At the bedside stood his bewildered daughter. Her bonnet was still in place and the giant black sash tied under her chin gave her a mournful air. She looked down at the ground.

"I won't have it. I have a say in who treats me and I refuse to have you do it." He tilted his chin upward.

"Father," his daughter whispered. "How can you speak to the doctor that way . . ."

"Don't tell me what's right, girl," he snapped. "She's probably here to clean the bedpan. No such thing as a lady doctor."

"It is quite all right," Lydia said. Her student Eleanor Petrie stood at her side. She had brought Eleanor along for attending rounds at Pennsylvania Hospital. Their presence elicited stares from patients and staff alike as they moved through the wards. It was still rare for women doctors to be granted privileges at this bastion of the medical establishment. The affiliation had been made possible through the tireless efforts of Harlan and other like-minded physicians, many of them Quakers, who had pioneered women's medical education in the city. Lydia was grateful for those who had eased the path; still, she resented that she was not judged solely on her ability. But it was part of the long road to acceptance and for now her work would have to speak for itself.

But lofty aspirations aside, there was the reality of one Mr. Josiah Brown who refused to be examined by a woman physician.

"I am Dr. Weston and this is my student Miss Petrie. We are here to help you. Are you in pain, sir?" Lydia asked.

He grunted in response.

"If you won't answer my questions, then your daughter will have to."

"He has been living on his own since my mother died, Doctor. I check in on him to make sure he has enough food and the like. But I couldn't last week, owing to my hours at the shop."

They were crowded together in the narrow space at the bedside. A thin drape separated Mr. Brown from the next patient. The beds were close in this section of the ward, where emergencies and high-acuity cases were brought first. Farther down the hall, they could hear the clanging of a metal cup against the handrail of the bed in a patient's futile attempt to summon the nurse. Eleanor's eyes were wide in astonishment. It was a very different experience from Woman's Med. Here was the hurly-burly of humanity, the depths of pathology on full display. It was a large public hospital, with a robust inpatient psychiatric ward as well as the oldest operating theater in the city. The wards were full; at times it was difficult to concentrate with the din of conversation going on all around them. It was the reality her students would face: the need to think on their feet and make accurate diagnoses all while facing suspicion and outright belligerence from patients.

"I found him like this," Miss Brown continued. "He was hot, feverish. I am not sure what he has been eating or drinking."

"None of your business. I am a grown man and can take care of myself." Brown grunted again. His eyes were glassy but he seemed to be following the conversation. If he had been taking in little food or water and drinking alcohol, there was immediate concern for his kidney and liver function. His flushed appearance could be due to fluctuating blood pressure or an infection of some kind.

"Where did you find him?"

"He was on the floor by his bed. I am not sure how long he had been like that. He may have had a fall. He had a hard time getting up."

He pulled violently at the bedclothes as if he was too warm and the sheet fell away, revealing his torso. His right arm hung limply at his side. Lydia could see the effusion of the shoulder joint. The humeral head was displaced from its socket.

"Mr. Brown, may I examine your shoulder? It looks as though you have dislocated the joint."

Lydia moved closer to the bedside and reached out to palpate the joint. He hissed in pain, drawing his arm away as if it had been burned.

"Get away, then!" he bellowed. "Get your hands off me! Told you I won't have a lady doctor!"

There were cheers and snickers from his compatriots in the adjacent beds.

"Dr. Weston, isn't it?" A deep voice spoke behind them. "Surely it is not your practice to have patients begging for mercy?"

There was a twitter of giggles behind them. She turned to see Dr. Richard Harper flanked by a group of male students. This was one of the teaching hospitals for the University of Pennsylvania's medical school.

She hardly needed an audience at this moment. Lydia gritted her teeth and drew herself up to full height.

"No, it is not, Dr. Harper." She nodded to him. "I am here on rounds with a student and if you will excuse me, I am about to do an exam."

"No, she isn't." Brown stared up at her belligerently. "Told you I don't want you touching me. I want him. You seem to be the gent in charge."

"Right you are, sir. Clearly, the patient's mental faculties are intact." Harper turned to his students, ever the pompous showman. A few snickered.

Lydia's cheeks burned. Damn this bloody man for making her feel as uncertain as a student. But she would not give him the satisfaction of seeing her discomfiture. She suppressed her fury at Harper and his fawning minions, and at the patient, ill and dependent, yet still voicing his opposition to her. She wanted to lash out at them all, but she knew Eleanor was watching.

"If you insist, Dr. Weston. May I ask what your diagnosis is?"

"I am not a student, sir. I am an attending physician like yourself. But since it is our duty to teach, I will oblige," Lydia said. "Mr. Brown has a closed dislocation of his right shoulder. But that is not all, I am afraid. If your students care to observe, please gather in."

The patient seemed chastened by the large group gathered around him and Harper's obvious authority. He now cooperated as Lydia went through an exam, quickly noting his skin temperature and pallor. She examined the sclera of the eyes and the mucosa of the mouth for signs of jaundice and anemia.

"Note his elevated heart rate and shallow breaths. He will need fluids and laboratory work as a basic assessment. I recommend admission to monitor urine output and observe for signs of infection." She nodded to the nurse at the bedside taking notes.

"But first, Mr. Brown, if you will allow me, we shall put your shoulder back in place."

He shook his head. His daughter took his hand and held it. "Please, Father, listen to her."

Lydia leaned in. She sensed the fear beneath the bluster.

"There is no need to be afraid. I shall tell you precisely what I am doing," she said. "Does the arm feel weak?"

"No, just hurts to move it," he said quietly. She directed Eleanor to the bedside.

"Check the pulses and pallor of the right forearm and hand," Lydia said. Eleanor did this carefully and nodded to her.

"You must make sure it is normal before proceeding. It is a sign that the arterial circulation is not damaged. If it has been more than a week since the injury, one must consider involving the surgeon immediately. Now, please watch."

Lydia stepped in closer to the patient. With one hand she grasped his wrist and with the other, she held his arm above the elbow. At the elbow, she turned the arm slowly to ninety degrees until she felt resistance. She could feel him tense with pain but she kept on firmly. She lifted the upper arm up and internally rotated the shoulder as the arm moved back towards the patient's chest. The joint visibly reduced as the humeral head slipped back into the fossa. She stepped away from the bedside.

"Now then, you should feel better," Lydia said.

Mr. Brown looked down at his arm and then up at her in surprise.

"What are things to watch for now? Complications?" she asked the students.

"One must monitor pulses to make sure no damage was done to the axillary artery during the reduction," Eleanor said.

"Yes. And then?" Lydia asked.

"And assess for weakness to ensure no tearing of muscle, like the subscapularis. If that occurs, the surgeon must be consulted," Eleanor replied.

"Correct. That was a fine example of intellectual rigor. Wouldn't you agree, Dr. Harper?" Lydia said. "As you once told me, we are in the business of educating physicians, not teaching Sunday school, no?"

Harper stared at her, clamping his mouth shut.

"Good day, gentlemen. Miss Petrie and I must move on to our next patient."

Lydia and Eleanor walked down the front stairs of the hospital and angled through the gardens. The grounds were dotted with trees now beginning to lose their leaves. The square of the hospital grounds was bisected by orderly paths looking much the same as they did when the institution had opened its doors in 1751. Its board of governors had included Benjamin Franklin and Benjamin Rush, signers of the Declaration of Independence. Lydia wondered what they would have thought to see two women hurrying along to their day's duties as physicians.

"That was well done, Dr. Weston." Eleanor blushed as if instantly regretting the audacity of her statement.

But Lydia smiled. She regarded Eleanor, looking awkward in her ill-fitting gray dress. They had finished seeing the remainder of the patients on their list, with Harper and his students following behind. Harper had taken pleasure in grilling Eleanor over each patient's diagnosis, trying to flummox her. But she had stood her ground admirably, fielding his questions in a calm and steady manner.

"Thank you. Your studies are progressing nicely. Unfortunately, what we experienced is also a part of your education."

It was only a few years before that women students had been invited to attend a clinical lecture, on the surgical treatment of femur fracture, at Pennsylvania Hospital. The group from Woman's Med, over thirty strong, had walked into an ambush of sorts. The lecture had devolved into chaos as they were subject to a torrent of abuse by the male students, who had gathered from all over the city to loudly protest their presence. As the women left the hall, they were assailed by a line of tormentors, shouting catcalls and epithets, even spitting tobacco onto the hems of their dresses. The "jeering episode" was now legend at Woman's Med, told and retold as veterans would regale one another with stories of the battlefield, only strengthening the resolve of students and faculty alike.

"It is natural to feel rattled by these encounters. I certainly do. But do your best work. Then you will do honor to yourself and to all of us."

Eleanor flushed again, her pale skin turning pink.

"Now, remember to go and write up the case histories while they are fresh in your mind," Lydia said.

They had emerged through the gates onto the corner of Spruce and Eighth.

"Will you be coming back to college now?" Eleanor asked.

"No, I have an errand to do," Lydia said. "I shall see you later."

THE DAY WAS COLD AFTER the recent rain and Lydia pulled her cape tight around her shoulders. She wanted to return to the Blake Trust. It was several blocks south and if she walked briskly, she could be there in half an hour.

Surely someone would have noticed Anna's behavior towards Thornton. How had he convinced the sensible and assured Anna to be his mistress? For one who was so determined to rise above her situation, what future could she have had with a married man? But it was unfair to hold Anna to such a rigid moral standard, to fault her for wanting what other young women had so easily. Davies told her that Thornton had been released from police custody. He had been held briefly on a charge of obstruction, but there was no legal reason to continue to detain him. Davies had warned her again not to investigate alone, ostensibly for her safety. But Lydia needed to learn more about the affair. She couldn't sit idly by while the police continued with their work. Anna may yet be alive. If she was hidden or being held against her will, not a moment could be wasted.

The street was awash in activity. The fruit stalls were open and doing brisk business. People sidestepped teeming piles of rubbish as they rushed to their appointments and little boys jostled to sell newspapers. The shops proclaimed their wares in gold lettering on the glass front windows. A shopkeeper stood in the doorway to entice passersby. Lydia avoided the errant sprays of mud as horse carriages clattered down the narrow streets. She crossed South Street and was soon in the serpentine lanes near the water. She turned in to the now familiar alley and knocked on the door. She opened it without waiting for an answer.

Andrew Cole and Lewis Euston were sitting at a table in the center of the room. They looked up at the same time.

"Dr. Weston," Andrew said, rising to his feet. His cheerful demeanor was subdued.

The room was empty save for three young women sitting in the corner.

"There is no one here but us, I am afraid. Trying to keep the ship afloat, I suppose." He gave a weak smile. "Have you come with the police today?"

"No, I am alone."

"And there is still no idea who is responsible for Anna's murder?" Lewis asked.

Lydia shook her head. No one was to know that the body was not Anna's. Volcker was adamant that this information could not slip lest it compromise the investigation.

"Is Ida here?"

"No, not since the arrest. She looked as though she was taken ill when she got the news."

"And Paul?" Lydia asked.

Lewis sneered. "Paul is likely worried he'll be let go. He's made himself scarce."

"Would you mind if I spoke with those who are here? I am trying to see if anyone noticed anything between Anna and Robert Thornton."

"We surely didn't. It beggars belief," Andrew said.

"But there is no reason the work of the trust should be brought down as well," Lewis said. "Please ask your questions, Doctor, if it will help. Only a few came in today. The news has spread around the tenement."

"Thank you."

Lydia approached the table in the corner. A young woman sat with an embroidery hoop neatly placing stitches in a circle. She looked up at Lydia warily. She had a blunt nose that looked as though it had been broken, with a smattering of freckles across it. Two other girls sat beside her. They were pale images of one another, with blond hair tied into tight buns. All of them looked to be the same age as Anna.

"You're the lady doctor?" the young woman asked.

"Yes."

"We saw you with the police. You helping them?"

"I am."

She nodded. "You needn't hedge. The others are staying away. We all know what happened with Mr. Thornton."

The girl extended a stout fist in a handshake.

"Josey. It is just me taking care of a passel of kids. Father is too drunk to care so I need to earn. This is the only place that offered help with jobs. So here I am. Same goes for those two over there."

"Did you know Anna?"

"Oh, we all did. A breath of air she was, what we all might have been." Josey smiled. "She said she understood what it was like to be poor. I don't know if I believed that. But it felt more honest than the way the others carry on."

"How so?" Lydia asked.

"I don't mean no offense. They mean well, Mrs. Ida and the lads here. But it's foolish to think all we need to do is learn a few sums and our troubles will be solved. Most of us here know better."

"But what of Mr. Thornton? Do you not include him in that group?"

Josey looked over her shoulder to make sure she was not being overheard. Andrew and Lewis were speaking at the center table, oblivious to the women's conversation.

"He is a wily one, Mr. Thornton. He puts on a show for Mrs. Ida to be sure: the savior of us poor folks and helpmeet to his wife. But he is up to no good."

"What do you mean?"

"I mean that if you are a pretty girl here, you best be careful. Isn't that right?"

The thin girl at the edge of the table looked up from her book. Her sister put an arm around her and squeezed.

"You know of the affair he had with Anna. Were there others?" Lydia asked.

"I don't know for certain," Josey admitted. "But it could be, the way Mr. Thornton carried on! He would always be touching a girl's hair or giving a pat on the back. He made it seem jovial-like. Some who come here don't have much. It was nice to be paid attention to by a man like that."

Lydia thought of that first meeting she and Davies had had with Thornton: the sense of bravado put on for their show, the overbearing presence towards his wife.

"Did you see how he behaved with Anna?" Lydia asked.

"He would call her into the office to talk to her alone, laughing and playful. One time she was trying to get away from him, but he wouldn't have it. He was carrying on right in front of us. Poor Mrs. Ida."

So the flirtatious relationship between Anna and Thornton had been noticed by others. And the unknown dead woman: was she involved in any of this?

"Josey, is there anyone else who noticed what you saw? I must know."

Josey nodded. "Kate Tierney. She sees everything around here, quiet but sharp. That day the police came, she was the one who showed them the way to Mr. Thornton."

Davies had told her of the young woman who had appeared in the alley during the chase and led them straight to Thornton's flat.

"She's in the kitchen. Come with me."

Lydia rose and followed Josey towards the back of the room. The door to the small office was firmly shut. The huge slate of windows looked out into the darkening alley behind them.

"Here she is, ma'am. Kate, the lady doctor is here. Needs to ask you some questions about Anna," Josey said.

A teapot was whistling on the hob in the little kitchen, the soft hiss piercing the quiet. Kate was so startled at the sound of Josey's voice that she dropped the teacups she was holding.

"Come now, no need to be skittish. Doctor won't bite," Josey said.

Kate hastily wiped her hands on the apron. She turned to face them.

"Beg your pardon, I didn't see you there."

It was the girl Lydia had seen each time she had been at the trust. The deep pockmarks etched like a tattoo on her face were unmistakable. She had served them lunch on that first day.

"I am just here to talk," Lydia said. "Josey tells me you helped the police when they were looking for Mr. Thornton?"

She nodded.

"How did you know where to find him?"

Kate looked at Josey before answering.

"She's not with the police. She wants to find out who hurt Anna. You can trust her," Josey said.

"I have lived in the tenement since I was a child," Kate said. "I know all the byways, the places to hide. I saw Mr. Thornton once on my way home."

"Did you follow him?" Lydia asked.

She nodded. Her face had the polished sheen of a red apple, but it was the flushed look of poor health. A few waxy strands of hair fell forward onto her face.

"Yes. I know the Thorntons live far from here. What was he doing in the neighborhood late at night or early in the morning? So I watched him. He went into the flat and didn't come out for a long time. He would tell Mrs. Ida he was out on an errand and be there instead. That's when I saw him with Anna . . ."

But Lydia was able to ask no more questions.

"Dr. Weston! What are you doing here?" The voice behind her was unmistakable. It was Beatrice Curtis.

"Do you now fashion yourself an amateur detective? I think you and the police have done enough damage."

"I did not expect to see you here . . ." Lydia said.

"No, I imagine you didn't. Do tell me, what other sordid details have you uncovered?" Her blue eyes glittered in anger. "I am merely here to support Ida's work, before it is undone completely."

Mrs. Curtis looked at the two young women.

"You have no authority to question anyone here, Dr. Weston," she said coldly. "You should be ashamed of yourself, trying to entrap these two. There is nothing more for you to do."

27

Lydia exhaled forcefully. "I feel as though I am trapped in a vise! Do go on, please!"

The woman's reflection stared back in the mirror that ran from floor to ceiling. She pulled the hood further over her face, like a regal queen of old. The silver gown pooled at her feet like the cascade of a waterfall.

"Oh, for goodness' sake, hold still!" Anthea said.

"I do like it. Rather *Idylls of the King*: maids of the mist, fog-shrouded moors and the like." Victoria Bailey regarded her thoughtfully. "What do you think?"

"She is a fine Queen to my Arthur. My lady." Anthea bowed comically, the scabbard of her sword swinging against her hip.

They burst into peals of laughter as Victoria tightened her corset.

It was the night of the yearly Halloween party, a time for the students and faculty of Woman's Med to enjoy an evening of exhilarating disguise. When she was a first-year student, Lydia had been astonished at the social life of the college: the round of parties, music recitals, and theatrical performances. She was used to solitude, single-minded in her devotion to her studies. But the students enjoyed life as well. Lydia had been slowly drawn out of her shell by the two friends who stood before her. Much time had passed since those early days. They all now held impressive positions and led busy lives as professors, but the bond of their friendship remained.

Lydia had planned to miss the festivities, longing for a quiet night at home. But Anthea had arrived at her flat, costumes in hand, refusing to leave until Lydia could be coaxed out. Lydia could see the concern on her friends' faces. It would do her good to be with them and forget her worries for the night.

"Shall we set out?" Anthea asked.

"Yes, indeed," Lydia said, trying to muster more cheer than she felt.

They stood together, Guinevere flanked by her king and knight. Victoria and Anthea had procured ingenious costumes from a friend in the theater. Both wore silver jersey, reminiscent of chain-mail armor, over pantaloons. Anthea had a bejeweled crown propped atop her head. Victoria's face was visible only through a slit in the knight's visor perched on her head.

Though the actual holiday was a few days away, Pine Street overflowed with revelers, a section of the street transformed into a commedia dell'arte carnival. At the corner, costumed buskers gathered, singing to an appreciative audience. Many shops were still open. There had been a light rain earlier in the day and the cobblestones shone under the glow of gaslight.

The party was being held in an assembly hall across from Independence Square. It was a quick jaunt from Lydia's place and they decided to walk. At the corner of Pine and Sixth Street, in front of a fruit stand, they passed a small girl clutching her mother's skirts. The child was pointing to a pile of misshapen gourds, covered in nodules that looked like warts on a witch's nose. She held a pumpkin in her tiny hands, a perfect orb, begging her mother to buy it. Lydia saw the child's face light up with pleasure. She thought of Anna's family, Sarah and John, the little joy in their lives gone, deadened by worry.

Lydia walked in silence, only half listening to her friends' talk. Her mind churned. She usually confided her most private thoughts, the joys and the worries, to Anthea and Victoria. But not now. She was fearful of drawing them into the case.

They arrived in front of the hall. They opened the creaking gate and stepped into the small courtyard.

By day the main hall was used for lectures. But now the large room was transformed: black and orange bunting adorned the banister of the staircase and jack-o'-lanterns leered at them with toothless grins from the landing above. In the entrance, plaster skeletons hung gaily from the lamp fixtures. "Madame Elsa" the fortune-teller had set up business in an alcove, complete with planchette and tea leaves, to predict the future for unfortunate guests. Lydia delighted in trying to identify her students, disguised as sorcerers, witches, ghosts, fair maidens. Robin Hood and Maid Marian stood in conversation with Scheherazade and the Rani of Jhansi. She marveled at the creativity on display.

Lydia pushed her way through the crowd with Anthea.

Any attempt at conversation was interrupted by the booming voice of the master of ceremonies, which rose above the din. "Ladies and gentlemen! May I have your attention, please!"

All eyes turned to him standing on the dais against the far wall.

"Our annual Halloween party shows itself to be more marvelous each year! Now the moment you have been waiting for: prize for best costume. I look out and see sorcerers, noblemen, and queens! But who shall win the grand prize?"

He surveyed the room, walking across the stage slowly.

A ripple of excitement went through the audience as people turned to compare costumes. Lydia felt the pleasant jostle of the crowd.

"I say, I see Merlin here. Now, is that Marie Antoinette? Shall we say,

Let them eat cake? And what of her husband, the poor king? Off with his head!" A ripple of laughter at the weak joke.

He peered out, shielding his eyes with a cupped hand as if trying to see at a distance. "Now there is a fine specimen in the back."

He covered his face in mock horror. "Let us all have a look at him," he said. He pointed to the back of the room, above the murmur of the crowd, as people craned their necks to see.

"Sir?" the master of ceremonies asked loudly. "Could you show us your face? We are intrigued."

Lydia turned to look. A man was in costume, wearing a black suit and an ebony top hat. It reminded Lydia of postcards of an English funeral procession, a cortege drawn by elegant horses. The carriage driver would be dressed in a morning suit, a velvet armband cinched on the arm. But under the hat, this man's face was covered by a black scarf.

"Sir, what creature of the night are you? A harbinger of Death? Have you come to us on this All Hallows' Eve, the night of ghosts and spirits?" The master of ceremonies looked around to the audience, drumming up amusement.

The figure nodded his head.

"What a clever costume. You can't see his face at all," Anthea whispered. "Do you have any idea who that might be?"

"I say," the master of ceremonies said. "It is all in jest here. Could you please show your face?"

Lydia could hear the rustling of fabric as people turned to see.

The man slowly shook his head.

An onlooker called out. "Speak up, man! It is just a bit of fun."

Again the dark figure said nothing. There were nervous murmurs in the crowd.

Anthea frowned. "He is taking it too far."

Lydia stood on her tiptoes, stretching to see. The mysterious man in the back of the room was gone.

It had been a curious interlude, but it was Halloween and tricksters of all sorts abounded. Lydia went on to enjoy herself, admiring the costumes of her friends, eating warm chestnuts out of newspaper cones. The laughter and drink flowed, and several hours passed. Lydia sat on a velvet settee to massage her feet, longing for her bed, but her friends were having a wonderful time and she did not want to interrupt their evening. Lydia collected her velvet cloak from the front hall and touched Victoria on the shoulder.

"Lydia, don't leave by yourself. Let me find Anthea and we will go together. It is late," Victoria said.

"No, no. I will take a hansom right to my doorstep. I promise," Lydia said.

"Very well." Victoria could see she was determined. "But be careful."

Lydia stepped into the cold night. The front of the hall was empty, no hansoms to be seen. She looked up and down the side lane. The streets would be empty at this hour but the streetlamps were still lit. It was a well-known route. She had walked so many times from Pennsylvania Hospital back home. She entered the square and directly ahead were the curved arcs of the windows of Independence Hall, the panes of glass gleaming in the moonlight.

The bell tower clock struck eleven as she passed through colonnaded arches. The heels of her boots clicked smartly against the brick, the low whistle of the wind rustling leaves around her feet. At first Lydia did not hear the footsteps behind her. She had come to the edge of Independence Square, to the corner of the footpath. It was empty save for a vagrant leaning against a shanty at the end of the street, a glowing ember from his cigarette visible at a distance. She looked over her shoulder, suddenly aware of the profound silence. She cut across the narrow lane, a path that would take her directly to Washington Square, just a block from home. The cumbersome hood of the cape was obscuring her vision. It was quiet save for the wind and the steady sound of footsteps. She walked quickly now, tripping in her haste, her heart beating faster. There were no houses in the lane, just the windowless backs of buildings, each a forbidding expanse of gray stone.

She saw the stone archway at the end of the lane. It must have been a carriage door leading to a courtyard, a remnant of colonial times. It was like walking through a long tunnel, the sound of footsteps echoing off the walls, one set rushed and quick, the other slow and steady. She stopped and the footsteps stopped. The only light came from a lamppost at the end of the lane, standing like a sentry. She made herself turn around, opening her eyes wide like a child confronting a hobgoblin. A figure stood stock-still, not twenty yards from where she was. The man's silhouette was framed in the arch of the doorway. She could barely see the outlines of his coat. Why did he stand still?

Lydia cursed herself for leaving the party alone. She lifted the silky hem of her skirt and started to run. She came to the end of the narrow lane and turned the corner: there was Washington Square. She leapt up the steps into the park, the way she had done as a girl running breathless through the woods, yet now her heart pounded with fear. She knew every inch of the park: the walking paths that bisected the square, the neatly placed benches, the trees denuded of their leaves. Lydia reached the edge of the park, only three steps down to the street. She was a few feet from home, where she would pound on Mrs. Boylston's door and rouse the neighborhood.

But the flimsy heel of her boot caught on an uneven brick. She fell hard onto her knees, the pain searing as she hit the ground. The loping, steady footsteps behind her stopped. She braced herself and closed her eyes. He emitted a low chuckle.

Lydia crouched on her knees. The pain was sharp as she tried to stand.

"Not so fast, Doctor," he said.

She turned to look up at him. She could make out the edges of his suit and the top hat covered with crepe. His face was in darkness, obscured by the upturned collar of his coat. The night was a pool of luminescent black. She could not tell what was real and what was an illusion.

With a swift movement, he put his hand on the back of her neck and applied pressure. She gasped in pain. The compression was so forceful that she started to see white specks clouding her vision. If he kept on, she would lose consciousness.

"Listen carefully," he said. "Keep away if you know what's good for you."

His voice was deep and muffled. He put his right hand over her mouth to stifle any screams.

"*Understand?*" He jolted her head backwards and she winced in pain. She nodded, trying to hold in her rising panic.

"Next time will be worse."

At that moment, a few revelers stumbled out of the pub on the corner. The man stood abruptly and, as quickly as he had come, receded into the darkness. Lydia closed her eyes in relief. She stood and pulled the remnants of her costume cape around her. She walked towards home, the last few steps to her sanctuary. She did not see him illuminated in the circle of light from the streetlamp. He was watching her. Yet he made no move to follow.

28

Davies poured a cup of coffee and handed it to Dr. Weston. Her hands trembled as she took the cup but she clasped it tightly, as if drawing comfort from its warmth. The morning sun poured in the station house windows as uniformed officers sat at their desks, shuffling papers and filing reports. Through the paned glass door, Volcker's office appeared empty.

"It was the man from the party. The costume was the same, save for the mask," she said.

"Could you recognize him at all? His voice? His clothing?" Davies asked.

Dr. Weston shook her head.

"But he knew who you were," Davies said. "He came to the party for the express purpose of accosting you."

"Yes. It is someone who knows how involved I am with the case."

"Are you all right?"

"Yes," she said quietly.

Davies regarded her but said nothing more.

"We know that Thornton has not returned to his home. He is supposed to have been under police surveillance for the last few days. But how and why would he plan something like this?"

Dr. Weston shook her head.

"Are there any leads about the blackmailer?"

"No, but I traced the reporter from the *Inquirer*. His name is John Briscoe," Davies said.

Davies had sent a message and Briscoe was eager to talk. They were to meet in a pub near the station at half past ten. The reporter's name sounded familiar.

"May I join you?"

He looked at her in surprise.

"Perhaps it would be better for you to rest," Davies said.

"Nonsense." She brushed off his concern. "Let us go now."

IN THE STREET A FEW carriages clattered by, dredging up sprays of mud onto unsuspecting pedestrians. Davies slowed his stride but Dr. Weston kept pace. He looked down at her as they walked. Her usual brisk manner was subdued. Davies knew many seasoned officers who would have been afraid after a targeted attack like she had experienced. It certainly would have given him pause. But she did not complain. Whatever fear she must be feeling, she had put it aside to get on with the job. Dr. Weston had nothing to gain by continuing in the investigation. Yet here she was, carrying on. Davies knew nothing of what was involved for a man or woman to become a doctor, the years of education and sacrifice it took; but whatever it was, he could admire it in the mettle of her character.

He stopped in front of a squat building on the corner. The façade of the building was an expanse of brick except for a solitary window, the mullioned glass providing a discreet shield for the interior of the pub.

Davies opened the door and they were enveloped in the fug of cigar smoke. It was as if they had stepped into the convivial atmosphere of a gentlemen's club. The tables were full and groups of men clustered around the bar placing orders. In the corner, shouts of encouragement could be heard over a robust game of dominoes. Davies ducked as a barmaid swung a platter of lager pints towards his head. The pub was frequented by the police and their assorted coterie: journalists, magistrates, and the odd informant. It was a place strangely suited to private conversation; amidst the din, they were ignored by the occupants.

The bartender raised a hand in greeting.

"Sergeant, what can I get you and the lady?"

"Nothing now, Sam. We are looking for John Briscoe," Davies shouted above the noise.

At that, a man turned from his stool and stood. He towered above Davies.

"Charlie Davies, as I live and breathe!"

The man clapped a hand against Davies's back. The force of it sent Davies stumbling a few steps forward. He took hold of the bar to steady himself.

"Jack! It is so good to see you!" Davies recognized the man immediately. He was genuinely pleased.

"Dr. Weston, may I introduce to you the great hope of our neighborhood? The man who came within a hairsbreadth of winning the city title in heavyweight boxing? And, I might add, the one that all the girls were sweet on."

Briscoe grinned at him; his sandy hair was streaked through with gray. Davies could see the weariness of age: dark circles under his eyes, like smudges of ash; the sallow tinge to his skin from too much drink. But he was full of good cheer. If Curtis and Thornton had their University of Pennsylvania and rowing club cronies, then Davies had the same on a humbler scale. He doubted their bond would be any less in loyalty and help for one another.

"Come into the back. It is better to talk," Briscoe said. He looked at Dr. Weston with approval. "You are keeping much better company these days."

They moved into a back room off the bar. Davies followed Briscoe, who walked slowly, with a limp. He had a sidelong gait and leaned heavily on a cane.

There was an unofficial office set up at the table in front of the wood-stove. The surface was covered with loose papers, haphazardly arranged in piles. Briscoe was well on his way through a pint of bitter.

"Now tell me how you are involved in this dreadful business," he asked.

Davies filled him in on the details of the case.

"How did you get involved in the story? A reporter, you?" Davies asked.

"I will take that as a compliment." Briscoe smiled. "I needed something to do after I got this souvenir from the war."

Davies could see the fold of the pant leg fall away. The leg was amputated above the knee.

"Where did it happen?" Dr. Weston asked quietly.

"Antietam," he said.

They were places he might never visit, Davies thought. Yet in those single names—Antietam, Fredericksburg, Gettysburg—the memories of horror were immediate for those who lived with their wounds and the loss of loved ones.

"I volunteered early on. Pennsylvania Light Artillery Battery F, the finest group of men you could hope to meet." Briscoe grimaced in pain as he lifted his leg up to sit in a chair. "I am more fortunate than most, I know that. But it means my days in the boxing ring are over."

"When did you come home?"

"End of 'sixty-two. A friend from the regiment got me a job in the mailroom at the paper. That's how I met some of the other Bohemians."

The infamous Bohemian Brigade, war correspondents and noncon-
formists of the first order, writing dispatches from the front. Davies remembered how the *Inquirer* was handed round the tenement, the black newsprint
smudging off on his fingertips. He would patiently read the accounts to his
illiterate audience, feverish for news of his brother-in-law's regiment.

"They were deep into reporting on the war, so the paper was short on
coverage for the local beats. It gave those of us with little training a chance
to try our hand at reporting," Briscoe said. "I was assigned to some of our
old neighborhoods in South Philly: robberies, local elections, small-time
news."

"How did you get the tip on the Curtis story?"

"In those days, I had a few lads on the lookout for story leads, at the
police stations, the fire brigade, City Hall. I would pay a bit of money and
get a tip."

Briscoe pushed a heavy book across the table towards them. It was a
bound folio with past issues of the paper. The page was open to the late
edition for December 3, 1863. There was Briscoe's story, with the headline
LEADING IRON FOUNDRY FOR UNION DECIMATED IN BLAZE, THIRTY FEARED
DEAD.

Davies told him of the blackmail, the mysterious letters alluding to
the past.

"Edward Curtis is sure it is related to this fire."

"Is he now? Interesting." Briscoe paused to take a long draft of ale.
"Do either of you know how the Curtis foundry came to be where it is?"

They shook their heads.

"Indulge me a bit." The reporter gestured to the stacks of notes on the
table. "The story consumed me for the better part of two years."

He sat up straighter and leaned in towards them. It was the manner
of an expert discussing his subject.

"They started out at the turn of the century, a family business making
decorative items for the home. It was comfortable but not lucrative."

It was what Curtis had told them, a company built from modest beginnings, Davies thought. No doubt many of the cast-iron railings and friezes that adorned the town houses around tony Rittenhouse Square owed their existence to the foundry.

"Then in the mid-forties, Curtis's grandfather makes a shrewd move. He contracts with Matthias Baldwin of the locomotive company. They move into large-scale production, winning accounts with all the railroad firms."

"How did they make the shift to munitions?" Davies asked.

"It was happening in other places too, like Tredegar in Richmond. They bought up land next to the original factory and consolidated the site: furnaces, rolling mills, boiler, and locomotive shops. Soon the ordnance departments of the Army and Navy come calling. They supplied iron for everything from small arms, like rifles and cartridges, to heavy artillery, like the huge cannons used for coastal defense."

"And an unending supply is needed," Davies said.

"Quite the setup, eh?" Briscoe said. "You start out as a humble shop peddling garden cherubs. In one generation, you catapult to spectacular wealth, all by profiting from the greatest death machine the country has known."

"Surely accidents had occurred before."

Briscoe shook his head. "The fire in 1863 was on a different scale altogether. It erupted out of one of the main furnaces, a billowing tower of flame in the dead of night. You could hear the creaking of the wooden scaffold around the furnace as it gave way, like the groans of a giant beast dying. A few men ran from the building engulfed in flames. The worst was the shouts of the men trapped inside, scrabbling like animals to get out."

His words, like his writing, were vivid. Davies felt as though he was watching the scene unfold on that December night.

"I watched as they pulled bodies, still burning like charred meat, out of the smoking debris. Some of the corpses were riddled with pieces of smoldering metal. They were so disfigured they couldn't even be identified."

"Was there an investigation?"

"Yes and no. You can't shut down one of your best producers at the height of the war. The Curtises made generous payouts. I am sure they convinced themselves they took the right course of action."

"Did you speak with any family members at the time?"

"I did. It was just Edward and his father at the helm. Curtis's elder brother had been killed the year before. He was the obvious heir to the firm. Edward was the ne'er-do-well younger son who stayed behind, drinking and carousing. He had a medical condition that made him unfit for military service."

"Do you know what it was?" Dr. Weston asked.

"A tremor of some kind. Apparently his hands shook so badly, he couldn't load a rifle, let alone hold it steady enough to shoot a target."

Briscoe smiled ruefully.

"Lucky sod. No one I joined up with could claim such a convenient ailment."

He placed his hand on his thigh, just above the amputated limb, and massaged it gently.

"He had already caused a ruckus in the family a few years before," Briscoe continued. "His only act of distinction, I would say. He married Beatrice Alford, the daughter of a pharmacist. She wasn't the sort of bride an up-and-coming socialite family wanted. I rather liked her myself. She was the most intelligent of them all."

"Beatrice Curtis told me her father had lost the family business," Dr. Weston said.

"Oh yes, in quite a disgraceful way. Beatrice was the eldest daughter and often helped her father. He started a side business selling medicinal tonics. I am sure you have seen the type, Doctor, hucksters peddling cure-alls. He made a lot of money."

"What happened?"

"Five children died from taking the tonic. It turns out the main ingredients were mercury and laudanum. Alford was tried for murder and let off by a lenient judge. But he was lacerated in the court of public opinion. Her marriage to Curtis must have been a welcome escape."

So Mrs. Curtis had not been entirely truthful about her past, Davies thought.

"Much of this information I got from different sources. The family stopped talking to me as I got closer to the truth," Briscoe said.

"What do you mean?" Davies asked.

"A few of the men wouldn't stay silent. They insisted that the fire had been deliberately set, by someone who knew how to manipulate the machinery."

"But who would want to do such a thing? And why?" Dr. Weston asked.

"A good question. The government investigation determined water had come into contact with the molten iron in one of the furnaces, causing the explosion. The Curtises produced witnesses who testified that there were wet rags and pails of water lying unattended on the furnace floor. But some of the old hands insisted that the supervisor would never have made such a novice mistake. He was a brilliant fellow, a West Point engineer with a degree in metallurgy. His safety standards were exacting. And yet . . ."

"Yet?"

"After the investigation was over, the Curtises vilified him. They claimed it was his carelessness that caused the fire. He could no longer defend himself. The poor lad died in the explosion. He was only twenty-six years old," Briscoe said.

"Did anyone come to the engineer's defense publicly?"

"No. But he had damning evidence to take to the authorities. There were men working double shifts on the puddling crew; cracks on the main furnaces ripe for metal fatigue; old scaffolding around the towers. It was like a match to a pile of kindling, so to speak."

"So a fire was set deliberately, but it raged out of control and caused more destruction than intended," Davies said.

"The Curtises wanted to stamp out any union sentiment completely. It could serve as a forceful deterrent," Briscoe said.

"But who actually set the fire?"

"One of Curtis's minions, no doubt. If you set the price high enough, you could pay someone to do anything," Briscoe said.

"But what of the young man's family? Surely they demanded answers?" Dr. Weston asked.

Briscoe nodded.

"I visited every single family. God knows how many weeping parents I sat with. Many had accepted defeat, but not this engineer's mother. She spoke to anyone who would listen: the investigators from the fire bureau and the police, the contractors from the government. William Curtis hired a lawyer to pay her off, a gag clause of sorts. But she refused."

"Were you able to publish any of it in the *Inquirer*?" Davies asked.

"No," Briscoe said bitterly. "My editor canceled the story, at the family's behest, of course. It was the reason I left the paper."

"What was the young man's name?" Dr. Weston asked.

"Michael Warburton. The men all called him 'Burt' for short. I never forgot it because of the way his mother pronounced it. She had left England as a young woman, but still had a trace of the accent. She had come from Coventry, I believe."

Part Five

SUTURING

29

"I demand to know what you are doing, Volcker. There are policemen swarming all through this house," Curtis asked.

"We are asking them to sign written statements. The statements can be used in court to corroborate their accounts to the police."

"Is that necessary? Some of them can't write much more than their names," Curtis said.

"I must insist," Volcker said. What he didn't say was that it was a ruse to get a sample of Mrs. Burt's handwriting.

Dr. Weston's and Sergeant Davies's tenacity had proved prescient. Volcker had been dining at home when Davies burst in with the news. A search in the city records had confirmed what Briscoe told them. There was no trace of Mary Geneva Warburton in Philadelphia after December 1863. She had been born on March 10, 1816, in Burton Green, a small village outside Coventry. Her past residential records showed a few addresses in South Philadelphia, the occupants listed as her and her son, Michael Andrew Warburton. His death certificate confirmed "death by accident" on December 3, 1863, aged twenty-six years. They scoured the city voting and tax rolls for information after that, but she had disappeared. Then in

1866, they found Geneva Burt, with the same birth date and place but a new address: 10 Winfield Place, the Curtis home.

"Sir, we need you immediately," he said.

"Wait! Inspector, what is happening?" Curtis's voice faded as the two policemen strode down the hallway.

"We found it, sir, in Mrs. Burt's office," Davies said.

"Excellent," Volcker said breathlessly. They clattered down the main staircase, round and round, almost slipping on the marble parquet floor in the lobby. Two maids stood at the door to the dining room, brooms and dusters in hand, watching as they ran down the hallway. They heard the shouts as the men approached Mrs. Burt's office off the pantry.

"How dare you? You have no right to be here! Leave at once!"

Any semblance of order was gone. Mrs. Burt was crouched on the floor, scrabbling to collect pieces of paper. The papers were strewn everywhere: bureau drawers were open and spilling out sheets of stationery. Her dress was covered in chimney soot, gray smudges marring the silk.

"Where are they?" Mrs. Burt shrieked, rifling through the open safe box. It was empty save for a few receipts and pencil stubs.

"I have them here, sir," Davies said. He held the cards aloft, high above Mrs. Burt's head. "We found these two letters, along with the box of stationery. There is a removable panel underneath the hearth grate. It was hidden there."

"You have no right to search here!" Mrs. Burt's face was a deep scarlet.

"We have a warrant to go over every inch of this house," Volcker said coldly. "Please stand down."

He opened the envelope and read the card:

When the truth becomes known, you will suffer just as greatly as those who died.

And the next:

Only a terrible punishment will come to those who murder innocents.

"Did you write these, Mrs. Burt?" Volcker asked. He held the card in front of her.

She said nothing.

"Very well. You can answer me at the police station," Volcker said. He nodded to Davies.

At that moment, the door to the office opened. Beatrice Curtis stood on the threshold. Her husband was trying to restrain her.

"We must leave it to the police, Bea," Curtis muttered angrily. She stumbled into the room unsteadily, as if in a daze.

"Mrs. Burt, it cannot be! How could you have done this? You have lived so closely with us, as one of the family."

She looked on the verge of hysterical tears, shaking with anger.

"Is it true, Mrs. Burt?" Beatrice knelt on the floor.

Mrs. Burt met her gaze without fear.

"I am ready to go to the station with you, Inspector."

Davies gestured to the small pair of cuffs he had. Volcker shook his head.

"May I take my belongings with me? I shall not be returning," Mrs. Burt said. Volcker nodded.

The housekeeper walked out of the room, past her shocked employers. The policemen followed her through the kitchen. The cook and maids watched her being led away.

30

Lydia was enclosed in her warm office at the medical college. She had closed the door firmly behind her for privacy. The case was wearing on her. Her nerves were on edge since the attack, far more than she cared to admit. The brush with violence had made her involvement terrifying and very real, Davies's warning come to pass. But she would not give in to fear. The intent of the attack was not to harm but to scare her. What truth were they getting close to?

The sharp turns in the case had left her reeling. Mrs. Burt was the blackmailer and her arrest by the police was imminent. Thornton had been released and was at large. Anna was still missing. Only Volcker seemed cheerful, seeing the developments as a hopeful sign.

Lydia pulled a stack of exam papers towards her. If there was one constant in her life, it was the never-ending pile of papers that needed attention. She had to make progress as her office hours started soon.

A soft knock came on the door.

There was no escape, likely a student needed help.

Lydia went to the door and opened it. It was the young woman she had seen on every visit to the Blake Trust, the distinctive pitting of her skin making her instantly recognizable. She looked chilled to the bone, covered only in a threadbare shawl wrapped tight around her shoulders.

"Kate! How did you find me?" Lydia said.

She reached her hand out in greeting and Kate grasped it. Lydia could feel the hard nodules in her joints, bulging like an old woman's.

"I found out your address from Mr. Cole at the trust."

The girl hesitated on the threshold. She eyed the steaming cup of coffee and fragrant sandwich on the desk.

"Please come and sit down. Would you like something to eat?" Lydia asked.

"Oh no, I couldn't," Kate said.

"I insist. I am not hungry and it will go to waste."

The girl needed no further encouragement. Lydia watched as she eagerly finished the food, wiping her mouth with a napkin.

"There, that must be better." Lydia knew she would have to put the young woman at ease. "I am sorry we did not have a chance to speak more. When Mrs. Curtis interrupted us, I had to leave."

Kate nodded.

"Why have you come?"

"After you left, I talked to Josey more. I don't know the other girls so well. I usually keep to myself. She said you were asking questions about Anna. That day Mrs. Curtis scared me off. But I had more to tell you."

"So you knew Anna?"

"Oh yes. She was ever so kind to me. She and Mr. Cole were teaching me to read better so I could get a job."

Kate hesitated.

"The thing is, I can't stop thinking about the two of them, Ellen and Anna."

"Who is Ellen?" Lydia asked.

"My friend Ellen Smith. She was the one who brought me to the trust a few months back," Kate said. "I don't look too kindly on charity workers. But Ellen said this place was different." The food and coffee had revived her.

"Were Ellen and Anna friends?"

"No, ma'am, they only knew each other in passing. That's what's so odd. Ellen went missing the same time Anna left, three weeks ago."

"What did Ellen look like?" Lydia could feel her heart beat faster.

"She had long dark hair, about the same height as Anna. You know how you see someone from afar and take them for another? It was like that. One day I came up behind her, thinking it was Ellen. I did a double take when I saw it was Anna. We had a good laugh about it."

"And you haven't seen your friend in three weeks?"

Kate shook her head.

"She had never left like that before, with no word. She had the room next to me in the boardinghouse."

"Do you have any idea where she might have gone? Did she have any family?"

"No, and nowhere to go either. I have been on my own since my father died and Ellen was too. We looked out for each other."

"What do you think of the trust?"

"It is too cozy for my liking, with the ladies and gentlemen mixed up with us. Anna, too, talking as if she was one of them. But we aren't. I do better on my own."

Lydia understood. Kate survived by relying on her own counsel.

"I wouldn't confide in any of them."

Lydia wondered if the Thorntons knew what a shrewd observer of character they had in their midst.

"I was there when the police came. When I heard about what happened with Anna and Mr. Thornton . . ." she said. "I had seen them together before, at his flat."

Kate looked down at her hands, the skin cracked and roughened from work.

"One of the girls said Anna was expecting a baby and Mr. Thornton was the father," Kate said quietly. "I don't know if that was true. But Ellen was."

Lydia took a deep breath. She had to proceed with caution so as not to frighten the girl.

"Isn't that too strange, miss? They looked so alike. And both gone missing at the same time?"

Kate's eyes filled with tears.

"I was so afraid to say anything. Who could I tell? Not Mrs. Thornton, with her own husband carrying on right in front of her! Who would listen to me?"

"Do you know who the father of Ellen's child is?" Lydia asked.

"No." She shook her head miserably.

Could it be Paul or worse, Thornton? Lydia thought.

"I was out of my head with worry. But Ellen was so settled. She said she was going to be taken care of. By whom? She had no one."

"Kate, this is very important," Lydia said. "Did Ellen tell anyone about the baby?"

"I begged her not to breathe a word," Kate said, her eyes wide with fear. "But Mrs. Thornton knew. See how fast they will turn on you now, I said. She talked too much, likely told the whole lot of them at the trust. She even told the Curtises."

"The Curtises?" Lydia was surprised.

Kate nodded.

"One day we were sitting at the table, talking. Anna and Mrs. Curtis were there. Mrs. Curtis had brought her husband too. No doubt he wanted to see where all his money was going. So chummy, sitting about like one big family." Kate's lips turned down in distaste.

"They start asking questions and next thing you know, Ellen is talking about the baby, in front of strangers!"

"Did they offer her help?" Lydia asked

"Mrs. Curtis didn't say much but didn't seem too shocked neither. She and Mrs. Thornton went off together. Mr. Curtis stayed. It was the strangest thing for a gentleman to sit with us. He asked questions about how she was feeling. He said it was a gift to have a baby, no matter how you might come about it. He was talking as if we weren't there. He said that his two boys were the light of his life. But he had a son who died."

"Another child?"

"Yes. Mr. Curtis said he was never the same after that. He missed the boy so much. He seemed to snap out of it when his wife came back, like he remembered where he was."

So Anna had heard it too. Was this the child she had referred to in the diary, "Thou, straggler into loving arms"? But why was the child's death hidden?

"Something terrible has happened to Ellen, hasn't it?" Kate whispered as tears streamed down her face.

Lydia could feel a painful mix of emotions surfacing. She felt sorrow for the senseless death of another young woman who at last had a name, Ellen Smith. She thought of Kate, herself alone and vulnerable, and her courage in telling the truth to aid her friend.

But Lydia also felt a growing sense of excitement. At last, they had it. The connection to the dead woman led directly back to the Curtis family and the trust. She had to get an urgent message to the police so Kate could identify the body. But first Lydia had to know the truth of what had happened to the Curtis child.

There was one person she knew who could tell her.

31

Volcker spread the letters before Geneva Burt on the table. Curtis had given them the lot and they were now in evidence.

Mrs. Burt declined Volcker's offer of an attorney's presence during questioning. She sat across the table from the policemen in a windowless room at the station house. She had brought one small bag of clothing with her and it sat at her side.

She seemed to require nothing else. A glass of water sat untouched before her. She looked at them expectantly. It reminded Davies of when they had first met, sitting in her office drinking tea. Then as now, her intelligence was obvious.

"These letters are very similar to the two we found in your office today. Yet this is not your handwriting. We were unable to match it with a sample from the household account books," Volcker said.

She said nothing.

"Did you write them?" he asked.

"Mr. Curtis said these letters began arriving six months ago, referring to a tragic event in the past. The writer asked for money and Mr. Curtis decided to pay," Davies said.

"Mrs. Burt, there is no use in trying to hide this any longer," Volcker said. "The letters were found in your office in a box, hidden underneath a slab in the fireplace. The stationery is an exact match to the blackmailer's letters. Why don't you tell us what happened?"

Mrs. Burt looked down at her hands. The room was lit by a single oil lamp, hanging from the ceiling. The three of them sat in the shadows.

"I am weary, Inspector," she said at last. "I no longer have anything to fear. My life ended with Michael's death so many years ago. He was my reason for living. I had spent my whole life alone, in an orphanage and then the workhouse. I had no illusions about what my future would hold. I came to this country as a servant of eighteen, taking passage with a family who settled in Boston. I was much like these young maids now. Life was an endless round of work. I was foolish, desperate to escape the drudgery, even by my own low standards. Michael was born when I was twenty. My husband, if he could be called that, died soon after in a haze of drink and violence.

"Then it was just the two of us. Yet I was not afraid. For the first time in my life, there was someone for me to love and be loved by. I managed on my own, doing domestic work. Along the way, kind employers helped me set aside money to educate Michael. As he grew into a young man I could see the gifts God had bestowed on him."

Mrs. Burt's voice was warm and rich, filled with memories of the past.

"Anything he took a hand to he would excel at. He was accepted at West Point and then spent a few years in an Army regiment. When he was offered the post at the Curtis foundry, I was elated. He was being given the respect he deserved for his education. I could scarcely dare to dream of such happiness."

Mrs. Burt paused and closed her eyes.

"And then the fire. I couldn't believe it when the police came to tell me he was dead," she said. "He had been spared the worst of the war by his skill as a metallurgist. He was on the cusp of a life of great promise, and then this. I felt cursed.

"The superintendent of the foundry came to see me. A patronizing bastard. As if I could put a price tag on my only son's life?" She practically spat the words out. "Michael told me how dangerous the work was. He accepted the risks. That was what I raised him to be: a man of integrity."

The pride in her voice was unmistakable.

"He lived in rooms at the foundry to better supervise the crews. He would come home to our little flat on his day off and tell me of the lack of safety practices that were endangering his men. He felt he had a duty to report it."

"Do you know if he approached the superintendent? Or the Curtises?"

"I know how things work, Inspector, when you are poor and power-less," she said bitterly. "I tried to dissuade him, but he wouldn't listen."

"But he never took his evidence to a higher authority, say, the government inspectors?"

"No."

"After he died, the Curtises alleged that Michael had made a careless error. Jack Briscoe at the *Inquirer* told us the story," Davies said.

"Jack is a good man. I wasn't surprised when the Curtises laid the blame on Michael. It was a shameful lie. I was the only one left to defend him. But who would listen to an old woman?"

"You left the city a few months later. Where did you go?" Davies asked.

"There was nothing for me here. I was like a ghost. I barely ate. My hair had turned white from the shock and grief. I moved around, to Boston and New York, found odd jobs. No one took any notice of me so long as I did my work."

Her words were so compelling, Davies could barely look away. The need to tell this story had been weighing on her for many years.

"I don't know what brought me back. Curiosity, I suppose. It was easy to get a job in the house," Mrs. Burt said.

"You blamed this family for your son's death," Volcker said. "How can we believe you meant them no harm?"

"I didn't set out to." She hesitated. "The anger I felt, it was like a cold, hard part of myself that I lived with. I did not know what I wanted to do, except to watch them."

Keeping one's enemies close, Davies thought. It was a way to hold power when there was none.

"Did anyone recognize you?" Volcker asked.

"No. I used my best accent, a distressed English gentlewoman needing a job. In time, Beatrice depended on me to guide her. Despite her airs, she is a very common woman."

Mrs. Burt likely thought it demeaning, not in the work done but the person it was done for, Davies thought.

"But she is a devoted mother and for that I admire her. She would do anything to protect her sons."

"So you bide your time. Then six months ago, you started sending threatening letters," Volcker said.

She said nothing.

"There is no reason to hide any longer. Unless you suggest it was someone else. Are you shielding another?" Volcker asked.

Mrs. Burt snorted, as if the idea were preposterous.

"Yes, I started sending the letters."

"How did you do it?"

"Mrs. Curtis would have recognized my handwriting immediately, so I took the letters to a scribe. They are a dime a dozen in the tenement, ready to extract money from a poor, illiterate woman like me."

She hunched her shoulders forward and looked up at them, her eyes meek and submissive.

"Begging your pardon, sir, can you help a lady write a letter to her boy?" she said. The voice had changed instantly, to the tremulous quality of an old woman. It was like watching an actress: her features were protean and the delivery seamless.

"I would dictate the letters. Not word for word, mind you. I would make up stories as if I was writing a letter to my son, then carefully cut up the words and paste them onto the stationery. I would add the letters to Mr. Curtis's mail tray. It became a game to me. I enjoyed watching them suffer: the confusion and uncertainty when the letters first came, then the outright fear. The money was useless to me."

"When did Anna find out about the blackmail?" Davies asked.

Mrs. Burt looked at Davies with genuine respect.

"Did you kill her because she discovered you as the blackmailer?" he probed.

"No!" The answer was vehement. "I am not a murderer. Do not equate me with the Curtises."

Volcker poured himself a glass of water. She watched as he took a deliberate sip.

"Why now, Mrs. Burt?"

She looked at him in question.

"You joined the Curtis household nine years ago. Why did you decide to blackmail them now for your son's death? Why wait so long to extract your vengeance?"

Mrs. Burt's expression was one of astonishment as she looked from one to the other. Her lips parted in a slow smile, a snarl unraveling its full contempt. She raised her head. Her laughter was deep, full of satisfaction. The sound reverberated in the small room.

Davies looked at Volcker in confusion. Was she mad? Had the burden of grief taken its toll?

"Do you and Mr. Curtis think this is all because of the fire, because of my son's death?" Mrs. Burt asked.

"Yes," Volcker said coldly.

"Then you are fools, all of you." She sat back in the chair and folded her hands on her lap. "I have nothing more to say."

32

"Enough. I have bloody well had it with this investigation. Lunatics, the lot of them," Volcker muttered angrily.

It was early evening and they had halted their questioning. Mrs. Burt had refused to speak further.

"Perhaps she will reconsider after a night in a jail cell," Davies said.

"It is a game to her. I don't know what she can be thinking."

Volcker pushed himself back from a desk strewn with papers. He took off his glasses and rubbed his eyes.

"We are at an impasse. Thornton admits to having an affair with Anna. He is self-absorbed to the extreme and he certainly cares for keeping his wife's money. Although I doubt his wife would cast him off. God knows why, but she seems to love him. He is a despicable philanderer but is he capable of murder?" he said.

"Why do you think Mrs. Burt is behaving so strangely?" Davies asked

"I don't know," Volcker said. "Mrs. Burt's primary motivation would be to conceal the blackmail. But I think she enjoyed seeing the Curtises' reaction to her deception, the fruits of her revenge."

"Neither of them knows that Anna might still live. Yet no one has seen her for weeks," Davies said. "And what of Paul O'Meara?"

Paul had left the Curtis house. His belongings remained but no one knew his whereabouts.

"Yet Anna may still be alive!" Volcker said. "That is where our inquiry must focus now. We must go through everything again."

There was a knock on the office door.

"Come in," Volcker said. The desk officer, Constable Ross, was on the threshold.

"The lady doctor brought this for you earlier, sir. She said it was important." He handed Davies a letter.

Davies tore it open and read through it quickly.

"Sir, you must look at this," he said excitedly. "Dr. Weston says she knows who the dead woman is. A Miss Ellen Smith. She spoke with the woman's friend, who is ready to make an identification."

Volcker took the letter from him.

"Extraordinary!" he said.

He looked at his pocket watch. "It is not too late now. Let's go to the college now and see if we can find Dr. Weston."

They walked through the workroom of the station, row upon row of desks empty.

Constable Ross sat at the front desk in the lobby. He was on night duty.

"Good night. We'll be back first thing in the morning. Send a message if you need anything. Did Mrs. Burt eat her meal?"

"No, sir, she refused."

"Very well, we will see if she is ready to talk tomorrow."

Volcker and Davies went down the short steps to the entryway of the station house, their footsteps echoing on the stairs.

They didn't see the dark figure watching them from the alcove off the hall.

33

Lydia pulled down the brim of her hat as Davies and Volcker passed. She leaned into the side of the wall. The cold stone was like a slab of ice against her back. She watched as they got into a hansom cab together. She had been biding her time in the pub across the street, at a corner table by the window. She had to speak with Mrs. Burt, to know for herself.

It was half past nine. Constable Ross sat at the desk with the evening's *Ledger* opened to the racing pages. He looked up in surprise.

"Dr. Weston? Inspector Volcker and Sergeant Davies left for the evening. You just missed them."

"Oh dear," Lydia said. "I had hoped to speak with them."

"Could I help you?" Ross asked.

"There were a few questions that I wanted to ask Mrs. Burt. Sergeant Davies gave me permission to do so." Lydia lied blatantly, hoping for future forgiveness.

"I am sorry. They won't be back until tomorrow," Ross said.

"Oh, that is a shame," Lydia said.

"I could send a message to the inspector if you think it is important."

"No, no, I don't want to trouble anyone." Lydia paused. "Perhaps it would be all right if I spoke with her now?"

Ross hesitated. "I was told not to let anyone back to see her."

"Of course, Constable," Lydia said. "It is just that I must teach early tomorrow morning." She gave him a charming smile. "I promise it won't take but a moment."

"I suppose it would be all right. You are part of the investigation after all."

Ross removed the ring of keys from his belt hook. He took an oil lamp and led her down a hallway. He stopped in front of a stout wooden door that looked like the gateway to a medieval dungeon. He opened it and walked in.

"The cells are through there, Doctor. Just give a shout when you are done." Ross handed her the oil lamp.

He closed the door softly. Lydia held the lamp aloft. There were four cells facing each other. As her eyes adjusted to the darkness, features of the room became more distinct. She could see the outline of a high window in the wall. The moonlight shone through, etching a sharp black-and-white pattern onto the cement floor.

"Mrs. Burt? Are you there?"

There was no answer. Lydia peered into the cell. A shapeless black form sat on the bench. Mrs. Burt was wrapped in a shawl. The edge of it was pulled over her face, like a funereal shroud.

"It is Lydia Weston. I know about the blackmail."

Mrs. Burt was silent.

"The police think you did this to seek vengeance for your son's death. But it wasn't because of the foundry fire, was it?" Lydia said.

Mrs. Burt stood and came to the middle of the cell.

"You discovered a secret that the Curtises were trying to hide. It was about a child. A child who died a premature death," Lydia said.

Lydia could hear the incessant dripping of an open spigot. The drops of water into an empty bucket filled the silence.

"I have read Anna's diary. She knew it too. Please, Mrs. Burt, you must tell me. It could save Anna's life. She might still be alive."

"What?" Mrs. Burt spoke for the first time, the shock in her voice unmistakable.

Lydia hesitated. She had agreed with the police to keep quiet about the fact that the body was not Anna's. But now she had no choice. She told Mrs. Burt what they knew.

"You are the blackmailer and Anna found out why," Lydia said. "Whose child is it? What happened?"

Mrs. Burt retreated again into the far reaches of the cell.

Lydia cursed herself. Had she said too much? She turned away in frustration. When she looked back, Geneva Burt stood face-to-face with her.

"Six months ago a woman came to the house. She would not give her name but said to tell Mrs. Curtis that she came from the Infirmary on Long Island. That the mistress would know what she meant.

"Most of the other servants had gone to the country residence to help with one of Mr. Curtis's weekend parties. Mrs. Curtis told me to go to my rooms, to have a rest. She said she would talk to the woman and then see her out. She was very casual about it, as if an old friend had come to visit. But I could tell she was upset."

"And you had never seen this woman before?" Lydia asked.

"No. They had a private conversation in the morning room. There is an air vent that leads to the dressing room next door. I stayed there and overheard the entire conversation."

"What did you learn?"

"She was a nurse at a children's home in New York. She had come to speak with Mrs. Curtis about the death of a child in her care that had happened many years before."

Lydia gripped the bars of the cell.

"The boy's name was James. He was placed in the institution as a baby by his parents."

"Edward and Beatrice Curtis," Lydia said.

Mrs. Burt nodded.

"So they had a child that died in an institution," Lydia said. "It is tragic, but why hide it?"

"The child was illegitimate. Edward Curtis had had an affair with a young woman. She gave birth to the boy. It happened early in the Curtises' marriage."

"What became of the boy's mother?"

"She died when the child was a year old. But she extracted a promise from Mr. Curtis that he would support James."

"There would be the scandal of an illegitimate child," Lydia said. "But with the child and mother dead, it was long done. Why did the nurse come back?"

"She was racked by guilt over what had happened. The child did not die a natural death."

"What?" Lydia gasped.

"When James was five years old, he became ill with pneumonia. Beatrice and Edward Curtis came from Philadelphia to see him. The boy died in the night. But the nurse was adamant that it was not a natural death."

Mrs. Burt looked up at Lydia. The black hood of the shawl had fallen away from her face. She reveled in the raw power of what she was about to say.

"He had been given a sedative to make him comfortable. But he was given too much, deliberately."

"By whom?" Lydia whispered. She felt chilled to the bone.

"By his father. Edward Curtis."

"Dear God." Lydia closed her eyes. "The nurse was sure?"

"Oh yes. She accepted it. She thought of it as a merciful death for a child who had very little to live for. But as the years progressed, she changed her mind."

"So she came to confront the Curtises so many years later?"

Mrs. Burt nodded. "She was convinced a crime had been committed."

"And Mrs. Curtis didn't know of the suspicious circumstances of the child's death?"

"No. She thought, as did everyone, that the child had died of pneumonia."

How that must have shattered Beatrice Curtis and destroyed the careful, measured world she lived in.

"Afterwards, Mrs. Curtis was deeply disturbed, almost delirious. Everyone thought she was ill. No one knew the truth of it," Mrs. Burt said.

"But Mrs. Curtis never suspected that you overheard the conversation?"

Mrs. Burt shook her head.

"So then you started the blackmail?"

"It was the opportunity I had been waiting for," Mrs. Burt said quietly. "I had lived so many years in that house. The Curtises reveled in their happiness, untouched by the devastation they had caused others. My Michael was dead and gone. It gave me the greatest pleasure, sending those letters. Now I could watch them suffer. Mrs. Curtis became more and more fearful as their marriage frayed. I don't regret it for a moment."

"How did Anna learn of the blackmail?"

"Anna was a sharp one, very observant. She saw that Mrs. Curtis was becoming more anxious and tried to find out why. She saw me placing one of the letters in an envelope and putting it in Mr. Curtis's mail tray. She confronted me."

"But Anna thought the blackmail was about the fire."

"Yes. Her head had been filled with that nonsense by Abe Griffin. So I told her the truth, that it was about James's death."

"What happened next?"

"Anna was shocked. She wanted to tell Mrs. Curtis the truth about the letters. She truly had her welfare at heart, thought it her duty to protect her. Foolish girl."

"What did you do to keep Anna silent?" Lydia asked.

"Nothing," Mrs. Burt said sharply. "I did not kill her. But I knew about the affair with Thornton and threatened to reveal it. That stopped her."

"When was the last time you saw Anna?"

"It was three weeks ago, just before she disappeared from the house. She was very agitated, insistent on telling the truth."

"Do you know if she ever told Mrs. Curtis about the blackmail?"

"I don't know. I never saw her again."

Mrs. Burt slipped a thin envelope through the bars of the cell.

Lydia opened it. The paper said: "Celia Jackson, Children's Infirmary and Home, Long Island, New York."

"That is the name of the nurse. She can tell you everything."

Lydia left Mrs. Burt and returned to the front desk. She thanked Ross and hurried out of the police station. She stood on the front steps. There was a faint pattern of stars in the night sky, barely visible above the glow of the city lights. She had been in the station for less than an hour, but she felt she had emerged from a subterranean world where she and Mrs. Burt were the only inhabitants.

So that was what Anna had discovered: the child who had died, "a mute remembrancer of crime / long lost, concealed, forgot for many years." It made sense at last, the cryptic messages in the diary. It was Edward Curtis's illegitimate son, dead at the age of five in an institution, far from his family. Was he guilty of the murder of his own child? And what of Anna? What had she done when she learned the truth?

Lydia needed to speak with Volcker and Davies. But as she looked down at the paper in her hand, she made her decision in an instant. She consulted her pocket watch. If she caught an early morning train to New York, she could be in Long Island by afternoon.

34

It was a busy morning at the station. The fashionable ladies were buying tickets to New York and blended with the crowd of bankers in their dark suits.

"One round trip to Grand Central Terminal, please," Lydia said to the ticket agent at the window.

"Yes, miss, if you make haste, you can catch the seven o'clock."

"Thank you, sir. It is the first piece of luck I have had today." She tipped her hat and gave him a smile.

Lydia walked to the platform and caught the train in time. She leaned back into the seat. She was exhausted, having slept only a few hours the night before.

It was a stroke of luck that she knew of the Children's Infirmary. Each year graduating students struggled to find work despite stellar credentials. Many hospitals were wary of hiring women physicians, but the infirmary was not one of them. The college had sent four candidates to interview last year. Each returned with glowing recommendations of the place.

Lydia looked out the window as the train rumbled out of the station.

According to Mrs. Burt, Edward Curtis had directed the killing of his own son. How could a father bow to such depravity? The child's life was a secret, an apparent threat to no one. Did Edward Curtis know what Anna and Mrs. Burt had discovered? Someone in that house had gone to great lengths to hide the truth.

THE SUN WAS DRAWING CLOSE across the sound and a flock of geese lifted off the surface of the water. Their wings touched the crests of waves, releasing sprays of mist. The landscape was bathed in the pellucid light of afternoon. The trees glittered with red and gold leaves, the last vestige of fall. Despite the harrowing circumstances that had brought her, Lydia marveled at the beauty. The train ride from the city had felt long and she was glad to be on the final leg of her journey. The carriage she had hired at the village station made its way into the countryside and she caught glimpses of the shoreline through the trees, the slate gray surface of the water broken up by peaked waves. It reminded her of childhood, walking through the woods at Walden. The dense stand of trees would close in on her as she leapt over stones and branches along the path, obscuring the view of the pond. Often she would run and stop short at the edge of the shore, marveling at the water's expansiveness, its balm a constant. Lydia laid her head against the seat and closed her eyes, taking a moment of rest.

"HOW DID YOU FIND US?" The chief matron, Mrs. Walls, was astonished when Lydia presented herself at the front desk. The infirmary, or "Children's Branch" as the staff called it, was spread out over ten acres on a bank of Long Island Sound. The institution felt a world away from the city.

Lydia told the matron the reason for her visit, sparing no detail. There was no need to hide the truth now.

"I understand, Doctor. This has troubled us all greatly."

Mrs. Walls was a cheerful middle-aged woman. Her demeanor was calm and assured.

"Come with me, please." She gave Lydia an informal tour as they walked up a winding path to the hospital. The path followed gently rolling lawns sloping towards the water. They passed a nurse pushing a baby in a pram. Nearby two older children were sitting on a blanket, playing with wooden trains.

"We take children from birth to age five. Sometimes they are born here, else they are brought in by family members that cannot care for them. The infirmary was started as a foundlings' home. It was meant to be a temporary place, but sadly we have grown to meet demand."

She pointed to a whitewashed cottage. A woman sat in a rocking chair on the porch soothing a baby.

"The children live in groups, each overseen by a matron. It is rather like a small village. The children have schooling. Of course, it is simple for the little ones. There is religious instruction, games, outdoor exercise. All our meals are taken together."

"Do families have to pay?"

"Yes, there is a separate fee for those who live in the cottages. The children in the hospital require medical care overseen by a doctor. No one is turned away. Our benefactors see to that."

They walked up a hill to a brick building.

"My office is just here. We will have some privacy to talk."

Lydia followed Mrs. Walls into her dark paneled office and sat in a chair in front of the large desk. The matron sat across from her.

"I need not even consult my files to know whom you speak of. I asked Celia to join us here. You know that the child died ten years ago?"

Lydia nodded.

"It was an unusual case. The family was very wealthy and not from the New York area. Usually, our referrals come from the city. I was not in charge then, of course.

"It was clear from the start that James could not be cared for at home." Mrs. Walls shook her head sadly. "I did not have much experience, but even I could see how his life would be prematurely shortened."

"What was the nature of his medical condition?"

"He was born with deformities of the skull and spine. His cry was unlike that of any other baby I have heard. He could not eat or nurse properly. The family consulted many physicians to determine what was wrong."

"How old was James when he came to you?"

"He was just a year old. It nearly broke my heart, the poor frightened thing. He was in the hospital at first, to make him comfortable. Eventually he went to one of the cottages and was happier there. But it is she who must tell you more."

Mrs. Walls looked behind her. "Come in, Celia."

A tall woman stood in the doorway. Her face was browned from the sun and her long ropy arms hung at her sides. Lydia guessed her age to be mid-thirties. She wore a black dress and a small gold cross on a chain rested on the bodice.

Celia took the chair opposite Lydia, fidgeting in her seat.

"It is all right, Celia. Dr. Weston is here to help. She has questions for you."

"I have spoken with Geneva Burt, the housekeeper at the Curtis house. She overheard your conversation with Mrs. Curtis. I know about James," Lydia said.

"The child's death has worn on me all these years. It is a relief to unburden myself," Celia said.

"Tell me about James," Lydia said.

"He was the first baby I cared for. I was as new as he was. I was in charge of a little group of four."

243

"What did you do with the children?" Lydia asked. She could see that Celia would need to be drawn out.

"Oh, all sorts of things, ma'am," Celia said. "We were like a family, together for the best and worst days. I would comfort them when they cried or when they fell ill."

"Did his parents come to visit?" Lydia asked.

Celia shook her head.

"So many of the little ones are orphans. But just after his second birthday, a couple came to visit. The talk was that the lady wasn't his real mother, he had been born a . . ." Celia hesitated. She decided against saying anything further after a look from Mrs. Walls.

"The matron at that time told me to mind my own business. Besides, what did it matter how my baby came to me?" Celia asked.

"Did James recognize the couple?"

"He just lit up with happiness to see them. They would bring treats, oranges and chocolates, enough for all of us. As he got older, he looked forward to the visits."

Beatrice Curtis presented a picture of idyllic family life to the world. How had she accepted the existence of an illegitimate child? Had Edward Curtis loved James's mother? Lydia thought of the maids she had spoken with at the house. They had described Mrs. Curtis's bouts of melancholy when she retreated to her room, how her husband fled the house to escape her moods.

"Then something changed. One of the last times, they had a terrible row. Mr. Curtis wanted to take James with them, to live in Philadelphia. He would hire a nurse to care for James so they could all be together. They were expecting another baby," Celia said.

This must have coincided with the birth of the elder Curtis child. Lydia could imagine Beatrice's patience depleted.

"What happened?"

"Mrs. Curtis refused to take him home. Mr. Curtis was angry but he gave in. Poor James wept his little heart out when they left."

"How was the boy's health at this time?" Lydia asked.

"He suffered. Sometimes he had a hard time eating, so he lost weight. We would all lie awake, listening to that cough, knowing he was in pain."

"Did Mr. Curtis know how ill he was?" Lydia asked.

"We sent letters. The money always came promptly for medicine but his father never came back to visit. All of us here tried to cheer him up."

"The boy died many years ago. What made you feel differently about his death now? Why did you come to Philadelphia?" Lydia asked.

"When James died, I was devastated. Yet I felt it was for the best. I believed it was a mercy, sending him home to God. But I was wrong."

Celia touched the small cross on the chain.

"What happened on the night he died?" Lydia asked.

Celia looked at Mrs. Walls. The matron nodded her encouragement.

"That last illness was different. His breath was short, just a ragged cry. I held my baby in my arms each night, to give him some comfort," Celia said. "I was afraid James might not recover. An urgent telegram was sent to Philadelphia. Mr. and Mrs. Curtis both came to be with him."

"Did you call for a doctor?" Lydia asked.

"Yes, there is a local doctor in the village who comes during the night if there is an emergency," Mrs. Walls said.

"Dr. Bates came. He gave James an injection of morphine, a very small dose," Celia said. "It was like a miracle. The crying stopped. I knew the medication would wear off after about four hours, so I watched him closely. But even then, his breathing remained steady and comfortable. He slept peacefully."

"What happened next?" Lydia asked.

"Mrs. Curtis was upset from all that had happened, so she returned to their inn to rest," Celia said. "Mr. Curtis stayed overnight, in James's room. I was just next door. I slept soundly for the first time in days. I was so relieved that James was better."

She paused.

"I went to check on him early the next morning. It was only a few hours later. And he was gone. He had died during the night."

Celia wiped away a few tears from her cheek.

"Mr. Curtis was there, sleeping on the cot. I woke him. He was almost inconsolable, so grief-stricken. It was a terrible moment, bound together in our sorrow."

"Did the doctor come back to examine the body?" Lydia asked.

"Mr. Curtis said no. James was finally at rest."

"But there is more. You must tell her," Mrs. Walls said.

The younger woman nodded.

"James's body was to be taken away, to prepare for burial. I was brushing his hair, arranging his clothes. And I noticed something unusual. His skin was clammy, it felt almost wet. I could see his lips were tinged blue. His eyes were closed, so I lifted the lids to see. The pupils were like pinpoints."

Lydia drew in a breath. The unmistakable physical signs of an overdose from an opioid compound. It was most likely morphine, given by injection, which would provide an immediate effect. The medicine from the doctor would have long worn off, as Celia had observed. Someone else had given him a large dose of morphine, with a clear intent to kill him.

"I checked the medicine cabinet," Celia said. "It is kept locked. There were no missing vials of medicine or syringes. Nothing was out of order."

"And you are sure no one returned during the night?" Lydia asked.

"Yes. The doctor was not called back. Mrs. Curtis stayed at the inn," Celia said. "Mr. Curtis was the only one with James all night, right there in the room. There was no one else."

Mrs. Walls shook her head. "Mr. Curtis must have brought the morphine with him. But how could he know how to dose the medication?"

But none of that mattered. Lydia knew Edward Curtis couldn't have done it. His tremor caused an uncontrollable shaking of his hands, wreaking havoc with fine motor skills. She had observed it herself at their first interview, when he abruptly dropped the cup of water in front of them, the glass shattering into pieces. His condition was so severe that he needed the help of a valet to get dressed, and he had been excused from military service, his hands too unsteady to load or shoot a rifle. Abe Griffin and Jack Briscoe would be able to corroborate. This type of tremor was triggered by intentional movement, not visible at rest. It was often exacerbated by stressful circumstances. Even if Curtis knew what to do, he couldn't have managed the small, very precise movements that would be needed to draw up the morphine into the needle of a syringe and then inject it into a vein in the child's arm.

Celia was speaking.

"I was convinced that James's death was for the best. But I was a coward, I know that now," she said bitterly. "So I went to Philadelphia six months ago and I told Mrs. Curtis what her husband had done. She was upset but said she needed time to think about what to do. She promised she would go to the police."

But Lydia barely heard the woman's words as the realization took hold.

There was someone else who could have returned during the night and given the fatal injection to James, someone to whom the child's existence was a dire threat. Beatrice Curtis, the pharmacist's daughter.

35

───────◦───∨───◦───────

T he clamor of the station went on around her, but Lydia was oblivious. She dictated the telegram to the agent:

```
Have new evidence to murder. Return Philadelphia
on the 8:00 train from Grand Central.
```

"Please mark it urgent," she asked the agent, addressing it to Inspector Thomas Volcker of the Philadelphia police. Mrs. Walls had insisted she stay the night but she had refused. She had to return immediately.

Lydia climbed into the empty carriage. It had been only that morning when she left Philadelphia, but it seemed a lifetime ago. She leaned into the plush seat, her mind racing with all she had learned.

Both Mrs. Burt and Anna thought Edward Curtis had killed James. Anna thought of Beatrice as someone to trust. Had she confronted Beatrice with her erroneous suspicions and threatened to go to the police? Anna couldn't have known that Beatrice would be willing to do anything to protect her position, her family, her security. Beatrice stood to lose everything she held dear if the truth came to light.

Lydia looked out the window as the lights of the city receded. The landscape was retreating into darkness as the train passed into the countryside. In the windowpane she could see her own reflection: a somber figure wrapped in a coat. She thought of her first trip to Philadelphia so many years before, to begin medical school. That journey had also been a solitary one, but full of hope and anticipation. She had sat by the window, her feet propped up on the luxurious steamer trunk bought for the occasion. Lydia had balked at the expense, but her mother had insisted, limited funds be damned. Of course, you shall have it, she said, a journey like this requires some extravagance. Lydia remembered the pleasure they took in packing the books and clothing that she would take with her, each item emblematic of a new beginning. How they had dissolved in laughter at the sight of an outdated hat or moth-eaten petticoat, culled immediately so as not to taint the undertaking.

But now Lydia felt only desolation. The depths of the inky night seemed to close in, broken only by the light of a lonely signal lamp on the track. She pulled her cloak tight around her for comfort as she felt the steady rhythm of the train rattling along the rails.

There was a rap at the door. Lydia sat up abruptly. How much time had passed? She must have fallen asleep. The train was slowing, beginning its arrival into the terminus at Philadelphia. She could see an attendant in the corridor. He held up a basket covered in a linen cloth. She motioned for him to enter. He was bearing sandwiches. Lydia bought one, realizing she had not eaten since the morning.

"That will be ten cents, madam."

"Thank you," Lydia replied. As he left, she gathered her bag and coat and moved to disembark behind the other passengers. The train came to a stop on the platform and steam pooled below as the engines cooled down. She hurried through the station and caught a hansom for home.

The cab rattled down the empty streets. It was starting to rain heavily, a gray fog obscuring the buildings and park squares they passed by.

She thought that the death of James Curtis, an innocent harmed by those charged to protect him, would have wounded Anna in a particular and acute way. He was a child in many ways like her own brother, John. Yet John was treasured by his sisters, their existence centered on his care. Lydia doubted Anna would have accepted anything less than telling the police the truth. She had to get this information to Volcker and Davies as soon as possible.

"Here you are, madam."

Lydia looked out. The hansom was at the corner of her street. She reached into her bag for a few coins and paid the cabbie. She walked up to the front porch of her building with her key in hand for this late hour. The rain was drumming down behind her. She did not hear the rapidly approaching footsteps or feel the presence of the intruder until it was too late. She only felt the searing pain at the base of her skull before darkness took over.

36

"Harlan, will you stop that infernal pacing, please!" Anthea said irritably. The fire was dying down and the front parlor was growing colder.

They were waiting for Volcker and Davies. Harlan stood in front of the window that faced the street. A steady rain fell outside the window. It was ten o'clock at night.

Harlan peered over the half shutter. He could just make out two figures hurrying down the lane.

There was a pounding on the door and Harlan opened it.

The policemen stepped into the hall, shaking off water from their coats. No greeting was offered.

"We have identified the woman," Volcker said.

"At last! Who is she?" Harlan asked

"Her name is Ellen Smith. Dr. Weston was approached by her friend. She was a seamstress who did piecework for several factories. Apparently, she came to the Blake Trust to learn how to read; a few weeks ago, she abruptly stopped coming to the classes. A friend went to her rooms to inquire after her and she was gone. She hasn't been heard from since," Volcker said.

"And you are sure she fits the physical description?" Harlan asked.

"To the mark. She was the same height and build as Anna, with dark hair. The friend will make an identification of the body."

Davies looked around the room.

"Where is Dr. Weston? I thought she would be here," he asked.

"I could ask the same of you, Sergeant," Anthea said. "She was expected to dine with us and she is over three hours late."

"When was the last time you saw her?" Volcker asked.

"At the college yesterday. She was going to the police station to meet you."

"Now let us think for a moment before we rush to conclusions," Harlan began.

There was a sharp rap at the front door.

"Whoever could that be, at this hour?" Anthea exclaimed.

"It must be Lydia," Harlan said.

Volcker opened the door. Constable Ross stood on the doorstep in his dripping black mackintosh.

"Ross! What are you doing here?" Volcker said.

"Sir, I have been trying to find you. This telegram came to the station two hours ago. It is marked urgent."

Volcker opened the telegram and read it. He handed it around to the others.

"Why is she in New York? What does she mean about new evidence to murder?" Volcker's voice was tight with worry.

"Do you know the meaning of this?" Davies looked at each of their faces.

"Of course not! What if something terrible has happened to her?" Anthea said, her voice rising. Harlan put his hand on her shoulder.

"So none of us have seen her since yesterday morning," Volcker said.

Ross shifted uncomfortably from one foot to the other.

"Sir . . . sir . . ." he stammered.

"What is it? Spit it out, man," Volcker said.

"She came back to the station, sir, after you and Sergeant Davies left. She told me she needed to speak with Mrs. Burt, to ask her some more questions."

"And you let her do so, without telling me?"

"Yes, sir." Ross nodded miserably. "Dr. Weston was with her for almost an hour. Then she left in a hurry. She didn't say where she was going but she was in a rush."

"Damn it, Ross, I should dismiss you for good! She may be in grave danger thanks to you," Volcker said.

"Right, sir," Davies said. "I will go to the train station and search for her. Perhaps the train was delayed or she got off early for some other reason."

"Yes. Send a constable round to her home and to the medical college, anywhere she might have possibly gone," Volcker said.

"I will come with you," Harlan said.

"We must find her tonight," Volcker said. "Ross, make yourself useful for once. You and I are going back to the station right now to talk to Mrs. Burt."

37

Lydia awoke in darkness. She winced with pain as she turned her head, sparkling shards of light obscuring her vision. She was lying on her side and beneath her fingers she could feel an earthen floor. Her mouth felt thick, as if her tongue was covered in cotton.

It was very cold. She breathed out deeply and a fine cloud of mist appeared; her chest expanded freely. It was a good sign. She pushed herself up and felt the rippling ache in her joints. It was like being plunged into the depths of night, but slowly she began to make out shapes. In one corner of the room, she could see the faint outline of a string of onions hanging from the ceiling. There were strange misshapen lumps covered in burlap sacks. It was a cellar of some kind. She brushed the dust and grime off the front of her dress. She gingerly felt the back of her head. It was tender and swollen, with crusted blood over a small wound.

Where was she? How much time had passed? Her last memory was of reaching the entrance to her home late at night. A cold rain had been falling. She looked up, and felt sharp pain with the head movement. There was a wooden floor above her. She could see tiny holes in the floorboards;

shafts of faint light shone down through open whorls in the wood. She had to get out. Her assailant could return at any time.

There was no window in the cellar. The only way out must be up. Lydia felt growing panic but she had to think clearly. The stone walls were impenetrable and the ceiling was at least six feet above her head. She had seen it before in farm cottages. There was usually a square of the floor that contained a thin staircase, pulled down from above, collapsing and unfolding like the pleats of an accordion. She crawled, feeling her way along the earthen floor and came upon her bag lying in a crumpled mass. No doubt her assailant thought its contents to be of little use. She put her hand into the bag. The silk pouch was there, nestled in an inside pocket.

Even in the pitch darkness, she could feel the familiar items instantly. She ran her hand over the coiled silk rope and came to the arrow tip, heavy and dense. Mother. She felt unwanted tears prick at her eyes. That the thought of that magical time should come to mind now, in this dark place. It was the summer she was twelve years old and they had sailed to India. Mother had called it a homecoming, a return to her childhood abode at the remote edge of the British Empire. They had made the long sea crossing from London to Bombay, then the overland journey to Calcutta. As they traveled up through the misty foothills of the Himalayas towards her grandfather's tea estate, everything familiar upended.

She had been agog at the wonders on display: monkeys hanging by the tail from trees, watching them shrewdly; the sound of morning prayers in the temple; the teeming bazaar redolent of spices and food. She had spent hours roaming the hillsides under the shadow of the Eastern Himalayas. Her mother had taught her to ride and shoot, just as she had done as a young girl. Her mother's pride in her was obvious. But Lydia remembered her grandfather had been unimpressed at her reserve.

"Timid child, eh, Mary? So unlike you."

"Not timid," her mother replied. "She doesn't know herself yet."

255

Lydia felt the packet of matches. There were only three. She cursed herself for not refilling the box. She struck one and the flare of light burst forth. She turned in a circle, quickly surveying the room.

And then through the silence, she heard a quiet, ragged breathing, like the soft panting of an animal. Dear God, was there someone in the room with her? Her heart pounded and her hands went clammy with fear. In the corner, there was a writhing shape, the long tendrils of dark hair unmistakable.

"Anna!" Lydia gasped, stumbling over to her. She could feel the warmth of the girl's body radiate through the gunnysack she was covered in. She was alive! Lydia felt a moment of ridiculous elation. But as she turned Anna over, she could see how dire the situation was.

"Anna!" She shook the girl, the hair falling away from her face. Her skin was flushed a cherry red. Lydia searched her eyes. They were glassy, unseeing.

"Can you hear me? Can you see me? I am here, Lydia Weston."

Lydia felt a faint squeeze on her forearm, then the hand went limp.

There was little time. The girl was severely dehydrated and near death.

Lydia had to find an opening in the ceiling. She held the last dregs of the match up. She walked up and down the length of the room, craning her neck back to see. She ignored the throbbing pain in her head.

She saw it at last. There was a wide metal ring hanging down from the ceiling. It was the latch.

The match died out. In the darkness, Lydia unwound the silk rope, using her hands to feel the length. It was thin but had a heavy coil, with tensile strength. She tied one end to the arrow tip, to serve as a weight. She lit the precious second match, holding it in her left hand. With her right, she threw the arrow tip into the air. She watched it sail upwards, missing the mark. She threw it again. The arrow tip clanged against the metal ring. Again it dropped to the floor, a dead weight. It was like threading the eye of a needle.

She had only one match left. Behind her, Anna turned, agitated and moaning. Soon they would be in darkness.

"Come now, Lydia." She heard her mother's calm voice. They had spent hours learning archery on the wide lawn that faced the snowcapped peak of Kanchenjunga. Her mother had stood behind her patiently. Over and over again, Lydia had practiced hitting the center of the mark, putting the arrow into the target. She could still feel her mother's hand, pressing softly against her shoulder, guiding her hand to the right path. Her presence had made Lydia feel that she was capable of anything.

"Hold steady, my dear. You can do it."

Lydia closed her eyes. She focused her mind's eye on the ring, seeing it in the darkness. She ran her finger over the groove of the arrow tip and with one gentle arc of the arm she lifted it into the air. The tip gave a satisfying clang as it went through the hole. It was done! She grasped the end of the rope and tied a loop. Using all her strength, she pulled down. Please don't let it be locked from above, she thought. But she felt the movement of the panel, and with a fearsome groan, it opened. The ladderlike staircase swung down and daylight poured into the dark cellar as if the heavens had parted.

Lydia listened. There were no footsteps above. It was silent. Were they alone in the house? Had no one heard the trapdoor open? Anna wouldn't be able to get up the stairs. Lydia lifted the girl. She was as light as a child. Step by step, rung by rung, she pulled Anna upwards.

They collapsed onto the floorboards of a kitchen. The room was bare, save for a gas hob in the corner and a table and chair. On the table sat an empty mug and a piece of half-eaten bread. There was someone in the house.

Lydia peered through the window. They were likely in a clearing in the woods. The bright sun was almost blinding after the darkness of the cellar. She could see the edge of the forest about thirty feet away. The woods could provide the perfect hiding place.

Then she heard it. It was the unmistakable sound of boots. It came again, steady and forceful, then a slight pause. The sound came from another part of the house. The footsteps stopped.

There was no time to pause or get her bearings. She gathered Anna up in her arms. The girl moaned softly in pain. Lydia kicked open the back door, a gust of cold air greeting her like a slap in the face. It gave her a burst of strength. They stumbled down the stairs and into the clearing.

Lydia looked back over her shoulder towards the cottage. She could make out the figure of a man in the window. She felt fear surge through her, igniting every fiber in her body towards one purpose: escape. She turned to the woods, running and half dragging the girl along. She would never surrender Anna. He would have to kill her first. If she could just get into the darkness of the trees. But she could feel her strength fading. She felt nauseous from the sharp pain in the back of her head. Anna pulled at her like a dead weight, but she would not leave her.

They made it to the edge of the woods. She could see the man walking towards her across the clearing. He started to run.

"You cannot take her away. She is mine."

He reached them and wrested Anna away from her, shoving the girl down. Lydia could feel his hot breath on her neck as he pulled her up violently. She yelped in pain, her vision blurring from the force of his hand on her neck.

"You should have stopped when I told you to," he whispered into her ear.

Lydia closed her eyes as he leaned in closer to her. She could feel the cold blade of a knife pressing into her neck. The pain in her head was unbearable.

He released her and she fell heavily onto her knees. He moved towards Anna.

Lydia put her hand in the pocket of her dress and felt the smooth handle of her penknife. She had taken it from her bag. She removed the knife and pressed the circular catch. The long blade released and she ran her finger along the sharp tip.

Anna lay motionless on the ground. The man bent over the girl, tying her hands with a rope. His back was turned to Lydia.

Lydia lunged forward. In one swift motion, she grasped him at the knees and pulled up the leg of his trousers. With every ounce of strength she had, she plunged the razor-sharp knife into his calf. She drove the blade down through the muscle, slicing into the Achilles tendon.

He roared with pain and fell onto his back. He clutched his leg in agony as bright red blood bubbled from the wound.

She recognized him. It was Paul O'Meara. He had been the man at the Halloween party.

Behind her Lydia heard shouts in the clearing as she sank to the cold ground.

38

It was Mrs. Burt who alerted them to the location of the country house. It was used for grand events like balls and shooting parties but often stood empty. It was a favorite place for the Curtises to retire for the weekend. Mrs. Burt seemed genuinely fearful for Dr. Weston's safety. She told them of their conversation and the link to the Children's Infirmary in New York.

They had reached the house just in time. It was a brick mansion set back on a gravel drive, surrounded by acres of rolling lawn and copses. The nearest neighbor was at least a mile away and had noticed nothing unusual. Volcker and Davies and a team of constables fanned out through the house and across the property. At last, they reached the small cottage in the clearing and raised the alarm.

Davies found Anna first. She had collapsed at the edge of the woods. As he lifted her up from the ground, she clutched weakly at his shirtsleeves. Her skin was burning, her eyes sightless as she lapsed in and out of consciousness.

Dr. Weston was beside her. Davies put his arm under her shoulders, supporting her neck. He could feel her hair matted with blood.

"Come, give a hand here! We need help!" he shouted to the uniformed policeman behind him.

"Sergeant, I am all right." Her voice was hoarse but strong. "I stabbed him in the leg."

"*What?*" Davies cried.

"Paul. It's Paul. He can't have gone far. You must stop him." Her eyes closed.

39

Davies moved quickly through the dense stand of trees, impervious to lashings from errant branches. The clearing had given way to the wild and overgrown terrain of a forest. He pushed on, navigating a narrow path forward.

He stopped and leaned against a tree trunk. He guessed he had come only fifty yards from the clearing. It was like the chase in the tenement, when Paul had led them to Thornton, and then vanished without a trace. Here again it was the hunter and his prey. But if Paul was wounded, he would be close by.

There was a stillness to the woods, save for the soft murmur of his own breath. He soon spotted crimson droplets of blood, stark against the dun-colored leaves on the forest floor. He strained to hear any subtle sound, searching the thicket for signs of Paul. He followed the trail for a few feet, stepping on a large branch that snapped under his weight. The sharp crack startled a pair of hawks in the upper branches of a tree, keening as they soared upwards.

"Charlie, look out behind you!" Volcker shouted as he burst through the underbrush.

Davies turned swiftly as Paul leapt from behind a tree, grasping him around the neck with a length of rope. Despite their difference in size, the younger man was surprisingly strong. Davies struggled to break free from his grasp.

"Stand down! You are under arrest!" Volcker shouted and drew his gun. But Paul wouldn't relent. Davies could feel the pressure tightening around his neck.

Volcker fired and the shot grazed the boy's shoulder. Paul recoiled in pain. Davies was released from Paul's hold and he stumbled forward, gasping for air.

The boy's eyes were wide as he looked at his shoulder; the corner of the shirt was shredded by the bullet, blood soaking through the fabric. He turned back towards them, his mouth parted in surprise. He clutched the bloody wound with his hand and fell to his knees.

Davies closed his eyes. He tried to banish the images from his mind, like a recurring nightmare.

40

Lydia saw a gauzy film in front of her, like the slow parting of a curtain. She blinked as her eyes focused on the scene: the white walls and crisp sheets. Her feet were tucked up against the iron bedstead. She turned onto her side, wincing from the sharp pain in her head. She gingerly touched the gauze dressing.

Anthea and Harlan sat at her bedside.

"Thank God! You are awake. My dear, don't move too quickly." Anthea leaned in towards her. She took Lydia's face in her hands as tenderly as a child's. "We were so desperately worried."

"Where am I?" Lydia could feel a thick lump in her throat. She was grateful to be alive and in the care of her friends.

"Ward one in Philadelphia's finest." Anthea smiled.

It was the same ward in the Woman's Hospital where she taught her students. Now she was here as a patient.

"You were brought in by the policemen," Harlan said.

He told her what had happened. She and Anna had been held by Paul O'Meara in a small cottage at the Curtises' secluded country property.

"The pain medications should be wearing off soon. Your head wound is superficial. But you need rest."

"Is Anna alive?"

"Yes, she is recovering in the next ward. You will be able to see her soon."

"And Paul?"

"The police apprehended him. He is being treated for his wounds and then he will be taken into custody."

Lydia leaned back on the pillow and breathed deeply. It was as if a terrible weight was lifted at last.

"Volcker and Davies are here. They want to see you," Harlan said.

"And I have kept them in the waiting room," Anthea chided. "It is too soon. Let her rest."

Lydia pushed herself upright in bed. "No, please, Anthea. I must speak with them."

THE TWO POLICEMEN ENTERED THE room cautiously. She was touched to see their concern. Davies's round face broke into a grin when he saw her sitting up.

"We are so glad to see you in health, Dr. Weston." Volcker removed his hat. They sat in the two chairs by the bedside.

"How are you?" Davies asked.

"Here safe and sound, thanks to you," Lydia said.

Davies blushed. He took her offered hand and squeezed it briefly in response.

"Mrs. Burt confirmed your conversation with her. An urgent telegram was sent and Celia Jackson is coming from New York to give her statement," Davies said.

"Edward Curtis is in custody," Volcker said. "He vehemently denies any wrongdoing in the child's death. But not to worry. We will wear him down through questioning."

Lydia sat bolt upright and threw aside the covers. She swung her legs onto the ground unsteadily and moved to stand up. She could feel a dull ache at the base of her skull.

"Lydia! What are you doing?" Anthea said.

"Edward Curtis is telling the truth. It was Beatrice who killed the boy," Lydia said.

"*What?*" Volcker looked astounded. Davies stood up in surprise.

Lydia told them of her conversation with Celia Jackson and Mrs. Walls, sparing no detail.

"But both Mrs. Burt and Anna believed that it was Edward Curtis," Davies said.

"Yes. I suspect Anna then confronted Beatrice, thinking she was revealing to her what her husband had done. Anna truly wanted to help. She feared that Edward Curtis was dangerous and could be a threat to Beatrice and her sons. Beatrice must have played along. But she realized that Anna might get closer to the truth."

Volcker's expression was incredulous.

"But why? Why would she harm a child?" Davies asked.

"Curtis refused to give the boy up," Lydia said. "Beatrice could never accept that. She had fought to rid herself of what she perceived as the shame of scandal and poverty. She would protect that future for herself and her sons, at any cost."

"Even murder . . ." Volcker said.

Lydia nodded. She closed her eyes. The light in the room had provoked an agonizing headache. But she continued.

"Beatrice must have returned during the night, to James's room. Jack Briscoe told us she had helped at her father's pharmacy, that she was adept at the work. She realized an injection of morphine would be fast acting and she had the skill to administer it. It was almost perfect. But she knew if Anna discovered the truth, she would never relent about going to the police. The only way to silence her would be to kill her."

"So it is. Now to prove it," Volcker said.

41

Edward Curtis paced back and forth like a caged animal, unable to keep still. Davies and Volcker sat across from him in an interview room at the station.

"My attorney is on his way to meet with the chief superintendent. You are finished, Volcker!" Curtis said. His features were blanched with rage.

"Sit down, sir," Volcker said. "That is quite enough."

"Quite enough? Is that all you have to say?" Curtis said angrily. "You have been intent on destroying my family from the beginning, interrogating us, harassing us in our own home. I am done with your bloody questions."

"That is your right, sir. But there is a new development in the case."

He stopped pacing. "What is it?"

Volcker did not answer.

"Tell us what happened the night your son James died."

"How do you know of James?" Curtis put his hand over his mouth, the fingers curling into a fist. Davies could instantly see the fine tremor, so obvious now that he knew what to look for.

"We have Celia Jackson's account of what happened. Dr. Weston

267

spoke with her in New York. Now answer the question. Why didn't you let the doctor return the next morning, to determine the boy's cause of death?"

"There was no need." Curtis sat down wearily. "James's death was a merciful release. That is all."

They sat in silence. Curtis stared at the wall behind them.

"It is useless for me now to think what would have happened if James's mother had lived," he said.

"You betrayed your wife," Volcker said. "Yet we are to believe that she would have accepted your illegitimate child as her own, without question?"

"I know you think her unfeeling," Curtis said quietly. "And I don't deny it was difficult for Bea at first. But she loved James. I know she did."

Curtis met Volcker's gaze.

"Why else would she have returned to check on him during the night, just as a mother would? I was sleeping on the cot in his room and I woke up. Bea was at the bedside. She was leaning over him, gently touching his brow. She gave me a drink of water and told me to go back to sleep, that all would be well from then on."

42

The two policemen sat across from each other, sliding to and fro on the plush seats of their conveyance. Volcker had obtained an urgent arrest warrant for Beatrice Curtis. The chief superintendent had loaned them his personal carriage to make haste back to Winfield Place.

Davies looked out the window as they passed through the streets. Dr. Weston remained in the hospital. She was still weak from her injuries, unable to join them. He thought of how bitterly he had opposed her involvement in the case at the outset. Now he was surprised to find himself longing for her calm presence. It did not feel right to him to be here only with Volcker. She deserved to be part of this moment. It was her keen insight, her tenacity, and ultimately her courage that had brought them to the end of this arduous case.

Volcker was subdued.

"I have been a policeman for many years, almost half my life now," he said. "My first case was investigating the death of a baby. Did I ever tell you the story?"

Davies shook his head.

"It was the mother who did it. She tried to pass it off as an accident but it was obvious she had drowned the baby. It was the youngest of eight, and she couldn't take on another mouth to feed. A neighbor reported her. It was a simple case.

"I went to make the arrest, my first one. It should have been a moment of triumph for cracking the case, eh? Something to show the chief."

Volcker smiled ruefully.

"But it wasn't. I stood in that stinking hovel, so smart in my uniform. All I can remember is the faces of her children, huddled and fearful in the corner. They watched me take away the only mother they had known.

"We have come to the end of a long chase, Charlie. But I can only think of James Curtis and Ellen Smith, of Beatrice's own children, the innocents whose lives have been destroyed by this crime."

"Do you think she will admit to what she has done?" Davies asked.

"I don't know, but I will do all I can to get a confession. I want to hear her say it."

DAVIES AND VOLCKER ALIGHTED FROM the carriage in front of the Curtis house. A uniformed police officer was stationed at the gate. He spied them from across the street and came running.

"Inspector!" He stopped short in front of them. "You must come at once! She is leaving!"

"What? Where?" Volcker said.

"The old gentleman at the door said she is leaving for New York. Their train departs within the hour."

"Now, Davies! We must stop them," Volcker ordered. They raced down the path at the side of the house and turned the corner into the courtyard.

Davies's heart sank as he saw the two boys. They could not have been more than eight or nine years old, dressed in traveling coats. They were surrounded by suitcases as if departing for a long voyage. Beatrice Curtis was climbing into the compartment of her carriage and reaching out to the boys to follow.

"Stop!" Volcker shouted.

"Inspector Volcker! What are you doing here?"

"I must ask you to stand down," Volcker said.

"Why are you trying to stop us? Are you mad?"

"No, I assure you I am not. Please," Volcker said.

The boys looked at the policemen curiously.

Dear God, Davies thought, please let it not end this way, not in front of these children.

But something in Volcker's urgent tone made Mrs. Curtis pause.

"Find a place for us to speak now. Or else we will have to take you into the station for questioning, Mrs. Curtis."

BEATRICE CURTIS STOOD AT THE fireplace.

"What is the meaning of this?" she said.

"What I have to tell you I did not want to say in front of your sons," Volcker said.

"And what do you have to tell me, Inspector? My husband is being held for a crime he has not committed. I trust our attorneys will do their job. I am taking my boys to New York to have a rest with my sister." She remained in her coat.

"No, Mrs. Curtis," Volcker said. "You know very well why we are here."

"Anna Ward was found at your country home," Davies said.

"What?" She looked up sharply. "How can that be?"

"Paul O'Meara has admitted to abducting her."

"I have no idea what you are speaking of, Inspector." Her voice was cold with anger.

271

"He told us that you instructed him to kill Anna," Volcker said.

"That is a lie! Paul is only trying to save himself."

"Anna has confirmed it. She survived," Volcker said.

They had interviewed Anna in the hospital. She'd told them what happened the night of her abduction from the house, when Paul had forced her into the carriage and taken her to the river. In their final moments together, Beatrice Curtis had told Anna that it was she who killed the boy, not her husband. She had to exert her superior cunning until the last. And that admission, a final act of hubris, would be her undoing.

"You are under arrest, for the abduction and attempted murder of Anna Ward and for the murder of James Curtis," Volcker said.

If Volcker's words registered, she showed no visible sign. Her face was impassive. But her lips were compressed, ashen in suppressed fury.

She turned away and regarded herself in the mirror above the fireplace. A pale reflection looked back at them. In one fluid motion, she swept her hand across the mantel, taking crystal decanters and figurines in its wake. The dainty figures crashed onto the marble floor, the glass shattering into pieces.

Davies stepped back in shock.

Volcker pressed on.

"You may have your attorney present, Mrs. Curtis," he said.

She shook her head.

"No. I shall finish this."

Beatrice sank into a chair by the hearth. She did not speak for a long time. The fire died down and no one moved to stoke it.

"Edward is weak, Inspector. He always has been. He has no idea what it is to protect something at great cost," she said quietly. "I suppose I shouldn't have been surprised. Why should I be immune from sorrow?

"It was a girl he had met at one of his charity regattas with that idiot Robert Thornton. Edward was suitably repentant. But she wouldn't relent. She wanted to give birth to the child."

"Did you ever visit James?" Davies asked.

"Yes. When James was a year old, his mother died. I was relieved. I could barely tolerate the child's existence. But then Edward insisted we visit him in the institution, that we were the only family he had."

Beatrice stared ahead as she spoke.

"Soon we were expecting our first son. Edward wanted to bring James home with us. And that is when I knew. He had been in love with the child's mother," she said.

"Were you afraid of what others would think, the scandal of an illegitimate child?" Volcker asked.

"No!" she said. Her expression changed in an instant, her beautiful features twisted in a rictus of anger.

"But the child could not come into our lives. Why should my sons suffer for their father's stupidity? It reminded me of my own father and his pathetic weakness. He had delusions of grandeur far above being the petty shopkeeper he was. Always the fool, Father was. He decided to sell medicinal tonics, only the huckster he worked with had heavily laced them with mercury and laudanum. A few children died and Father was tried in court. We were shunned by those who knew us.

"Do you know what that is like, Inspector, living in fear every day, covered in the stench of poverty? My sisters and I were reduced to two rooms in a boardinghouse, fending off the advances of lecherous men. On most days, I was weak from not having enough to eat. Yet Father was oblivious to our suffering. He gave every last cent of ours to the victims as compensation, begging forgiveness of those he had harmed. He was just like Edward. Why should this child, this bastard, take what was our due? I promised myself that my own children would never suffer as I did."

"What did you do?" Volcker asked.

"James was frequently ill. When the last telegram came, we went to New York. Edward insisted. I brought the morphine vials with me. It

273

was simple to administer it. He died quickly. It was to look like a natural death. I never thought the nurse would be so observant."

"And you heard nothing until Celia Jackson came to see you, here in Philadelphia?" Volcker asked.

"Yes. The woman had had some sort of religious awakening. She thought we should go to the police."

"And then Anna discovered what had happened at the infirmary so many years before."

"She came to my dressing room late one evening and told me. But like the nurse, she thought it was Edward who had done it. I appeared suitably shocked. I begged her to give me time to make sense of it. She was so concerned, fearful for my safety. If Edward could harm a defenseless child, who knows what he was capable of?"

She barked out a short laugh.

"Stupid girl. But I knew Anna would not be persuaded. I was not going to lose everything I had because some sanctimonious little maid thought it her duty to act. She had to die."

"Did you try to kill her yourself?"

"Don't be ridiculous, Inspector. Paul helped me, as he always has. He owes me his life and that is a very useful thing."

"What did you tell him?"

"I told Paul to kill her and dispose of her body in the river afterwards. A distraught young woman kills herself over an affair gone wrong."

A malicious smile appeared on her lips.

"So many people loved our dear Anna, Inspector. I knew about Robert Thornton, of course. It was very satisfying to see Paul's reaction when I told him."

Davies could imagine the rage and desperation Paul would have felt when that news was cruelly delivered.

"Yet Paul could not kill her. He defied you."

"I did not know that."

"When the body was found, you assumed your plan had worked perfectly," Volcker said.

"Yes. It was only an added boon that she was pregnant."

"How did you kill Ellen Smith?" Volcker asked.

"I have no idea of whom you speak," she said coldly.

So it was Paul who had done it, Davies thought. There was no other explanation.

Beatrice Curtis had a last question for them.

"When did you know that the body was not Anna's?" she asked.

"It was Dr. Weston who discovered it. Anna had a medical condition that prevented her from having a child," Volcker said.

"She also correctly deduced that only you could have killed James. She knew your husband's severe tremor would have made it impossible for him to give the injection," Davies said.

She nodded. It was as if she had to know who had bested her.

"It no longer matters for me, Inspector. Edward will take care of the boys." Her voice broke as she choked back tears. "Will I be able to see them? To say goodbye . . ."

She was repentant only because she had been caught, Davies thought. She cared nothing of the suffering she had inflicted on others. How would she protect her sons now, amidst the shattered remnants of their lives without their mother?

"No, Mrs. Curtis. It is over. You must come with us now," Volcker said.

43

Paul O'Meara was too weak to sit up in a chair. His wounds had been dressed but he had lost a significant amount of blood.

He lay on a cot in the small cell, propped upright against a pillow. Davies and Volcker sat on small stools. The cell was in near darkness, the only light coming from a small window at the top of the cell wall. It reminded Davies of the first time they had met him, in the stable at the Curtis home.

Then as now, Davies was struck by Paul's youth. His thick hair fell over his face, but he looked haggard. The expressive dark eyes were vacant.

Paul was in shock, barely aware of their presence.

But he had asked to speak with them.

"Where is Anna?"

"She is recovering in the hospital. She will be fine."

Paul nodded.

"Why did you hide Anna?"

"Like I told you, Beatrice told me to kill her. But I wouldn't do it."

"But Anna's affair with Thornton made you angry."

Paul gripped the sheets on the cot, his knuckles blanched as he twisted the fabric.

"Yes. When Beatrice told me, I thought I could do it. Anna betrayed me. So I took her to the river. But she tried to run away from me, to jump into the water."

He looked at them as his eyes welled with tears.

"I saved her. She needed me to protect her. He couldn't love her like I would."

It was only in his depraved state that he could see this as love, Davies thought. Anna had been his captive, near death from lack of food and water.

"How did you meet Ellen Smith?" Volcker asked.

"At the Blake Trust. I knew Beatrice would realize that I didn't follow her plan," Paul said. "Ellen was like all the others, lonely and afraid. I gave her food and some money. It was so easy to gain her confidence. She thought I was her friend. It helped that she looked like Anna. I took her body to the river after it was done."

The stark, matter-of-fact way he told them belied the horror of what he had done. He had killed an innocent woman, a horrific act of violence born of desperation.

Paul propped himself up further on the cot.

"When will I see Anna? I must be with her. She needs me."

"Sir, we must await the attorney," Davies said to Volcker. "He can't answer more questions in this state."

Volcker nodded. "Stay with him, Charlie."

Davies placed a chair just outside the cell. He sat watching Paul through the bars as darkness cast them both in shadow.

44

The mundane bustle of the coffeehouse went on around them. Lydia could smell the rich aroma of food and hot drinks being borne on trays. The warmth of the close quarters steamed up the windows, obscuring the view outside. Lydia breathed it all in as if she were seeing life anew. It was only a week ago that she had left the hospital. While there she had been lovingly cared for by her friends and students. She had continued her recovery at the Stanleys' home, fussed over by Anthea. She was feeling stronger each day and would soon be back to her teaching duties.

Beatrice Curtis had been arrested. The newspapers were full of lurid accounts of the murders. Edward Curtis was doing everything in his power to attempt to clear his wife's name despite the overwhelming evidence against her. Whatever he thought privately of her treachery, in public he was the faithful husband, sure of his wife's innocence. Paul O'Meara would stand trial but only after it could be determined he was competent to do so. Mrs. Burt was awaiting sentencing. Lydia hoped that she would be granted some leniency as she had directed the police to their rescue.

"I trust that you have no more surprises for us, Dr. Weston?"

"No. I assure you I have revealed my hand completely," Lydia said.

Volcker nodded and lifted his mug of coffee in salutation. Davies smiled at her.

"I must say I understand why your lectures are so popular with students. You have quite a flair for the dramatic," Volcker said.

"We returned to the Blake Trust," Davies said. "Thornton has gone to Boston to be with relatives. There is no word on when or if he is returning. Ida Thornton is determined to carry on her work with or without him."

"Good for her, I say," Volcker said. "Kate Tierney was there. She asked us to give you her thanks."

Ellen Smith had no living relatives. Lydia and Anthea had arranged a burial for her, so that there would be a place of remembrance for her friends to pay their respects.

"And what of Paul?" Lydia asked.

"According to Beatrice, his loyalty was sacrosanct. She saved him from a life in the workhouse where he was beaten and starved. When she needed an accomplice, who better than Paul, who owed his life to her generosity?" Volcker said.

"Beatrice told him about Anna's affair with Thornton. But Paul loved Anna. When it came down to it, he couldn't kill her," Davies said.

"Yes. But he had to avoid drawing Beatrice's suspicion," Volcker said. "So he befriended the vulnerable Ellen Smith at the Blake Trust. No one knew who the father of her child was. She was a perfect substitute for Anna. It was so easy to make her disappear."

Lydia shook her head in sorrow.

"Paul killed her with a blow to the head, in her rooms at the boarding-house," Volcker continued. "He waited until night. Then he transported Ellen's body to the river. He made scratch marks on her face to suggest that the body traveled through the water, catching against branches and rocks. But he didn't think to do the same to her hands."

The sequence of events explained what they discovered at autopsy, Lydia thought.

She imagined the desolation of the river in the dead of night; Paul's cold-blooded calm as he had watched the girl's body go into the icy water and how he had arranged Anna's clothing and shoes on the riverbank.

"As you told us, Doctor, Beatrice's terrible gift was to understand where the point of weakness lay for those she manipulated."

Beatrice Curtis had created a web of vulnerable people, exploiting them for her own wicked gain. Yet they had all been drawn in, Lydia included, by her charm and calculated intelligence. She had been masterful at concealing the murderous cruelty underneath.

They took their last sips of coffee and paid the bill. Davies and Volcker stood to leave.

"Well, it is a case closed," Volcker said. "I wish I could say there was more satisfaction in the outcome. Paul O'Meara will face the consequences of what he has done. And I think Beatrice Curtis may know better than her husband what she will have to face. I hope she will stand trial eventually."

"Thank you for your help, Dr. Weston," Davies said. "We couldn't have done this without you."

Lydia smiled at the policemen. She understood the respect behind those words and what it had taken for Davies to say them.

"Can we walk you back to the college?" Davies asked.

"No, thank you. There is someone I must say goodbye to."

45

Lydia walked onto the platform. The engine sat at the ready, steam pouring from its underbelly in preparation for departure. She passed through clusters of passengers waiting to board the train.

From a distance she could see Sarah Ward, who stood with her hands protectively on the handles of John's wheelchair. The wind ruffled the boy's hair. He was bundled up in a snug coat, a scarf wrapped smartly around his neck. His legs were covered with a plaid blanket.

"Our grand adventure begins at last," Anna said. She approached Lydia with her hands outstretched. "The train leaves in half an hour."

"Then you will arrive in New York this afternoon. That should give you time to settle into your cottage," Lydia said.

"Yes. There are three other children in our home, two boys and a girl. They will keep us quite busy," Anna said, smiling. "John is looking forward to having playmates."

Mrs. Walls had responded to Lydia's request with great kindness. Sarah and Anna were to be installed as caretakers for a group of children at the infirmary. Sarah's needlework would be in great demand. Anna would be able to use the skills she had discovered at the Blake Trust, her

RITU MUKERJI

nurturing disposition ideal for caring for children. More important, the
two sisters would be able to live with their brother, free from financial
worry, for however long that may be.

Anna clasped Lydia's hands. Her face was pale, dark circles etched
under her eyes. Her recovery would take time.

"Thank you, Dr. Weston. If you had not come when you did, God
knows what would have happened."

"I am only sorry that I did not know the truth until the end," Lydia
said gently. She put her arm around Anna. She could feel the thin bones
of the girl's shoulders protruding through the wool coat.

"This belongs to you," Lydia said. She took out the blue diary from
her bag. "It connected us through the investigation. I felt as though I
could hear your voice."

Anna took the book in her hands.

"I must know," Lydia said. "What happened the night Paul took you
to the river?"

Anna nodded.

"I had told Mrs. Curtis what I thought to be the truth, that Mr.
Curtis had harmed James. She was so upset. We were to go to the country
house together, so she could think what to do next. It was odd. She was
insistent that we leave late at night. I knew something was wrong when I
saw her arguing with Paul."

Anna paused.

"That's when she told me she had killed James. She relished saying it,
almost took pleasure in telling me." Anna looked up at her, stricken. "You
should have seen her face, Doctor. She said I was a fool to interfere, and
now I would pay for what I had done.

"Then Paul forced me into the carriage. I had never seen him so angry.
He said I had deceived him."

Anna's affair with Robert Thornton was the blow that had shattered
his fragile psyche, Lydia thought.

282

"I knew then that Paul was going to hurt me. I slipped away from the carriage and ran blindly. I ended up at the waterworks, at the river's edge."

Anna took a shuddering breath as she relived the moment.

"I jumped into the river, desperate to get away from him. But I fell short. I went into the deep water just above the dam. Paul dove in and pulled me to the shore. He was sobbing, saying that he was sorry, that he would protect me always. That's when he took me to the cottage and held me there."

Anna closed her eyes.

"I still can't believe what Mrs. Curtis has done. I trusted her. And Paul . . ."

"It is only because of you that James and Ellen will have a small measure of justice," Lydia said quietly.

Anna put her hands to her face and sobbed, the weeks of pent-up fear and terror releasing their hold on her.

Lydia stood beside her in silence.

"It is over now," she said after a moment. "Come, let us get you on board the train."

Lydia thought of James Curtis and his unforgivable death at the hand of one he trusted. She thought of the senseless and cruel death of Ellen Smith. Her grief was for the young people whose lives were prematurely taken and for those left behind, like the Curtis boys, faced with the loss of their mother and the knowledge of her terrible crimes. Paul O'Meara was also a victim of Beatrice Curtis; she had preyed mercilessly upon his vulnerability and loneliness. At least for Anna, there was the possibility of starting anew.

Lydia watched as the porter carefully lifted John's chair onto the train. His two sisters followed behind. Sarah tucked the edges of the blanket around the boy's feet.

Anna boarded last and turned to wave goodbye.

Lydia raised her hand in return. How different a parting it was than that day at the clinic. It was one of the glorious days of early winter. The sky was shot through with a deep blue. The rays of the sun glittered on the surface of the black engine as the light speckled in a thousand directions.

EPILOGUE

L ydia walked along Pine Street. The footpath was covered in a blanket
of snow from the recent storm. The city felt hushed, as if taking in the
peaceful lull after the holiday season. The few trees were bare, luminous
icicles hanging from denuded branches.

She turned in to the narrow lane and stopped in front of the bookshop. She peered into one of the panes of the bay window, steamed from
the warmth inside. Mr. Kohler was sitting by the fire.

Lydia opened the door and stamped her feet on the small carpet.
She removed her hat and gloves and felt her face flush with the welcome
warmth.

"Dr. Weston, it is good to see you." He stood and grasped her hands.
"Happy New Year."

"And the same to you, Mr. Kohler."

"Please sit down. I thought the day called for something more cel-
ebratory than our usual fare."

She settled into the chair opposite him. He handed her a small glass
of port.

"To 1876. May it be a year of new beginnings, met with hope."

She raised her glass to him.

"Your letter only hinted at your exciting venture. Do tell me more," he said.

It was the year of the Centennial Exposition, the World's Fair to be held in Philadelphia in celebration of the hundredth anniversary of the signing of the Declaration of Independence. The organizers' intent was to showcase American industry and scientific innovation, but it was also a moment to celebrate patriotic unity after the painful rupture of war. The opening date was May 10, and a sprawling city unto itself was taking shape over two hundred acres in Fairmount Park. The elegant triumph of London and Paris was in recent memory, and the architects' renderings of the vast exhibition halls were coming to life. The fairground itself would be a place of beauty, grand avenues bisected by fountains and flower gardens, statues and art interspersed amidst walking paths.

The medical college had been invited to exhibit in the Woman's Pavilion, a unique forum that would house the work of women inventors, engineers, scientists, and artists. Elizabeth Duane Gillespie, a great-granddaughter of Benjamin Franklin and masterful civic organizer, was chairwoman of the Women's Centennial Executive Committee. Through her indefatigable efforts and an endless round of benefit recitals, teas, and bazaars, the funds had been raised for construction of the pavilion.

"And I understand your friend Dr. Stanley will be guiding the college's efforts?" Mr. Kohler asked.

Leading the charge was a more apt term, Lydia thought. After they had paid a visit to the committee's headquarters on Walnut Street to discuss ideas, Anthea had been galvanized into action. She had called an immediate meeting of the clinical faculty to begin planning. The eyes of the world will be upon us, Anthea had told them. Why should we be content with staid displays in a vitrine case? It is a moment to be bold, to show what we are capable of.

"My students are preparing a display on the evolution of anatomy as a clinical subject, from antiquity to the present day," Lydia told Mr. Kohler. "Some of the books we need are quite rare, illustrated atlases and the like. Could you help us?"

Mr. Kohler perused the list that she handed him.

"Certainly," he said. "I will inquire with publishers in Paris and Berlin."

"Dr. Stanley envisions a more robust presence for us, given that many in the medical community will be gathered. There may be opportunity to present practical work, in clinical and surgical demonstrations."

"Surgical demonstrations? How fascinating."

"Yes." Lydia knew he was something of a polymath, endlessly curious about scientific advances. "More experimentation is being done with anesthetic techniques, to enable the surgeon to perform longer and more complicated procedures. The patient falls into a painless state, so to speak, and awakens with no memory of what has happened."

"Aah, such a marvel to consider," he said. "A way to mimic eternal sleep, yet under the direction of human hands.

Where sunless rivers weep
Their waves into the deep,
She sleeps a charmed sleep:
Awake her not . . .
Rest, rest at the heart's core
Till time shall cease:
Sleep that no pain shall wake;

He stopped short.

"Forgive me, Doctor," he said, shaking his head. "With all that you have endured over the past months, perhaps it is time for a respite from poetry."

"No, Mr. Kohler." Lydia smiled at him. "Never."

ACKNOWLEDGMENTS

This is a work of fiction, but I hope readers will be inspired as I am by the story of Woman's Medical College of Pennsylvania. Drexel University's Legacy Center Archives and Special Collections was a wonderful resource and fount of inspiration. The work of historians Regina Morantz-Sanchez, Susan Wells, Steven Peitzman, MD, and Ruth J. Abram provided rich context about the lives of these extraordinary women physicians and the world they inhabited.

This book would not have been possible without my literary agent, Nicki Richesin. Her unwavering support sustained my efforts over many years, and I am so thankful for the literary journeys that we have taken together. Thanks to the remarkable team at Dunow, Carlson & Lerner, especially Arielle Datz.

I am deeply grateful to my editor, Tim O'Connell, and for his vision of what the book could be. His keen insight and guidance, delivered with kindness and good humor, shaped the book and made it better at every turn.

I appreciate the care that brought these pages to life, and my heartfelt thanks goes to the excellent team at Simon & Schuster: Maria Mendez, Samantha Hoback, Amanda Mulholland and Lauren Gomez, Beth Maglione, Jackie Seow and Alison Forner, Rex Bonomelli, Wendy Blum, Danielle Prielipp and Hannah Bishop, Sienna Farris and Imani Seymour. Thank you to Jonathan Karp.

I am indebted to Veronique Baxter at David Higham Associates; Marei Pittner, Juliana Galvis, Sabine Pfannenstiel, Olga Lutova, Anna Jedrzejczyk, and Ludmilla Sushkova at Andrew Nurnberg Associates. Immense gratitude to Claudia van der Werf at Uitgeverij De Fontein.

Katie Herman provided invaluable help, as did Louise Aliano, whose graceful intuition as a reader and a writer is woven into the pages of this book. Thank you to Maddee James for her wonderful artistry.

I am grateful to Swati and Aditya Mukerji, and to Ratna Sen, for wholeheartedly encouraging my bookworm habits since childhood, with love. Thank you to Lynee Bradley, Sonia Bodilly, Jane Doherty, and Renee Tremmel for friendship and laughter; and to the Gupta, Bose, and Metzger families.

To my family, who cheered me on with love and enthusiasm, as this book took shape over many late nights at the kitchen table. Lucas, Noah, and Nila: you bring so much joy to my life. And to Alex, my first and best reader. A thank-you cannot encompass the depths of loving support and the countless ways, large and small, that he embraced my dream and made it ours.

ABOUT THE AUTHOR

Ritu Mukerji was born in Kolkata, India, and raised in the San Francisco Bay Area. From a young age, she has been an avid reader of mysteries, from Golden Age crime fiction to police procedurals and the novels of P. D. James and Ruth Rendell. She received a BA in history from Columbia University and a medical degree from Sidney Kimmel Medical College of Thomas Jefferson University in Philadelphia. She completed residency training at the University of California, Davis, and has been a practicing internist for fifteen years. She lives in Marin County, California, with her husband and three children.

ABOUT THE TYPE

This book was set in Adobe Garamond, which was designed by Robert Slimbach. Adobe's first historical revival, it is a digital and contemporary interpretation of the original Garamond typefaces. It is of interest to note that Adobe Garamond has historically been used in the world of desktop typography and design.